"I wish ....).

He chuckled. "Why, because you can't seem to keep your eyes off me?"

Her gaze flew to meet his, and she could feel a flush tinge her cheeks. She didn't know if he was joking or not. "Well, no," she managed. "I just don't want to see you get chilled."

"And here I thought I was turning you on."

The heat spread. There was something disconcerting about sponge-bathing an almost-naked man whom she'd known only a couple of days, especially when that man had the broadest chest and shoulders she'd ever seen. As she ran the sponge across Riley's chest, his brown nipples hardened. Her stomach dipped and fluttered in response. Goose pimples rose across his hard, flat belly, and she raised apologetic eyes to his.

"How many times are you going to do this?" he asked.

"As often as it takes to bring your fever down."

"Know what I think?" he said. "I think you like doing it."

WHAT ARE *LOVESWEPT* ROMANCES?

They are stories of true romance and touching emotion. We believe those two very important ingredients are constants in our highly sensual and very believable stories in the LOVESWEPT line. Our goal is to give you, the reader, stories of consistently high quality that may sometimes make you laugh, sometimes make you cry, but are always fresh and creative and contain many delightful surprises within their pages.

Most romance fans read an enormous number of books. Those they truly love, they keep. Others may be traded with friends and soon forgotten. We hope that each LOVESWEPT romance will be a treasure—a "keeper." We will always try to publish

LOVE STORIES YOU'LL NEVER FORGET
BY AUTHORS YOU'LL ALWAYS REMEMBER

The Editors

READY-MADE FAMILY

CHARLOTTE HUGHES

BANTAM BOOKS
NEW YORK · TORONTO · LONDON · SYDNEY · AUCKLAND

READY-MADE FAMILY
A Bantam Book / November 1995

If you would be interested in receiving protective vinyl covers for your
Loveswept books, please write to this address for information:

> Loveswept
> Bantam Books
> P.O. Box 985
> Hicksville, NY 11802

ISBN 0-553-44496-4

Published simultaneously in the United States and Canada

Bantam Books are published by Bantam Books, a division of Bantam Dou-
bleday Dell Publishing Group, Inc. Its trademark, consisting of the words
"Bantam Books" and the portrayal of a rooster, is Registered in U.S.
Patent and Trademark Office and in other countries. Marca Registrada.
Bantam Books, 1540 Broadway, New York, New York 10036.

PRINTED IN THE UNITED STATES OF AMERICA

OPM   0 9 8 7 6 5 4 3 2 1

PROLOGUE

Widower, 35, desperately seeking wife and mother with old-fashioned values. Must love children and enjoy small town life. Will provide good home, stable environment. Excellent references. Write to R. Locke, Box A, Gull Island, South Carolina.

ONE

The town of Pinckney was a peninsula, rising like a monument out of the surrounding wetlands. The tide was out, creating whimsical tidal pools and exposing oyster beds. Salt marsh, seared golden from the sun, rippled in the breeze.

Savannah Day prayed she'd made the right decision by coming. After having spent the past fifteen years in an overcrowded, crime-ridden city, this small Southern town was a refreshing sight and made her think of the town in which she'd been raised. She smiled and sucked in the salt-kissed air, still nippy for spring. It was a perfect day for fresh starts.

Her smile faded slightly as she drove past an antiquated, two-story brick building with boxy, cumbersome-looking air conditioners stuffed into the windows. The surrounding lawn consisted mostly of hard-packed red earth. A rusted flag pole stood bare and forlorn next to a weather-beaten sign bearing the words, PINCKNEY H GH.

Savannah glanced across the seat where her fourteen-year-old son stared out the window in what could only be described as mixed horror and disbelief. In the backseat, thirteen-year-old Melody remained silent. The look on the girl's face told Savannah her thoughts were elsewhere; she shuddered to think where.

"I know it doesn't look like much," she said, hoping to snap her daughter out of her silent reverie and appease her son, "but I'm sure it's a good school."

"You should have called Grandma and Grandpa," David said.

They'd had this conversation before. "You know better than that," Savannah replied.

"They would have helped us. They can't stay mad at you forever."

"You don't know my parents." It was sad but true. Her parents had never laid eyes on her children. Savannah considered it their loss.

"How can somebody be mad for fifteen years?"

"They're very rigid in their beliefs," Savannah told him, remembering what it was like growing up under their strong Southern Baptist influence. "I broke their hearts when I ran away with your father. They had already picked someone out for me, a nice, average sort of guy who was studying to be a minister. Instead, I took off with a musician who swore I was going to be the next Loretta Lynn."

"So what happened?" David asked.

She had told her children the story before, but they never seemed to tire of hearing it. She supposed it had something to do with how they saw her now, dedicated and hard-working, but very dull. To think she had, for one brief period, traveled with a band and sang onstage in front of hundreds of people, well, that was not the mother they'd come to know and love.

"Things just didn't work out the way I'd planned," she said at last. "I liked singing and all, but I still wanted a home and family." She had never told them how their father had insisted on her retiring when she got pregnant with David or that she'd discovered he was having an affair with the new lead singer shortly after Melody was born. Her children didn't need to know all the facts; they had enough to deal with knowing their father wanted nothing to do with them.

David grunted and shook his head sadly. "I'll bet this town draws some fine rock concerts," he muttered, sarcasm ringing loud in his voice.

"Oh, well," the girl said from the backseat, her tone hostile, "there goes *my* reason for living."

Savannah tried to ignore the comment. It was only one of a handful the girl had tossed her brother's way during the journey. It was obvious she hated him at the moment—not to mention the whole world and everybody in it.

David said nothing. Like his mother, he was trying to be patient with his sister's infrequent but cutting outbursts. Guilt motivated him. He longed to have the old Melody back.

He scratched his neck and inside his collar. "I'm still itching from that fleabag motel we stayed in last night," he said.

"Perhaps if you hadn't been so stubborn and slept on the floor," Savannah reminded him gently.

"I'm not going to sleep with my mother," he told her, scrunching his face in such a way, one would have thought she'd suggested he sleep on a bed of cow dung. "Melody should have slept with you so I could have the other bed, but nooo—"

"That's enough." Savannah's look warned him not to so much as utter another word about his sister. Melody had absolutely refused to share a bed with her the night before. Worse still, she shunned all physical contact, even something as innocent as a pat on the shoulder. She had fought the young doctor in the emergency room two weeks earlier when he'd tried to examine her injuries after her attack.

It was hard to believe that Melody had once been a happy, well-adjusted child with an active social life. Unlike David, who surrounded himself with underachievers and less favorables, Melody had hung out with the popular crowd who dreamed of going to the best colleges after graduation. Her brother had floundered through eighth grade, passing literally by the skin of his teeth, while she'd passed the seventh with honors. And while David had the hygiene practices of a polecat—smelly sneakers, torn jeans, day-old shirts; Melody was persnickety to a fault and refused to leave the house until she was just so.

Until the attack, of course. An attack that had robbed her of a full mane of blond hair, but more importantly the sparkle in her eyes. An attack that had her brother's name all over it.

David had been honored when the ruffians in the neighborhood had invited him to join their so-called gang. Then he discovered they were planning to rob a liquor store, got scared, and dropped out. You didn't simply drop out of a gang when you knew their secrets, he'd soon learned. The members cornered Melody in a dark alley one afternoon and roughed her up, whacking her waist-long hair almost to the scalp.

The police made feeble attempts to locate the boys responsible; ringing doorbells, asking questions. But with the ongoing drug problem and the alarming homicide rate in Nashville, they simply couldn't spare the manpower.

It could have been worse, Savannah knew. It could have been rape. She'd made up her mind then and there it was time to get out of the city.

"We're going to make a fresh start," she'd told her daughter the week before. "You won't have to worry about people in the new town knowing what happened." She knew the girl was embarrassed to have the other kids whispering behind her back about the attack. She'd even taken her to a hairstylist to see what she could do with the hair that was left. All she'd been able to do was shape it a bit. They all hoped it would grow back quickly.

"It doesn't matter where we go," Melody had replied. She was sullen and frightfully depressed. "I'll know what happened."

Savannah had cried until she was sure there were no tears left in her body. She felt better knowing she was taking action; getting her children out of the city, away from the bad neighborhood and its influences.

She nudged her thoughts aside gently as she crossed a bridge that lifted high out of the water like a bow. That same water was shot with silver from an already brilliant sun. Shrimp boats dotted the horizon, surrounded by fluttering seagulls looking for breakfast. Breathtaking was the only word Savannah could find to describe it.

They left the bridge. There would be one other before they reached their destination, she knew. Riley Locke, her intended, had supplied her with a hand-drawn map listing in detail what she could expect once she left the interstate. She had gazed long and hard at the neat handwriting and wondered what kind of man he really was.

The brief but businesslike conversations she'd had with him had given her few clues other than the fact that he sounded educated and nice enough, but very harried. She had one photo of him holding adorable twin toddlers; she took it out whenever her children weren't looking and studied it. He looked average—okay maybe a little better than average—but she was trying not to romanticize. His hair was brown, cut in a conservative style. He had nice eyes; she supposed they were brown as well. At least she wasn't marrying an ugly man.

He had excellent references. A letter from his banker hinted that the Locke brothers could stop farming today and wouldn't miss the revenue. Still, she didn't know everything about him, and he certainly didn't know everything about her. Her anxiety level rose at the last thought. Would he understand why she'd kept some things from him or would he boot her right out the minute he discovered she hadn't been completely honest?

Once over the bridge, the two-lane highway grew narrow. They passed various service stations, bait stores, and bars with such names as the Oyster Reef, High Tide Bar and Grill, and the Thirsty Gullet. All the buildings were in various stages of neglect or disrepair, weather-worn and drooping like week-old Easter lilies.

The fields, when they came into view, were vast, the dark soil rich looking and ready for planting. "This is it," Savannah said, noting the Locke Farms sign. She shifted in her seat, suddenly excited as well as nervous. Imagine living in such a place, where the neighbors didn't fight half the night and you weren't jolted from your sleep by wailing sirens.

"What kind of farmer is he?" David asked, squinting at the bare fields.

"He and his older brother grow soybeans and tomatoes," Savannah told him, hoping to spur his interest with what little information Riley had shared with her about the farm. "The soybeans help enrich the soil after the tomatoes are harvested. And for the past couple of years Riley has been experimenting with cotton as well; some special variety that can only be grown in this climate." She glanced at her son to see if he was at all interested. He looked bored; she might as well have been talking about the mating practices of the boll weevil.

She checked the rearview mirror to see if Melody had crawled out of her shell long enough to check out their new surroundings. The girl's face was expressionless. Savannah turned off the highway and followed a series of paved roads that cut through the fields and marshy area like arteries.

Tall pines, palmetto, live oak, gum trees, and scrub brush flanked the fields and provided a fence of sorts. There was still plenty of swampy area or wetland; the whole area had a tropical flavor to it. She drove on, following the narrow road. They seemed to drive forever. Just when Savannah feared she was lost, another Locke Farms sign appeared.

She spied the house from a distance; a massive, two-story farmhouse with a red tin roof from which almost a half dozen chimneys jutted out. As she got closer she saw it was built on a tabby foundation, concrete and oyster shells.

Panic seized her. For days she'd thought of nothing else but this moment. Now that it had arrived she was tempted to turn her old clunker around and drive off in the opposite direction. Without warning, she pulled to the side of the road and cut the engine. She was trembling; she couldn't seem to catch her breath.

"Mom, are you okay?" David asked.

She was going to marry a perfect stranger! "Give me a minute," she said, chiding herself for the attack of nerves. This marriage had been in the works for weeks now, and she'd had ample time to adjust. Still, with all that she'd had to do to prepare she hadn't had much time to think about what it would mean to her personally. At times, it had felt as if it were happening to somebody else. Now, looking at the house, it all came rushing to her with the clarity of a frying pan in the face.

Savannah realized her son was watching her, a worried look on his face. "I'll be okay," she said after a moment.

"You're awfully white," he pointed out.

Surely the man would give her time to get used to him before he expected any form of intimacy. "Yes, well, this is a big step."

"Roll your window down farther, Mom," David said. "You look like you need air."

She did so and was greeted with the smell of fresh dirt.

Of course, once Riley found out she hadn't been completely honest, he might not want to marry her at all. "We have to talk," Savannah blurted out.

"Oh, great," David grumbled. "Last time you used that tone of voice we ended up eating Beenie-Weenies for a week so you could have the muffler replaced."

"This is serious, David," Savannah said. "Now, listen up." She propped her right arm along the back of the seat so she could gauge her daughter's reaction to what she was about to say. The last thing Melody needed was more stress in her young life, and Savannah felt guilty for having to deal her more. "Before I go any farther, I want you both to realize how much I love you. I know you haven't had the greatest life so far."

"What are you getting at?" David said, beginning to look uncomfortable.

"Why don't you just shut up, maggot, and let her finish," Melody said from the back.

Savannah took a deep breath. As soon as they were settled, she was going to get her daughter into counseling. Until then, she simply had to be patient and loving like the emergency room staff at the hospital had advised. "All I'm trying to say is, everything I do, I do for you two. I would never, ever have agreed to this if I didn't think we were going to have a better life."

"You don't have to go through with it, Mom," David said. "Nothing is worth you having to marry some old geezer. We can turn this car around and go someplace else. I'll quit school and get a full-time job."

Savannah shook her head. "He's not a geezer. Actually, he's only a couple of years older than me. And you're not quitting school, David, no matter what. How do you ever hope to get into an art school without a high school education?"

"We don't have the money for that."

"Yet," she replied. "That doesn't mean I won't have it by the time you're ready to enroll."

"Well, the guy can't have much going for him or he wouldn't have run that ad to begin with."

Savannah was genuinely offended. "That's not a very nice thing to say considering I answered the ad."

"Yeah, but you're desperate."

"So is he. His wife died last year and left him with twin boys. He claims he doesn't have time to meet women."

"You still shouldn't have to marry someone you don't love."

"There'll be a brief probationary period," she said, "during which time we'll see if we're compatible. If not, I'll receive a fair settlement."

"Yeah, right."

Savannah was growing irritated with his negative attitude. "I have a signed contract. If things don't work out here, we'll have enough money to start over."

David wasn't convinced. "He'd better not touch you. I'll kill him with my bare hands."

She was touched that her son was willing to go to battle for her. At the same time, she didn't want him starting trouble. "I've checked this man out carefully, Son," she said. "I wouldn't have agreed to go through with it otherwise." She paused. "I shouldn't have to remind you how desperate we were to get out of Nashville."

For her it had been a nightmare, working two jobs, fourteen to sixteen hours a day, and she'd still been unable to make ends meet. Her car had lost every vital organ beneath its hood in the last six months, which meant she was often short on the rent or groceries or both. She seldom saw her children, and the recent attack on her daughter had devastated her. She couldn't eat or sleep, and she feared losing her jobs because she was unable to concentrate.

"You need to get away for a while," her boss at the

insurance company had advised. He was a stern, unyielding man who didn't tolerate personal problems on the job. Savannah, who knew it was a dead-end position anyway, decided she needed to get away permanently.

"I suppose we have no other choice," David said, sounding resigned.

Savannah hesitated, knowing there was no time like the present to tell them what she'd done. If nothing else, it might lighten her burden. "One more thing," she said. "Mr. Locke doesn't know I have children. I'm going to have to ask you to stay in the car so I can break it to him gently."

Riley Locke had not slept all night, and it showed. The tired lines around his eyes and mouth marked the hours he'd spent pacing the floor, first with fifteen-month-old Travis, then with his twin brother, Trevor. Thankfully, the children had just fallen into an exhausted sleep.

Riley slipped out of the nursery and made his way down the hall and into the kitchen where the coffeepot waited like an old friend. He'd made it strong, knowing he'd need it to get through the day. The house was a wreck. His present baby-sitter was good with the kids, but she didn't know the first thing about housekeeping. Damned if he didn't have the worst luck with sitters. First, Mrs. Hammel had gone and broken her ankle, just when the boys were getting used to her. Then, eighteen-year-old Jennine Carpenter had caught the flu.

Half the folks in town were sick. And now his boys had the strange ailment. He'd already called the doctor, who promised to call in a prescription. If only he could reach his sister-in-law, Jessie. Perhaps she wouldn't mind driving into town for the medicine. Poor Jessie. With three kids of her own and all the community work she did, she didn't have time to help him raise his boys.

Hopefully, that would end soon. He had a wife coming in a couple of weeks, thanks to Jessie's insistence that he run that ad. He'd put up a fuss in the beginning, of course. Advertising for a wife seemed like a crazy thing to do, sort of like running an ad for tomato pickers. But what choice did he have? Gull Island wasn't exactly brimming over with eligible females. He'd have to drive to Pinckney if he wanted to meet a woman, then spend six months to a year courting her. That left a bad taste in his mouth. Any woman who needed that much wooing didn't belong on a farm with a ready-made family.

Riley sipped his coffee on the back porch, noting the perfect spring day. He felt antsy knowing his fields were ready for planting. He'd been working for weeks getting the soil just right, only to have some of his best workers come down with this new flu virus. Poor old Doc Henly was beside himself trying to treat it; said he hadn't seen it this bad since the mid-seventies when the Swine Flu had swept the country.

Truth to tell, Riley wasn't feeling so good himself. But he never got sick, and he blamed the achy tired feeling on losing so much sleep the past couple of nights. At first he'd thought the boys were cutting more teeth, and he'd rubbed that smelly gunk on their gums and wondered why it wasn't helping. Leave it to him to treat them for the wrong thing. He decided not to tell Jessie about his mistake. She'd give him one of those looks that suggested he didn't have enough sense to raise chickens, much less twin boys.

Back inside, he dialed his brother's house. Again, no answer. He left a brief message on the recorder and decided to clean the kitchen while he waited to hear back. He grabbed an apron and grimaced at the sight of ruffles. Wouldn't his brother, Ben, get a kick out of that. Still, he didn't want to mess up the shirt Jessie had given him for Christmas so he tied it on and surveyed the room. It was a mess; dirty dishes covered every conceivable spot. It gnawed at him that he hadn't bought the dishwasher his wife had asked for three years before. Well, asked wasn't exactly the right word. Kara Wentworth Locke had never asked for anything in her life. She'd demanded. And he'd refused to be ordered around.

Still, he should have modernized the place, made things easier for her. Maybe then she would have been happier. Maybe she wouldn't have spent so much time in town. He sighed heavily. Shoulda, coulda, woulda. The story of his life as far as his dead wife was concerned. But he hadn't wanted to tear out the antique heart of pine cabinets that his grandfather had built by hand, nor had he found time to insulate and heat the room off the back porch where the washer and dryer sat. He'd been a bastard for not doing it, but damned if Kara hadn't brought out the worst in him at times.

The sound of the doorbell tore him from his thoughts and made him frown. He hadn't even heard a car pull up. Where was Bo, the rangy stray who'd wandered up some months ago and pretended to be a watchdog? he wondered. Probably in the woods chasing rabbits.

Riley checked the old-fashioned wall clock and saw it was barely nine o'clock. He'd string the visitor up if the bell woke the boys. Unless it was Jessie, of course. She knew how to handle the toughest emergency. But Jessie didn't bother with doorbells; she just walked in . . .

He dried his hands quickly on a dish towel that was gummy with oatmeal and hurried toward the front of the house. It rang again before he reached the door, and he muttered a cuss word under his breath. He wrenched the door open and regarded the blond woman on the other side.

"Don't even think about ringing that doorbell again, lady," he said.

Savannah took a step back and gazed at the big man in the frilly apron. He stood tall and straight as a towering pine. She was acutely conscious of a wide chest and broad, powerful-looking shoulders. His snapshot had not done him justice. "I beg your pardon?"

Riley frowned. She looked familiar, but he couldn't place her right away. Too little sleep, too many worries. "What do you want?"

"Are you Riley Locke?"

"Yes."

She offered him her nicest smile. "Savannah Day."

It took a moment for her name to sink in. Shock rendered him speechless for a moment. "What's the date?"

"April first."

"You're two weeks early."

"I finished up earlier than I thought." She didn't want to tell him her landlord had rented her apartment right out from under her. The fact that she'd been late with her rent these past two months and had been forced to pay by the week probably had something to do with it. Her boss had found her replacement almost immediately, and Savannah had been hurt that he seemed so eager to be rid of her. Seven years wasted.

"I decided to come as soon as I received your check," she told Riley after a moment, stopping herself when she almost told him her children were out for school break.

He studied her. She was small, no more than five two or three, and skinny as a beanpole. Why hadn't he noticed it in her picture? Even her features were dainty; small hands, narrow wrists. His twins were plump and big-boned, thirty-five pounds of flesh in motion. He doubted this tiny creature would be able to keep up with them, much less lift them.

"This is a bad time," he said. "The place is a mess, and the boys have the flu." He reached into his back pocket for his wallet and pulled out several bills. "There's a motel in town. You can stay there for a few days—"

"Why should I do that?" she asked. "You obviously need my help. That's why I'm here, remember?"

"Mom?"

Startled by the sound of her son's voice, Savannah swung her head around. "I specifically asked you to stay in the car, David," she said, giving him a ferocious look. Of all times for him to disobey.

"Who's this?" Riley asked.

"My son."

"You have a son?" he asked, frowning.

David didn't seem to notice the tension between the adults as he went on. "Melody's sick. She said she's been carsick since we left the Fleabag Inn, but she didn't want to say anything."

"Who's Melody?" Riley asked.

"My daughter."

"She's throwing up," David finished.

"You have a daughter too?" Riley asked. The frown deepened.

Savannah didn't answer. She left the front porch in a flurry and rounded the house, where she'd parked her car out of sight in hopes of hiding her children until she could explain their existence to Riley. Her daughter was standing beside the car, presently caught up in a fit of dry heaves.

"Honey, why didn't you tell me you were sick?" Savannah asked upon reaching her.

The girl simply shook her head and wiped her mouth on her sleeve. "I dunno."

Riley stared at the dark-haired boy who couldn't have been more than fourteen or fifteen years old. His hair was long and stringy, his jeans faded and torn at the knees. An earring hung from his left ear; attached to it was some kind of marble. Riley winced when he realized it was a plastic eyeball.

"Good God!" he said aloud, drawing a frown from the boy.

David shrugged. "You were expecting the Brady Bunch?"

Riley was about to answer when Savannah hurried onto the porch, clutching her daughter's hand. The girl wore so much black, she appeared to be in mourning. Her hair was cropped off almost to the scalp. He simply stared at the group and wondered what to do next. And to think, only a few minutes before, he'd felt things couldn't get worse.

"We need to use your bathroom," Savannah said hurriedly.

Wordlessly, Riley led them into the house and down the hall. He pointed to a door just off the kitchen. "You'll find clean towels beneath the sink," he said, then thought of the mountain of dirty laundry waiting to be washed. "Hopefully," he added.

Savannah ushered her daughter inside and closed the door.

Once again, Riley found himself alone with the boy. "Would you like a glass of juice?" he asked.

David shrugged. "You got any soft drinks?"

"At nine o'clock in the morning?" he asked quizzically, then turned for the refrigerator. "Sure." He grabbed a can and handed it to the boy. "How old are you?"

David popped the top, took a loud swig, and wiped his mouth on his shirtsleeve. "Almost fifteen. And you?"

Riley ignored the question. "Your mother didn't mention the fact she had children."

"She was afraid you wouldn't go for it. I told her that

didn't make any sense at all considering that you expect her to take care of your kids. What's fair is fair, right?"

Riley didn't say anything. The bathroom door opened, and Savannah peeked out. "Do you have something for an upset stomach?"

"Check the medicine cabinet."

Savannah closed the door once more and checked the small pine cabinet over the pedestal sink. Nothing to combat stomach trouble. She did find one prescription bottle for a Kara Locke containing nerve pills. "His late wife must've been the jittery type," she whispered to Melody.

"Maybe he made her that way," the girl replied, chewing a thumbnail.

They stared, wide-eyed at each other for a moment, then glanced at the door as though wondering what was waiting for them on the other side. Savannah realized she was being silly. "I don't see anything in here for a queasy stomach," she said. "How about I get you a soda cracker instead?"

The girl shrugged. "I'm okay now. As long as I don't have to get back in a car right away."

Savannah ruffled her short hair and opened the door, trying to appear more optimistic than she felt. Riley Locke might very well insist they get in the car and go back in the direction from whence they came. She found Riley and David standing in the kitchen staring at each other as if they'd each discovered a new species of man. "All better," she announced.

"That's good," Riley said, only to be interrupted by crying from the nursery. All the commotion had obviously woke his boys. "Excuse me." He gave a tired sigh and started in that direction. Suddenly the thought of dealing with his sick boys seemed less stressful than trying to figure out what to do with the strange family that had landed on his doorstep.

"Stay here," Savannah told her children, and followed Riley into a room off the hall that smelled of dirty diapers. She stepped inside and found a chubby towheaded boy standing in his crib. "Da!" he cried, the minute Riley walked into the room. Riley picked him up, just as the toddler in the other crib began to stir.

"Oh, how adorable," Savannah whispered, noting the boys were exact replicas of each other.

Riley, who'd not heard her follow him in, glanced over his shoulder as he picked up his son. "They have the flu," he said. "You might not want to get close—"

Savannah found herself staring for a moment at the broad back and shoulders that seemed even more powerful holding the toddler. The snug jeans made nice work of his lean hips and thighs. "Don't be silly," she said, coming up to stand beside him. He was a good twelve inches taller than her. "What are you giving them?"

"The doctor called in a prescription. I was going to have my sister-in-law pick it up, but I haven't been able to locate her."

Savannah pressed her hand against the baby's red cheek. "He feels hot. Do you have a thermometer?"

Riley motioned toward a built-in cabinet along one wall. "Everything should be in there. Use the side that has the blue sticker on the door."

"How about a vaporizer?" she said, going to the cabinet that was marked with a blue teddy bear.

He shrugged, bouncing the baby who was watching the strange new woman curiously. "Not that I know of. They don't get sick much, to tell you the truth."

She thought she noted pride in his voice as she reached for the thermometer. "Bring him over here," she said, motioning to the changing table. "And while I check him for fever, I want you to make a list of things to buy at the drugstore."

Riley hesitated. She'd been there less than five minutes, and she was already telling him what to do.

"Is something wrong?" Savannah asked, sensing a problem but having no idea what it could be.

"No, I reckon not," he said, deciding she was only trying to be helpful. What was he going to do after all, he asked himself. He couldn't find Jessie, and he needed someone to look after the boys so he could go for the medicine. This was not the time to be stubborn or discuss the fact that she'd lied to him about her children. He laid the baby down on the padded changing table and left the room in search of pad and pencil. He found Savannah's children sitting at the kitchen table looking miserable. They glanced up as he came into the room. "Would either of you like something to eat?" he asked.

David shook his head. "We just had breakfast. What's my mother doing in there anyway?"

Riley located what he was looking for. "She's taking Trevor's temperature."

"Trevor?"

"My son." He noted the baby was no longer crying. "She seems to know her way around babies."

David met his gaze. "That's what you advertised for," he said. "Someone who could do your cooking and cleaning and raise your children too."

Riley decided he didn't like the boy's attitude at all. The girl wasn't much better; sullen and downcast, she hadn't spoken one word. She hadn't even made eye contact for that matter. "You don't sound too keen on this," Riley said, thinking it would be a perfect reason to tell the woman in the other room that it wasn't going to work out.

"My mother didn't ask my opinion. She'd already made the plans by the time she told us."

Riley remembered the pad and pencil. "Look, nothing is for certain at this point. Your mother's probably already having second thoughts." He knew he was. He was going to ring Jessie's neck for talking him into such a foolhardy scheme. In the meantime, though, he had to see to the twins' needs. After that he would do whatever was necessary to get rid of this strange bunch.

Savannah had just finished taking Trevor's temperature when Riley returned to the nursery. "One hundred and one," she said, sticking the thermometer back into a container of alcohol. "If it creeps up any higher, I'll have to give him a cool bath." The boy saw his father and grunted. She picked him up and handed him to Riley, then made her list as the baby in the red crib opened his eyes.

"Who thought of the color scheme?" she asked.

"My sister-in-law. We kept getting the boys mixed up when we first brought them home from the hospital so Jessie bought each of them a bracelet, one blue, one red. Trevor's bed and cabinets are blue, and Travis's are red. Same thing with their personal care items," he said, pointing to the alcohol container she'd just used that boasted a blue sticker. He paused. "Look, I'm sorry things are in such a mess," he said, not wanting her to think he lived like a slob. "The baby-sitter got sick and—"

"I understand," she said, more interested in her list than his housekeeping skills.

The baby in the crib was starting to fret. Savannah handed Riley the list, then picked him up. He whimpered. "It's okay, fella," she said softly. "I'm just going to get you out of that wet diaper. So, you're Travis, huh?" The baby blinked several times at her through red, watery eyes. It was obvious he felt bad.

Riley watched her change his son and marveled at the

way she did it with such ease. He checked the list in his hand. "Is there a certain brand name of vaporizer you want me to buy?" he asked.

"Doesn't matter. Just make sure it's the cool-air type. Oh, and before you go, I'll need several pillows. I want to elevate these mattresses, help the boys breathe a little easier. You can tell they're congested. And clean sheets if you have them," she added, noting the beds were in dire need of changing.

Still holding Trevor, Riley made his way from the room to a closet in the hall. After a couple of trips he had enough pillows to do the job. Locating clean crib sheets was not as easy, but Savannah assured him she could make do with whatever he had until the others were washed. He finally found two full-size ones that were clean.

"Why don't you go on to the drugstore?" Savannah suggested. "I'll have all this cleaned up by the time you get back."

Riley set his son down on the rug and made for the door. The boy wailed. He hesitated. The woman was a stranger. How did he know he could trust her with his children?

"They really need that medicine," Savannah said, sensing his uncertainty. "I promise to take good care of them."

Something in her look told him he could count on her. "I'll hurry," he said, tucking the list in his pocket as he made his way out of the room.

David and Melody ventured to the nursery door as soon as Riley pulled out of the driveway. They found Savannah wiping down a plastic mattress cover with a sponge and a spray bottle of disinfectant she'd found in one of the cabinets. The toddlers sat on the floor with their blocks. Their halfhearted play was a clear indication of how crummy they felt; not to mention their coughs and runny noses. They gazed curiously at the teenagers.

"Oh, this is nice," David said, his tone thick with sarcasm as he watched his mother scrub a crib. "He couldn't wait to put you to work."

Savannah looked up. "Mr. Locke didn't ask me to do this."

"But he expects it. I mean, that's what this is all about, isn't it? You act as his maid and bedmate, and if he likes the job you're doing, he'll marry you."

Savannah gazed back at her son. "You've got it all wrong, David." She would have gone on to explain, but he left the room before she had the chance. She sighed and hoped her son wouldn't make trouble. Then she noted Melody had stepped farther into the room and was watching the twins play. Savannah didn't say anything for fear of chasing her out. One of the boys threw a block, and the girl retrieved it, then knelt beside them and built a tower. They were quiet as they watched her.

"What are their names?" Melody asked.

"Trevor and Travis."

"How do you tell them apart?"

"Trevor is wearing the blue bracelet. You might not want to get too close, they have the flu." As if to back up her assertion, Travis started coughing and wiping his nose with a chubby fist. "Mr. Locke went to the drugstore for medicine."

"Their little eyes are so red," Melody said. She reached for a block and handed it to one of the boys. He took it and brought it to his mouth. The girl smiled. "I think he's hungry."

"I'll feed them as soon as I get this room straight," Savannah said, laying a fresh white sheet in the scrubbed crib and tucking it around the sides. She watched her daughter from the corner of her eye. "I never knew you liked babies," she said.

The girl shrugged. "They're okay, I guess. I certainly don't want any of my own."

"How come?"

All the light went out of the girl's eyes. "Because I don't want some man pawing and crawling all over me, that's why. Nothing is worth that." There was a bitterness and worldliness to her voice that defied her young age.

Savannah raised up from her work and took a step closer to her daughter. "It doesn't have to be like that, Melody," she said gently. "When you love a man you want him to hold you in his arms. You don't feel dirty when he makes love to you, you feel cherished and protected and desired."

Melody's look hardened. "Is that how you felt with my father?" she asked, then went on before her mother could answer. "If that's the case, why'd he find a girlfriend as soon as I was born?"

Savannah was surprised her daughter knew the details surrounding the split but guessed she'd overheard it at some point. She was also saddened by the caustic tone the girl used when she spoke of her father. But who could blame her; the man had never once tried to see his children after Savannah left him. "We were very young at the time," she said, "and I'm sorry to have to tell you that, no, your father and I did not have that kind of relationship. But that's not to say it doesn't exist."

The girl looked thoughtful as she went back to playing with the twins. "Are you hoping to find that kind of love with Mr. Locke?"

Savannah pondered it. She couldn't imagine sharing an intimate relationship with the big man who was little more than a stranger to her. "I don't think Mr. Locke and I are interested in love and passion at this point in our lives," she replied truthfully.

"Then I'd say that both of you are wasting your time," a woman said from the doorway, startling mother and daughter so badly, they jumped.

Savannah lifted her head up and found herself looking into a pretty round face surrounded by bright red hair. The woman smiled and stepped into the room, and the twins squealed in delight and reached for her.

"So you're Riley's intended," she said, eyeing Savannah carefully as she swooped one boy up and kissed him loudly on the cheek. The other one stood and wrapped his chubby arms around her leg and began to cry. "He didn't mention you had children of your own."

Savannah saw Melody exit the room. The girl wasn't good with strangers these days. "Yes, I'm Savannah Day," she said, offering her hand and wondering who the woman was. They shook hands. "I'm afraid I never got around to telling Riley about my son and daughter."

The other woman looked amused. "I'm Jessie Locke, Riley's sister-in-law. So how'd he take it? The part about your having kids, I mean?"

"I think he's still in shock."

"I'll bet. Oh, my, this baby has a fever," Jessie said. "Doc Henly told me they were sick. I had to take my daughter in for her allergy shot this morning, and the waiting room was full of flu patients."

"I'm not sure when they came down with it. Riley's gone for medicine now."

"Blast him. He didn't tell me. I would have come right away. No wonder he hasn't started planting." She sighed in frustration. "That man has too much stubbornness in him if you ask me. He'd rather bite his tongue off than ask for help." She paused and gave Savannah a stern look. "That's something you need to know about him right away if you're going to make this relationship work." She set one boy down and picked up the other. "There's one more thing you ought to know as well."

"What's that?"

"You're a fool if you're willing to settle for a platonic relationship with my brother-in-law. Riley Locke is one of the most virile men I know. Don't force him to look elsewhere for love and affection."

TWO

By the time Riley returned from town, Jessie had fed the boys and Savannah had cleaned the kitchen and put in a load of white clothes to wash. Melody dusted and vacuumed the den and living room, and David, though he grumbled and complained bitterly, swept the porches and walks.

Riley stood in the doorway of the kitchen, holding a large sack and a box under one arm as he took in the spotless kitchen and wondered, not for the first time, how quick and efficient the opposite sex was. He'd never spent much time inside a house; the men in the family had had more chores outside than they could keep up with. It was the women, his grandmother and mother, who had done the cooking and the cleaning and the laundry, and the men were all ignorant as to how it was accomplished. He hadn't realized what a mistake that was until his wife had died and left him with two babies to raise.

Jessie turned from her work and frowned at the man. "Riley Locke, what in tarnation are you staring at?"

He smiled. She was only a couple of years older than him, but she acted like a mother sometimes. "Hi, Jess."

She stuck a hand in the sudsy sink water, pulled it out, and flicked water in his face. "Hi, yourself. Why didn't you tell me my nephews were sick?"

He chuckled and dried his face on his sleeve. "I figured you had enough to do with three kids and that lazy brother of mine."

She suddenly looked stern. "We've been through this before, Riley. What's a family for if we can't help each other?" She gave a huff of disgust. "You're not even listening to me."

"I am, darlin'. I'm just in a hurry to give the boys their medicine. They've been coughing and crying for two nights." He set the box down and reached into the bag, bringing out two bottles of cough medicine and two more containing a thick pink liquid. "The pharmacist said both medicines taste good, so we shouldn't have any trouble getting them to take it."

Jessie reached into a drawer and pulled out two measuring spoons along with red and blue bear stickers like the ones in the nursery. "Don't forget to put these on everything new for the boys. We certainly don't want to get their medicines mixed up. Why don't you give it to them," she told Savannah. "I've never been good at that sort of thing."

Savannah suspected that wasn't true. With children of her own, Jessie Locke had to know something about dispensing medicine. This was obviously her way of making Savannah feel welcome and reminding Riley how much he needed someone to help him.

"My kids are older now," Savannah said, taking the spoons, "but I think I remember how it's done." She had the medicine down the boys in no time. Then she filled the vaporizer with cold water and carried it to the nursery, placing it in a central location so both twins could benefit from the steam. Before long, they were rubbing their eyes and yawning, no doubt due to the elixir in the cough syrup. Riley tucked them into their cribs and closed the door.

"Well, that's that," Jessie said, dusting her hands. "I reckon you two can carry on without me. Riley, you're going to have to go to the grocery store before long. You're out of milk and applesauce, you know how the boys love their applesauce." She grabbed her purse and started for the door, then glanced at Savannah. "My number's in the phone book. Call me if you need anything or have questions. I'll drop by later. And make him be nice," she added, cutting her eyes toward her brother-in-law.

Savannah watched her go, feeling a strange sense of loss as the woman pulled away in her car and left her alone with Riley. The house seemed oddly quiet, the only sound came from the television set in the den where David and Melody were watching a *Barney Miller* rerun.

"We need to talk," Riley said. "Why don't we grab a cup of coffee and sit on the front porch."

Savannah nodded but remained silent as she poured two cups and followed him out. This is it, she thought. He was going to get rid of her before she even had a chance to prove herself. She was feeling defensive as she took a seat on the front porch swing. Riley, who'd remained standing, gazed out at the bare field across the narrow asphalt road that ran in front of the house. The dark whiskers on his cheek and jaw suggested he'd missed shaving that morning, but instead of hindering his good looks, the beard only enhanced his masculinity and the inherent strength in his face. She wondered what it would be like sitting out there with him in the evening, discussing their days.

Riley wondered at her silence, wondered what she could be thinking. Walking into a dirty house with sick children probably wasn't her idea of a fun time. "I appreciate all you've done this morning," he began.

"I'm glad I was able to help," Savannah replied, then

waited. It seemed as though she was always waiting for the other shoe to drop, so to speak. She had seen the big comfortable house and thought what a cozy home she could turn it into, but deep down she'd known it wasn't meant to be. Did she not measure up in his mind? Was she not what he'd expected? She chanced a look in his direction and knew by the rigid set of his jaw that she wasn't going to like what he was about to say.

He took a deep breath. "I don't like being lied to, Savannah. We've had several phone conversations. You could have told me about your children."

Savannah decided she would not give up without a fight, without having her say. "We had several brief conversations," she said, "during which time you discussed your needs. The only thing you wanted to know about me was whether I liked children and did I have a recent photo. I was wrong not to tell you about David and Melody, but I hardly think it's fair to expect me to raise your twins if you aren't willing to reciprocate."

"It's not the same. I was prepared to give you something in return for being a mother to my boys. A stable home, for instance. Financial security."

She lifted her chin. "You talk as though I don't have anything of value to offer. A house is not a home unless someone makes it one. And this house, if you don't mind my saying so, needs some work." She vaguely recalled the faded walls and scratched wood floors. The drapes in the living room were made of velvet, of all things. Of course, it wasn't really all that bad, and she could make changes over time, but she wasn't about to let him throw her children in her face without getting back at him over his house.

Riley was momentarily speechless by her matter-of-fact attitude. He studied her. She had certainly hit the nail on the head about the house needing work. He still remembered how homey the house had felt when his parents and grandparents had run the farm. His mother was the only one left now, but she was in a nursing home. He wanted the house to feel like a home again, he realized. He could paint and carpet and put all new appliances in the kitchen, but that had nothing to do with making it a home.

"Why did you really come?" Riley asked Savannah after a moment, realizing he had spent much of their phone conversations talking about what he was looking for and feeling selfish now because of it. But he'd been desperate. He still was. Was he desperate enough to take on a woman with two teenagers?

Savannah did not hesitate. "I didn't like the idea of my children growing up in a big city where crime is so prevalent. Also, my job kept me from spending the kind of time I wanted with them."

"You're willing to marry a man you don't love for those reasons?" he asked. "That's quite a sacrifice."

"Is there any sacrifice you wouldn't make for your own children?"

Riley pondered it. "Your son doesn't like me."

Savannah shrugged. "David's going through a rebellious stage. He doesn't particularly care for anybody. Trevor and Travis will go through the same thing when they're teenagers. The good news is, it doesn't last forever."

"And your daughter?"

She hesitated. How could she make him understand what Melody was going through? "My daughter will be okay in time," she said simply.

He sat down in one of the chairs and sipped his coffee in silence. "Look, you seem like a nice woman and all, but I need some time to think about this," he said. "I've pretty much had my hands full with running the farm and taking care of the twins; I wouldn't feel right taking on a wife and a couple of teenagers unless I was confident I could do it."

He paused and glanced at her, softening at the worry line
on her forehead. It was obvious she hadn't had it so eas
herself. "I don't think you want me to jump into some
thing, then change my mind when the going gets rough,"
he added.

She tried to read between the lines but couldn't. Thei
eyes met. His gaze was penetrating, as though the deepe
he stared the better his chances of discovering what she wa
really about. She was the first to look away. "Perhaps w
both need time to think it over," she said after a momen
and had the satisfaction of seeing his look of surprise. H
obviously suspected she would agree to just about anything
in order to stay. He was wrong. She wasn't about to bring
David and Melody into a situation where they weren'
wanted. "After all, you're asking me to raise your boys from
infancy. That's a tall order." She stood as though bringing
the discussion to a close. "We don't have to decide today."

There was a long, brittle silence. Riley wondered how
she'd managed to put him on the defensive. She might be
small but she wasn't about to be bullied. He drained hi
coffee and stood as well. "It's settled then. We'll give it a
few days. A trial run, so to speak."

"Fine. If it doesn't work out, you can always call your
regular sitter back. In the meantime, I'll be glad to look
after the boys so you can take care of business."

Relief shone on his tan face. "That'd be a big help. I
need to set those tomato plants out as soon as I can find a
few good workers. Everybody in town's got this bug. I've
never seen anything like it."

There didn't seem to be anything else to say so they
simply stood there for a moment. Savannah felt his gaze on
her, frankly assessing her. She glanced up as he continued
to stare. "Is anything wrong?" she asked.

Riley shuffled his feet, made uncomfortable by the fact
she'd caught him gawking. The cool air had put color in

her cheeks. "I was just wondering how you'd take to farm life," he said.

She shrugged. "I should do okay as long as you don't hook me up to a plow."

He saw the teasing glint in her eyes and relaxed. "Naw, I got modern machinery for that."

Once again, there didn't seem to be anything left to say. Riley shifted from one foot to the other. He wondered at the tension in the air, wondered if she felt it as well. He could feel it in the muscles at the back of his neck.

"Why don't you let me show you where you and your children can sleep?" he suggested, hoping to ease the strain between them. "I had someone clean the place last week. Nobody's been upstairs, so it should be okay."

"I'm sure it will," Savannah told him.

Back inside, she followed him to a staircase where a baby gate had been fixed in place at the bottom. Riley opened it and motioned for her to go first. At the top, Savannah found herself on a U-shaped landing flanked by old-fashioned four-paneled doors with brass knobs. All three bedrooms were large, with ten-foot ceilings. Antique quilts draped the beds and braided rugs adorned the wood floors. The largest bedroom had its own bath; the smaller ones adjoined a blue-tiled bath with a double vanity. The furniture was old, a bit battered in places, but more than serviceable.

"My parents had the place completely renovated when my brother and I were in high school," Riley said. "They added a large master suite downstairs, but I put the nursery in there after my wife died, because it was a pain carrying the boys up and down the stairs all day."

"Where do you sleep?"

"There's a library or sitting room of sorts attached to the master. I have a bed in there."

"It's a big house," she mused.

He nodded. "My grandfather built it. Nothing fancy, mind you, but it's rock-solid. My mother hired a landscaper to give the yard a parklike setting, which is nice for cook-outs and picnics. She also had a vegetable garden out back."

"Did your late wife enjoy gardening?" she asked, thinking how nice it would be to have one. His expression dimmed, and Savannah had a sudden sinking feeling she shouldn't have asked about his late wife.

"She didn't like living in the country," he answered abruptly.

Savannah tried not to show her bafflement. She'd fallen in love with the place the minute she'd laid eyes on it. But she wasn't about to tell him that and have him think she would go to any lengths to stay. She decided to change the subject. "One of us should probably go to the grocery store," she told him. "Jessie said you're low on food."

"I'll go," he said, "if you don't mind looking after the twins."

"I don't mind at all. Besides, they're going to sleep for a while now that they've had their medicine. So I'll have a chance to get settled." She saw his brow furrow the minute she said it and wished she hadn't. There was no sense trying to get settled until she knew for sure whether or not she and her children would be staying. "I mean, unpacked," she corrected.

Riley nodded and started for the door. He was in a bit of a hurry to get away so he could think more clearly about what was going on. "Is there anything in particular you want me to buy?" he asked. When she offered him a blank look, he went on. "What kinds of meals do you usually prepare?" When she didn't answer right away, he became insistent. "You can cook, can't you?"

"Of course I can cook," she said as though he'd just insulted her. "Buy whatever you like, and I'll cook it."

Savannah waited until she'd heard his pickup truck pull

away before she tackled the laundry once more. She checked on the babies, both fast asleep, then went about cleaning the downstairs bathrooms. She ventured upstairs to the bedrooms and discovered the rooms David and Melody were to sleep in had no sheets. She found two sets of full-size sheets in the linen closet. She was in the process of making one of the beds when her children came into the room.

"Where'd he go?" David asked.

"Mr. Locke went to the grocery store."

"For what?"

"To buy food, silly."

"Who's going to cook it?"

Her look was reproachful. "That's not funny."

"What were you guys talking about on the front porch?"

Savannah paused, then decided to level with them so there'd be no surprises later if things didn't pan out. "Whether or not this will work out."

"Mom, you can't be serious about staying," David said, leaning against the doorframe and looking every bit as petulant as the twins had when she'd taken their temperatures with a rectal thermometer. "Did you get a look at this town? There's nothing to do."

"I'm sure there's plenty to do once we get out and start meeting people. Let's give it a few days, okay? In the meantime, you two need to decide which bedroom you want."

"We get our own bedrooms?" Melody asked, speaking for the first time.

"Uh-huh." Savannah smiled. "Maybe later you can think about fixing them up just the way you want." She was probably making a mistake by building up her daughter's hopes, but she realized, at that moment, she would do or say anything to get the girl to smile.

David looked at his sister. "You can have first choice, Mel," he said.

Savannah watched quietly as the girl studied each room closely, then selected the one with an iron bed draped with a blue-and-white quilt. Pale sunlight filtered in through the open windows, warming a cozy window seat filled with throw pillows. Nearby, a pine bookcase was stuffed with books and piled high with old magazines.

"I love it," Melody said. "It's very peaceful. I'm going to get my stuff and start unpacking." She hurried out of the room, wearing an eager look.

David's mouth was hanging open. He looked at Savannah. "That's more than I've heard her say in two whole weeks. Wow!"

Savannah was equally thrilled. In fact, she felt very close to crying. "Maybe a change of scenery is what she needed," she said. She excused herself to check on the babies.

The twins felt cool when Savannah checked them a moment later. She left the room and went straight to the phone in the kitchen. She found Jessie's number and dialed. The woman answered on the first ring.

"I need to talk to you," Savannah said without preamble.

"What's wrong?" Jessie asked quickly. "Are the boys—?"

"No, they're fine. I'm the one who needs help."

"What's the matter, honey?" she asked.

"I need for you to teach me how to cook."

Jessie was quiet for a moment. "You don't know how to cook? Anything?"

"Oh, I can boil an egg or make toast," Savannah said, "but I haven't actually cooked a meal since—" She paused and tried to remember but couldn't. "I don't even know how to make coffee unless it's instant."

"You must know how to cook something," Jessie insisted. "What have you been feeding your children?"

"Frozen dinners." She explained how she had no time between jobs to come home and prepare meals, so she had Melody pop something into the oven. "I lived off fast food myself," she added.

"Riley hates frozen dinners and fast food," Jessie replied. "That's all Kara ever put on the table. These men work very hard all day, they need something substantial." She sighed into the phone, it was obvious she was upset. "Did you lie about everything in your letters and conversations with my brother-in-law?" she asked.

Savannah could hear the irritation in her voice and knew right away Jessie was very protective of Riley. "He never asked me if I could cook. He only cared about finding somebody who loved children. Which I do. I guess he just assumed I knew my way around the kitchen." She paused. "In all honesty, though, I suppose I would have lied had he asked. I was just that determined to get out of Nashville." She'd almost used the word desperate again, but pride kept her from doing so.

"Why were you so . . . determined?" Jessie asked, as though sensing there was more to it. "You weren't in trouble with the law or anything?"

"No, nothing like that. My children weren't safe. I was afraid for them."

Jessie was silent for a moment. When she spoke again, her tone was softer. "I have children, too, Savannah. I can understand a mother's need to protect them."

Savannah hesitated. "Then you'll help me?"

Another brief pause. "Riley likes to eat early, around six o'clock. I'll come by at four on the pretense of checking the twins. Do you know what he wants for dinner?"

"I have no idea. I just hope it's not something like fried chicken and gravy. The last time I tried to fry chicken I burned it so badly I set off the smoke alarm in my apartment as well as the one next door. And the gravy. Well—" She sighed. "We tried to flush it down the toilet and ended up calling a plumber."

"It's not so hard once you've done it a few times," Jessie assured her.

Savannah was about to say something else when she heard Riley's truck pull up beside the house. "He's here!" she whispered.

"Stay calm. I'll see you at four o'clock."

Savannah was wiping the kitchen counter down as Riley stepped inside carrying several large brown sacks. His hair was wind-tossed in a beguiling way that made her wish she knew him well enough to comb it back into place with her fingers. She called David to assist him in bringing in the rest of the groceries while she and Melody put the food away. She noticed several packages of lean hamburger meat, a turkey breast, a picnic ham, sliced bacon, and two chickens.

"I got the chickens for tonight," Riley said. "I hope you don't mind going to all the trouble of frying them. I'll even clean the kitchen afterward."

"You say you want them fried?" she said anxiously.

"If you don't mind. It'll be a real treat after all the frozen dinners I've eaten lately."

David chuckled and opened his mouth to speak, then, seeing the look on Savannah's face, kept quiet. Finally, when Riley went out for another load of bags, he grinned at his mother. "I can't wait to see how you're going to pull that one off," he said before he hurried out for another load.

The twins woke an hour later, as Savannah was folding laundry on the kitchen table and Riley was making phone calls. She followed him into the nursery to check on them. Once again the boys watched her with open curiosity.

"I think they look a little better, don't you?" he said.

She nodded. With their fevers down, their little cheeks weren't as red. Their coughs had subsided, thanks to the cough syrup. She picked up Trevor and carried him to the changing table. He was alert after his long nap; his blue eyes followed her every move. He whimpered briefly at being tended by a stranger, but Savannah soon had him smiling.

"I guess you weren't expecting to find things in such an uproar," Riley said, standing close by with Travis in his arms.

She glanced up. His smile was apologetic. She was vaguely aware of the scents surrounding her; warm baby smells of lotion and talcum powder and the tangy, woodsy fragrance of Riley's cologne. He was so close, she could see the tiny crinkles at his eyes, could see the rich brown shade of his irises. She noted he stared at her just as closely, and she immediately became flustered. She looked away.

"My life in Nashville was pretty hectic," she managed, deciding it was easier concentrating on the twins than their father. "I guess I'm used to it."

Once again, she glanced up at him briefly. He was still watching her curiously, as though wondering why any woman would want to take on the responsibility of an entire family. She thought he looked tired; the lines around his mouth were more pronounced than they'd been earlier. She suspected he was worried about getting his crop planted. He'd spent much of the afternoon on the phone trying to line up a crew.

"I appreciate your taking over so I could get some work done," Riley said at last. "You can imagine what it's like trying to take care of business with these guys under foot." He chuckled. "I call them my demolition crew."

Savannah laughed as well. "Yes, I'm sure these guys

could take a house apart quite nicely if left on their own for any length of time."

"Which is why everything's so bare around here," Riley said. "I used to have a lot of things sitting around, but I finally packed them up and put them in the attic."

"You'll be able to pull them out one day," she assured him.

He looked thoughtful. "Look, I've managed to scrape together enough workers for the planting," he said after a moment. "They'll be here first thing in the morning. I know we agreed on giving this, uh, situation a few days. I just wanted to make sure you would still be here tomorrow."

Savannah suspected it wasn't easy for him to ask for help, even from his sister-in-law, who seemed more than willing to assist. She could easily relate to that trait in him since she had always depended on herself for whatever she needed. Only in her case, there'd been no one else she could count on. "I'm not going anywhere in the immediate future," she said, and thought he looked relieved to hear it. She couldn't help but wonder how anxious he'd be for her to stay once he got his planting out of the way. "Would you happen to have a small pail I could fill with warm water?" she asked, changing the subject. "So I can sponge off the boys?"

"I'll be right back." He set Travis on the rug, handed him a toy, and hurried away. The boy's face seemed to crumple as though he were about to let out a cry of protest, then changed his mind abruptly as he became interested in the toy. Riley returned a moment later with a pail of water, then reached into the nearby cabinet for a soft washcloth and a bar of soap. "I don't usually let them go this long without a bath," he said. "But with them being sick and all—" He shrugged.

Savannah bathed Trevor first, taking care not to let him

get chilled. She dried him and put him in fresh pajamas while Riley went for clean water. Travis was next and seemed in no mood for a bath. He struggled and whimpered through it, despite all that Riley did to calm him. Savannah watched the boy grab on to his father's finger, and she marveled at the sight of the tiny white hand and the large brown one feathered with black hair. Riley stood uncomfortably close as she tended his son; it was all she could do to concentrate on the task at hand. Finally, when both boys were clean, they took them into the kitchen and fed them a late lunch and allowed them to play until it was time for their medicine. Before long, they were rubbing their eyes again and ready for another nap.

"Where are the others?" Riley asked once the twins had fallen asleep.

"David's listening to music, and Melody is reading."

"Do you believe it's almost four o'clock?" he said, rubbing the back of his neck.

"It is?" she asked, startled. Where had the day gone? "You look tired," she said, noting his weary expression. His eyes were red-rimmed with fatigue, and she remembered he hadn't slept much since the boys had taken ill. "Why don't you take a quick nap," she suggested. "I noticed a comfortable-looking recliner in the den."

"You wouldn't mind?" he asked hopefully. "I guess sitting up with the boys the last couple of nights has caught up with me." He disappeared inside the den a moment later.

It was almost four-thirty by the time Jessie slipped in through the back door with an armload of cookbooks. "Where's Riley?" she asked Savannah, who'd been pacing the floor waiting for her.

"Asleep in the den. He looked dead on his feet."

"I hope he doesn't end up sick." She shrugged out of

her sweater and draped it over the back of the chair. "Okay, what does he want for dinner?"

"You're not going to believe it." She pointed to the chickens on the sink that she'd washed.

Jessie opened a drawer, fumbled through it, and brought out two aprons. "Do you know how to cut up chicken for frying?" she asked.

"No."

Jessie shook her head sadly. "Oh, brother."

It was coming up to six o'clock when Riley opened his eyes to the smell of fried chicken. He raised up in the recliner and glanced around. It wasn't like him to take naps, and now he wished he hadn't. His head felt funny, as though stuffed with cotton. He got up and walked toward the kitchen, intent on a cup of coffee. He paused in the doorway and watched as Savannah and her children worked; David setting the table, Melody putting ice in glasses and filling them with tea. Savannah set a bowl of mashed potatoes on the table next to a plate of biscuits and a platter piled high with fried chicken. There were also green beans seasoned with bacon and onion, like Jessie made, and what appeared to be a squash casserole.

"Wow," he said, startling all three.

Savannah smiled at the sight of him. "How was your nap?"

"It left me feeling sort of groggy. You mind if I make a quick cup of coffee before we eat?"

"The coffee's already made. I'll pour you a cup while you wash up."

When Riley came out of the bathroom he found them already sitting at the table. A mug of coffee sat next to his plate. He sat down and raised it to his lips. He couldn't remember when he'd tasted better. They all seemed to be waiting for him to do something. "Is anything wrong?"

"I was going to have Melody say the blessing."

He nodded. "Sorry." He set his cup down, bowed his head, and waited for the girl to say grace. She had a pretty, clear-pitched voice. Afterward, he went back to sipping his coffee while the food was passed around. Oddly enough, he wasn't hungry, and he blamed his loss of appetite on exhaustion.

"Aren't you going to eat?" Savannah asked.

He met her gaze. She looked so hopeful. It was obvious she'd worked hard on the meal, and he hated to disappoint her. "Sure," he said, trying to sound enthusiastic. He accepted the bowl of mashed potatoes from David and dipped a hefty serving. By the time all the food came around, his plate was piled high. He felt his stomach revolt at the sight of it. The coffee wasn't sitting too well either. "Would ya'll excuse me?" he said. He left the table and hurried into the bathroom.

"Well, that's a fine how-do-you-do," David said. "You slave for two hours in his kitchen, and he takes one look at it and gets sick."

"I don't think Riley feels well," Savannah said. "Go ahead and eat your dinner."

David took a bite of his chicken. "This is great. When did you learn to cook?"

Savannah shot him a dark look. Finally, she got up and walked into the hall and knocked on the bathroom door. "Riley, are you okay?"

The door opened. He stood there looking wan and pale. "I'm sorry, but I don't think I'm going to be able to eat after all. I can't seem to hold anything in my stomach."

Savannah reached up and pressed her open palm against

his forehead. "You're hot as a pistol," she said. "Does your head hurt?"

He nodded. "Ever since I woke up from that nap."

"You've got the flu, Riley."

He shook his head. "I never get sick. Ever."

"Well, you're sick now, so you'd best get to bed so you can start getting better."

"I can't just go to bed," he said, his voice loud in protest. "I've got work to do. And a crew coming tomorrow. Not only that, there's the twins."

"I can take care of the twins." She prodded him toward the stairs. "I think you'd better sleep in my room so I can be close to them tonight."

He looked anxious and more than a little frustrated at the thought of someone sending him to bed and taking over his job. "I don't know," he said.

"Where do you keep your pajamas?" she asked.

"I don't—" He paused and looked at her. "I don't wear pajamas. I don't even own any."

She nodded but refused to let her mind wander. "Okay, go ahead and get in the bed, and I'll bring up something for your headache."

He turned for the stairs. Savannah heard him trudge up slowly as she made her way back toward the kitchen.

"What's wrong?" David asked as she filled a glass with water. She'd noticed headache medicine in the bathroom earlier. She'd grab it on her way back.

"Riley's got the flu."

"Oh, great. I guess that means you're expected to keep his house, care for his children, and nurse him."

"I'm getting tired of your negative attitude," she said. "I'm sure he didn't get sick on purpose. But since you're so worried about me, you and your sister can put the food away and clean the kitchen for me."

"Mom!" he protested loudly. "I've been working all day."

She paused at the door. "I'm disappointed in you, David. You whine as much as those babies in the next room."

THREE

When Riley opened his eyes the next morning, he noted the sun was already high. The planters! He bolted upright in the bed, and his head seemed to explode with the effort, sending needles of intense pain into his eyeballs. It reminded him of the time he and Ben had gotten their hands on a bottle of corn liquor in high school. Naturally, they'd gotten caught, and their parents made them do ten hours worth of chores the next day, despite the fact they were so hung over, they could barely move. Riley suspected that's why he and Ben didn't drink on a regular basis now.

He tried to edge off the mattress without causing further agony. He succeeded in swinging his legs over the side. The floor felt cold under his feet. He shivered and looked longingly toward the warm covers.

"Oh, no, you don't," Savannah said from the doorway as she carried in a tray. She paused slightly when she saw he wore only his underwear. She glanced away quickly, but not before she caught sight of a broad, slightly muscular chest feathered with black hair and an otherwise tempting male physique. "You're sick, Riley, so you might as well climb right back in that bed."

"What time is it?" he asked, trying to cover himself with a quilt. The mini explosions in his head had stopped, but the room seemed to sway as though he were traveling on some seafaring vessel.

"Nine o'clock."

"Nine o'clock! And you let me sleep—" He started to get up again, then remembered how he was dressed. He didn't have a modest bone in his body, but he suspected that wasn't the case with the woman before him. Not only that, he feared he'd throw up if he moved too quickly.

"I called your brother first thing this morning," Savannah said, "and he was here bright and early to get everything started. He's supervising the crew now."

"You called Ben?" he asked in amazement, and was suddenly caught up in a fit of coughing. His throat felt like someone had done a jig in it wearing steel spikes on their feet.

"That's right. He said you'd be madder than a hornet, seeing how stubborn you are about asking for help, but I told him that was just too bad. So you might as well lie back in that bed, because, believe it or not, the world is getting along just fine without you."

Riley frowned. He didn't know what to make of her, and he wasn't used to being told what to do. "You're quite the little spitfire this morning, aren't you?" he said irritably.

He watched her set the tray on a nearby dresser. She was wearing snug jeans, a simple pullover blouse, and white sneakers. Her blond hair was pulled back in a short ponytail that made her look more like a schoolgirl than the mother of teenagers.

"I just did what needed doing, that's all. I also phoned the doctor, and he's called in a prescription. They're calling this flu thing an epidemic now, you know. There's been outbreaks in Macon and Atlanta, and as far south as Jacksonville. Anyway, Jessie's going to drop your medicine by this morning. You still have that headache?" she asked.

He debated answering her. Who did she think she was, barging into his life with those fanny-hugging britches and taking over his farm operation? Wasn't it bad enough she'd shown up two weeks early bearing a couple of sullen teenagers? Now, she acted like she owned the place. What irked him further was the fact that he couldn't do a damn thing about it at the moment. He was too sick to lift his head much less run a household and a farm.

"Excuse me," Savannah said, noting his thoughtful expression, which was more of a scowl actually, and wondering what he was thinking. "I was asking if your head hurt this morning."

"Only when I breathe."

She could see he wasn't going to be an easy patient. "Take this." She handed him a glass of orange juice and two aspirin.

Riley accepted it gratefully despite his sour mood. His mouth was as dry as processed hay. But when he popped the pills into his mouth and took a sip of the juice, he winced at the rawness in his throat.

"You didn't sleep very well last night, did you?" she asked gently.

He tossed her a suspicious look. "How'd you know?" He had visions of her snooping around his bedroom as he slept.

"I could hear you coughing from downstairs. I looked for cough medicine but didn't find anything."

He felt a twinge of guilt for being so distrustful of her when it was obvious she only wanted to help. But it wasn't easy sitting there with a pounding head and aching muscles and having to look at her, all fresh and pretty and downright sexy, if he were to admit the truth. He felt his body stir and was amazed that he could be next to dying and still have urges. "Where are the twins?" he asked, deciding it was easier on his libido if he concentrated on his sons instead of her jutting breasts and narrow waist in a close-fitting blouse.

"Napping. They played for a while after breakfast, but dozed off shortly after I gave them their medicine. Dr. Henly says sleep is the best thing for them right now." She smiled. "I think they're getting used to me."

He nodded, then wished he hadn't when an arrow of pain shot through his temples. He realized he was frowning. This was not how he'd imagined Savannah's first days in his home. Unfortunately, nothing was turning out the way he planned, and the two of them were stuck with each other until he was better.

On the other hand, he wouldn't have blamed her for turning around and running, fast as she could, in the opposite direction. If he was disappointed, think how she must feel. She had shown up at his front door, and he'd welcomed her with the same enthusiasm he would a summer drought. It wasn't her fault he felt as if he'd been run over by his own tractor. He told himself he would be nicer until they decided what to do. Even if it meant going their separate ways. He hated thinking along those lines, especially with her being so nice and easy on the eyes, but he couldn't sit by and let them both make what might possibly be the biggest mistake of their lives.

Savannah felt the tension in the air. "You didn't tell me you had a pregnant cat," she said, trying to make conversation with him.

He shrugged, and his head hurt from the simple movement. "Must've slipped my mind."

"She had her kittens last night. Melody was touring the barn this morning and found several of them hidden in different locations. She and David are out there now searching in case there are more. By the way, they saw the horses in the pasture and wanted to know if it was okay to give them a carrot. I told them to wait until I found out if they were gentle."

Riley wished he didn't have to talk so much. He couldn't remember ever feeling so worn down. "They're gentle enough, I suppose, but they've gotten a bit skittish since nobody's ridden them in the last year." He paused. "They belonged to my wife. I don't have anything to do with them except feed them. I don't mind if they try to pet the horses as long as they don't get behind them. Even the most gentle horses kick from time to time."

"I'll be sure to mention it to them. I brought you some toast and tea," she said. "Do you think you could eat something this morning? You didn't have any dinner last night."

He shook his head and offered her the closest thing to a smile he had. "Maybe later, after this headache goes away."

"I'll bring the medicine up as soon as Jessie gets here." She started for the door.

"Savannah?"

She paused and looked at him questioningly.

"Look, I don't know what the future holds for us, but—" He paused. "You've been a big help."

She smiled prettily. "That's why I'm here."

He wondered at her remark. Did she think he was only looking for someone to perform chores and baby-sit? If so, she was sorely wrong. True, he wanted a good mother for his children, but he longed for someone to fill that empty side of his bed as well. He'd lost his wife over a year before. He thought he'd handled it well; then, she had shown up at his door and reminded him just how long the year had been.

"Riley?"

He blinked. Had he been staring at her all that time? "Huh?"

"Is there anything else you need?"

Her light brown eyebrows were arched in expectation, her compact body poised and ready to assist him in any way. Her lips were . . . full. He was tempted to tell her she could kiss all the achy parts of his body. But he wouldn't, of course. She would probably dump that cup of tea right on the spot that ailed him the most.

Besides, it wasn't right thinking along those lines when one part of him was thinking about getting rid of her. "I just need to sleep for a while," he said, feeling weary after all his pondering about her lips and body.

"Okay, I'll check on you later."

She left him then, and he felt she'd taken some of the sunlight streaming through the window with her. He told himself he was being silly; the sun had simply slipped behind a cloud.

Riley was sound asleep when he felt someone nudge him gently. He opened his eyes and found Jessie and Savannah standing beside the bed. "Hi, Slugger," Jessie said. "I hear you've got the flu. I guess that means you're not as tough as you think you are."

Riley could feel his head pounding so he didn't try to raise up. "Is that supposed to make me feel better?"

"No, but Savannah has something that might." She motioned to the woman beside her who held a couple of plastic prescription containers and a bottle of cough medicine.

"Do you think you can sit up?" Savannah asked.

Riley did as she'd asked. "Feels like my head is coming off."

Jessie grinned. "That's how come we know it's the flu, honeykins. Otherwise we might end up treating you for hemorrhoids or something."

Riley scowled. He didn't see anything funny about being flat on his back. "Where's Ben?"

"Your brother says he's not coming anywhere near this place till everybody gets well."

"Aren't either of you worried about catching it?"

Jessie shook her head as Savannah gave him a couple of pills and offered him water to swallow them with. "I take a flu shot every year, remember? Of course you do, because you and Ben make fun of me."

"I took one this year as well," Savannah said. "They offered them free at work." She poured cough medicine into a spoon and held it to Riley's mouth. He took it, then lay back on the bed, already exhausted by the small effort.

"By the way," Jessie said, dropping a bag onto his lap. "I brought a pair of Ben's pajamas over so poor Savannah doesn't have to close her eyes every time she comes into the room."

"Thanks." he mumbled, wondering if Savannah had complained to Jessie that he slept in his underwear. "Are the boys doing okay?" he asked.

Savannah started to answer, but Jessie cut her off. "They couldn't be better. Savannah is managing perfectly, although I fear she'll spoil them rotten by the time you're up and around. Which is exactly what the little dears need," she added. "She even made a big pot of chicken noodle soup for you."

Riley regarded the other woman who, for some reason, was blushing. "I wish you wouldn't go to so much trouble," he said. "If you can just see to the boys while I'm sick, that's really all I ask. I can call somebody to come over and clean."

His expression was so earnest that Savannah felt guilty for taking credit for the soup. Jessie had made it the night before when she'd called to see how dinner went and had learned Riley wasn't feeling well. She'd figured he'd managed to pick up the bug that half the folks in town had. "It's no trouble," she said at last. "I'll bring you a bowl in a bit."

A moment later, Savannah faced Jessie in the kitchen. "I can't keep lying to him," she said. "I feel so guilty."

"Just remember it's for a good cause," Jessie said. "He needs a wife and you need a husband. And there are four children who need parents."

"Yes, but we can't keep up this game. What are you supposed to do, drop by every afternoon on the pretense of seeing the boys so you can cook dinner for me?"

"I'm not going to cook it for you. I'm going to teach you. Have you ever had cooking lessons?"

"The answer to that should be obvious."

Jessie reached into a cabinet and pulled out the cookbooks she'd brought with her the day before. "Okay, first we need to talk about food measurements. You can study them in your spare time, but remember, they're very important when following recipes." She turned to the back of one of her cookbooks and showed Savannah the page.

"I'm supposed to memorize all that?" she said doubtfully.

"Not necessarily, but you do need to know where to look for the information." Once Savannah had studied the page briefly, Jessie turned to the front of the book. "Let's discuss cuts of beef, shall we?"

By lunchtime they were ready to prepare a pot roast. While Jessie sipped a cup of coffee on a tall stool beside the counter, Savannah gathered all the ingredients she would need. She put the roast into a Dutch oven to brown, then, hearing noise from the twins' room, turned off the burner and hurried in that direction. Both boys were standing in their cribs. They didn't look thrilled to see her, yet, they both smiled brightly when they saw their aunt.

"Don't worry, they'll get used to you," Jessie told Savannah. "Once that happens they won't let you put them down."

"They may not get the chance to get used to me," Savannah told her, then explained how reluctant Riley was to take on her own children.

Jessie looked sad. "My brother-in-law has a heart of gold, honey. He's not trying to be selfish. It's just—" She paused. "When Kara died, everything was sort of dumped in his lap at once. It hasn't been easy." She was thoughtful. "Maybe he's afraid your children won't like it way out here. Kara complained bitterly about it. She wanted to move to town, and to tell you the truth, Riley would've been glad to see her go if it weren't for the babies. From what I understand, Kara was moving out the night she died. Without the twins," she added on a whisper.

"How did she die?"

"Her car went off a bridge. She was angry at Riley and going much too fast. It'd been raining for days so everything was slick." She paused and looked regretful. "It was a terrible time. Riley blamed himself, naturally, for letting her go out in that weather. And because they'd argued earlier."

"He must've loved her a lot," Savannah said, surprised at the twinge of jealousy she felt over it.

Jessie picked up Travis and carried him to the changing table. "If only you could have seen her. She was absolutely one of the most stunning creatures I've ever laid eyes on. Riley adored her in the beginning, buying her lavish gifts, including that fancy Jaguar she was driving the night she died. But Kara got tired of playing house and living so far away from the city, and that's when the trouble began. Riley couldn't just pick up and move; this land has been in his family for years. Then she got pregnant, and it was all downhill after that."

"No wonder he isn't eager to get involved in another relationship."

Jessie looked sad. "Perhaps I shouldn't have pushed him to run that ad. But I was thinking of my nephews. I didn't want them spending the rest of their lives with baby-sitters. They need a mother. I figured by running that ad, Riley could find just the sort of woman he wanted."

Savannah looked equally dejected. "And here I show up with two teenagers, and I can't cook worth a flip." She sighed. "I should probably leave."

"Oh, no, you don't," Jessie said. "Now that you're here, I want you to hang around and see if anything can come of this. I'll never get Riley to agree to another ad. Besides, I handpicked you, so naturally I'd like to see it succeed."

"You picked me?"

"Riley didn't have time to answer all those letters. Lord, there were hundreds of them. So I picked the best of the lot and passed them on to him. He saw your picture, tucked it into his shirt pocket, and said he'd take care of the rest." She put Travis on the rug and went for his brother.

Savannah stood there, waiting to hear more. "That's all he said?" she asked.

Jessie glanced over her shoulder. "Yep."

By the time Jessie went home, Savannah had put the vegetables in the pot with the roast and had the boys playing on the rug on the kitchen floor. She asked Melody to watch them while she carried a tray upstairs. Riley was sleeping. He opened his eyes when she set the tray on the dresser. "How do you feel?" she asked.

"Like hell."

"Maybe this soup will help. First, though, you'd better take your medicine."

"Are they still working out there?" Riley asked.

"Yes, Ben is seeing to everything. You needn't worry."

Riley didn't miss the crispness of her tone or the fact

that she wasn't smiling. "What's the matter?" he said. "Are the boys giving you a hard time?"

"No, they're fine." She offered him a tablespoon of his cough medicine. He took it dutifully, but his brown eyes were watchful.

"Something's wrong," he said. "You're upset."

She didn't answer.

"Savannah?"

She paused and looked at him. The pajama shirt had come partially unbuttoned in his sleep, exposing a wide portion of his chest. He'd kicked the covers off, and the pants legs strained against his powerful thighs. Even in sickness, Riley Locke struck an imposing figure. "I shouldn't bring this up while you're sick," she said.

"Bring what up?"

She folded her arms across her chest. "I'm curious. What made you choose me out of all those women?"

So that was it. He shrugged. "I suppose I liked the way you looked."

Savannah knew this wasn't the time to discuss it, but she had to know. "Surely there were prettier women."

"I wasn't looking for pretty." He saw her frown. "That's not what I meant, dammit. Of course you're pretty, but I was looking for more." His gaze locked with hers. "Your eyes—" Even in her photograph he could see they were the eyes of a kind, loving soul. He wanted someone who could love his twins as much as he did. "I had to think of my boys," he said at last.

"So, basically, you were looking for a good mother and nothing more."

"I didn't say that. But my first concern had to be my sons. I wanted to find somebody who would raise them as her own. Like Jessie said, I couldn't have baby-sitters doing it. You have children, you should be able to relate to what I was feeling."

"Would you have gone along with this had your sister-in-law not pushed you into it?"

"Jessie talks too much." He sighed and raked his hands through his hair. "Probably not. I thought it an odd way to get a wife." He looked thoughtful. "But you sounded so nice over the phone. And your letters seemed sincere."

"You're squinting. Your head hurts, doesn't it?"

"Feels like somebody threw a brick at me in my sleep." He chuckled. "You?"

She smiled. "No, even though it might have crossed my mind." She opened the bottle of aspirin and dumped two in her palm, then grabbed the glass of juice on the tray and offered him both. "I shouldn't have brought it up while you're feeling so bad."

He took the pills and juice, noting how small her hand was next to his. He wondered how those hands would feel on his body, stroking and caressing him in places that had hungered too long for a woman's touch. He pushed the thought out of his mind as he popped the aspirin into his mouth and drank. Lying around had obviously given him too much time to think. Finally, he handed her the empty glass. "How do you feel about being here, Savannah?"

She didn't hesitate. "I'm uneasy if you want to know the truth. How do I know you won't send me packing as soon as you're on your feet?"

He lay back on the bed and gazed at the ceiling. "How do I know you won't walk out on me while I'm flat on my back?"

"I wouldn't do that," she said softly. She avoided looking at him as she returned the glass to the tray and lifted his bowl of soup. She set it on the night table in case he got hungry. "I have to go," she said, remembering she'd left Melody with the twins. She started for the door.

"Savannah?"

She paused. "If you want to take a break, go into town

or something, Jessie's good about watching the boys. I don't want you to feel stuck out here."

She shrugged. "Who says I feel stuck?"

Ben Locke looked very much like his younger brother except he was a few pounds heavier and his hair had more gray at the temples. Savannah noticed the resemblance as the tall man sipped a cup of coffee on the back porch. Although she'd met him briefly when he'd arrived that morning, she hadn't had the opportunity to get acquainted. Now, as she tried to coax him inside the kitchen, he refused the invitation, stating he had no desire to catch what was going around.

"So how's my little brother?" he asked Savannah as he finished his coffee and handed her the empty cup. "Think he'll live?"

"He's a bit on the moody side," she told him.

Ben chuckled. "Riley never has been what you'd call your ideal patient. I remember when we were kids and we'd get a bad cold, I was perfectly happy to lie on the couch and watch cartoons, but Riley would have none of that. The only way my mother managed to keep him still was to give him a teaspoon of paregoric."

"You're welcome to go up and see for yourself how he's doing," she teased.

"No thanks." He pushed open the screen door, then paused. "By the way, your kids asked about those horses out in the pasture—"

Savannah was instantly concerned. "I hope they're not getting in the way."

"No, nothing like that. I was just wondering. If you wouldn't mind, I could send my oldest boy over here, and he could teach them to ride. Give them something to do over spring break."

"Teach them to ride?" The way she said it you'd have thought he'd just suggested they do something illegal. "I don't know, Ben. My children have never been around horses. They don't know the first thing about them."

"Which is all the more reason to get Sam over here. He knows everything there is to know."

Savannah gazed thoughtfully out the window where David and Melody had stood by the pasture gate all morning. "I guess it wouldn't hurt. As long as they're careful."

Savannah heard a squeal from one of the twins and peeked inside to see what was going on. The boys were in the midst of a tug-of-war over a stuffed dog. "Well, I'd better get back inside," she said. "Otherwise, I'll be sweeping up stuffing the rest of the afternoon."

Ben chuckled. "Don't let 'em wear you out, Savannah," he said, then hurried back to his own work.

Riley didn't look any better when Savannah carried up the tray that evening bearing chicken noodle soup and crackers. He'd taken off his pajama shirt and had kicked the covers away. Savannah noted the sheen of perspiration on his forehead when she set the tray down. She hurried over to the bed and placed her hand against his forehead. He opened his eyes.

"Sorry for the mess," he said. "I was burning up."

"You're still burning up," she told him, going into the bathroom for a cloth. She wet it and returned a moment later. She pressed it against his cheeks and finally laid it on his forehead. His normally ruddy complexion was tinged bright red as though he had a sunburn. She filled his glass with water, and he drank gratefully. She pulled the covers over him. "I'll need to take your temperature." she said.

Riley remembered how she'd taken the babies' temperatures and looked anxious. "Oh, no, you don't."

Savannah realized what he must be thinking and stifled

the urge to laugh. "Oh, yes, I do. Do you have a thermometer around here for adults?" she asked.

He looked relieved and shook his head with eyes closed. "I couldn't say. I don't remember the last time I had to take my temperature." Finally, he opened his eyes. "I'll be okay. I just need to sweat this out. I don't feel much like eating right now, though."

Savannah sat on the edge of the bed, watching him, gnawing her bottom lip. He looked so big and virile, even flat on his back. It was hard to believe a simple virus was capable of bringing him to his knees, so to speak. "I should probably call the doctor," she said.

"Don't do that. Doc Henly's got more than he can handle right now." Riley reached over, grasped her hand, and squeezed it. "You're a good nurse, Savannah, but you worry too much."

She didn't quite know what to do about the fact that he was holding her hand. She could feel the strength in him, the power, but his touch was surprisingly gentle. She met his gaze; his eyes were bright with fever. "I've always been a worrier," she confessed. "It comes with being a mother, I suppose."

"Well, as long as you don't start thinking of me as your son, we'll get along fine."

She wasn't really listening. "You bought ice cream yesterday, didn't you?" she said.

The abrupt change in subject confused him. "Uh-huh."

She stood and reluctantly pulled her hand from his. "I'm going to run downstairs and get you a bowl. It'll help bring your fever down."

"I'm not really in the mood for ice cream," he mumbled.

She was almost at the door. "Tough."

Savannah was back in no time, having checked on the twins, who were now playing in a kiddie corral she'd found in a downstairs closet. They were good about entertaining each other except when one had a toy the other one wanted, then all hell broke loose. She'd thrown enough toys in so, hopefully, it would be a while before they reached that point.

Riley opened his eyes once more when she sat on the edge of the bed. She had to scoot closer in order to feed it to him. She took the linen napkin she'd brought and draped it across his chest. "I wish you hadn't taken off your shirt," she said.

He chuckled. "Why, because you can't seem to keep your eyes off of me?"

Her eyes flew to his, and she almost dropped the bowl. She could feel the blush that tinged her cheeks. The look in his eyes was hard to read; she didn't know if he was joking or not. "Well, no," she managed. "I just don't want to see you get chilled."

"And here I thought I was beginning to turn you on."

The heat spread. "Open your mouth, Riley," she said, all business now. "If you have to go to the hospital, they'll pack you in ice, you know." He took the spoon of ice cream and swallowed it, wincing slightly. "Throat sore?" she asked.

"Only when I swallow. Hell, yeah, it's sore," he added irritably.

She fed him another bite. "Are you always this much fun when you run a fever?"

"I dunno. Like I said, I don't get sick much."

"Well, you're sick now. Are you sure you don't know where I can find a thermometer?"

He shrugged. "My . . . uh . . . Kara kept up with that kind of stuff."

"Are you in the mood for a sponge bath?" she asked, grabbing the cloth from his head which had since turned warm.

"Not especially. Are you?"

She chose to ignore the question. "Riley, you're going to have to let me cool you down with a cloth, otherwise I'll have no choice but to stick you in a cool tub." Even as she said it she realized how ridiculous it sounded. The man was at least twice her size; unless he went willingly, there was no way she was going to force him into a bathtub. "Don't move," she said, using an authoritative tone and knowing he had to think she was in charge whether that was really the case or not. "I'll be right back."

"Look, I just want to be left alone, okay?" He saw that he was talking to empty air. She was already gone.

When Savannah returned, she was carrying the pail she'd used to bathe the twins as well as a sponge and a couple of large towels. She'd called Melody in to keep an eye on the boys since she had no idea how long she'd be. "I phoned Jessie. She's bringing a thermometer over. Good thing she lives close."

Riley opened his eyes and shook his head with effort. "See I told you you worry too much."

She put the bucket on the rug and stood there for a moment, gazing down at the man and wondering how she was ever going to do what needed to be done. "Okay, Riley, I don't know any other way to say this, but you're going to have to let me give you a bath."

FOUR

At first he thought he'd misunderstood, then decided she was teasing. But he took one look at her face and knew she was as serious as a two-alarm fire. He noted the pail and towels. She was going to give him a bath? The same woman who'd complained when he took off his shirt and who was probably responsible for Jessie bringing those pajamas. Had he not felt so damn bad he might find her idea of a bath amusing.

"I don't have the energy, Savannah," he said tiredly. "Just let me rest. Tomorrow, I'll be good as new."

Savannah heard footsteps on the stairs. A moment later, Jessie came into the room. The redhead looked concerned. She pulled a thermometer out of her purse and ordered Riley to open his mouth. She popped it in, then pressed her hand against his forehead. "He's hot as a woodstove. What can I do?"

"Help me get him out of these pajamas so I can sponge him down," Savannah said, pulling the covers to the foot of the bed.

Riley grumbled but did his best to help. Savannah draped a towel over his white underwear, then, with Jessie's help managed to put the other towels beneath him. Jessie reached for the thermometer. "One hundred and two," she said gravely.

"I'll bet it was higher than that before I fed him the ice cream," Savannah said, then wondered if he'd held her hand because he'd been delirious.

Savannah dipped the sponge into the pail of cool water and started bathing Riley's forehead before moving to his face and neck. She couldn't help but note the subtle sensuality in his features. His beard had grown during the night, darkening his jaw and giving him a rakish air. She tried not to notice. She failed miserably. She moved the cloth to his shoulders, and he started to object. "I don't want—"

"Hush, Riley," Jessie told him. "You either let Savannah do it, or you go to the emergency room." She looked up sharply. "Did I just hear one of the twins?"

"One probably has something the other one wants," Savannah said. "Melody's with them, but she's sort of new at this."

"Well, it's getting close to their bedtime. I'll go ahead and start cleaning them up. Call me if you need me." Jessie started for the door. "Riley, you behave yourself, you hear?"

Savannah would have preferred his sister-in-law stay and she go. There was something totally disconcerting about sponge-bathing an almost-naked man whom she'd known only a couple of days, especially when that man had the broadest chest and shoulders she'd ever seen. As she ran the sponge across Riley's chest, his brown nipples hardened. Her stomach dipped and fluttered in response. Goose pimples popped out across his hard, flat belly, and she raised apologetic eyes to his. "I'm sorry I have to do this," she said.

Riley sucked his breath in sharply as she ran the sponge along the waistband of his underwear. He realized when he'd fantasized about her hands on his body, this wasn't exactly what he'd had in mind. "I figured you were just trying to get even," he said.

She paused. "For what?"

He shrugged. "For my acting so gruff when you and your children first arrived. Not much of a welcome, was it?"

She turned back to her work. "I understand your reluctance, believe me. Teenagers aren't easy."

"It's not fair, though, is it? After all, my twins will be teenagers one day."

"Try to rest, Riley. We can talk about this later."

He smiled through chattering teeth, and she decided he was much better looking when he wasn't making that serious expression he always wore. "I can't rest when somebody's hosing me down with ice water."

She returned the smile. "I didn't put ice in it. It just feels that way because you're so hot." She moved to his legs. They were long and solid and slightly muscular, and sexy, too, if she let herself consider it. Not that it was easy to ignore. Unless maybe she was a seventy-year-old nun with poor eyesight. She started bathing his thighs, taking care not to move too close to the juncture covered by the towel. She could feel the power in them, the strength. He was clearly a man used to physical labor. She moved to his knees and calves, then his feet. They were well-shaped, feathered with hair; the soles tough as rawhide. Finally, she changed the water and started over.

"How many times are you going to do this?" Riley asked.

"As often as it takes."

He didn't look happy to hear it. "Know what I think?" he said. "I think you like doing it."

Savannah glanced up sharply, then, seeing the amused look on his face, realized he was joking. "Know what I think?" she replied, smiling at him. "I think you flatter yourself unduly."

When Savannah took his temperature a little later, it had already dropped two degrees. With his help, she managed to pull the towels from beneath him. They were damp, but the sheets were completely dry. She covered him. "Okay, I'm going to leave you alone for now so you can rest."

Riley looked relieved as he closed his eyes and fell into an exhausted sleep.

Savannah carried the pail downstairs and found Jessie entertaining the twins in their room. Both were dressed in Disney character pajamas with feet in them. David and Melody were in the den watching a funny sitcom on TV.

"How is he?" Jessie asked when Savannah walked into the nursery.

"Temperature is down to one hundred. I'll take it again in a bit."

"You look dead on your feet," Jessie said. "Why don't you take a break, and I'll make you a fresh cup of coffee."

Savannah slumped into a rocking chair. "It's been a long day."

"Well, I'll have to say the boys are looking better. You, on the other hand, look like something the cat would think twice about dragging in." She paused. "Instead of having coffee, why don't you take a little nap?"

"You can use my room, Mom."

Savannah looked up and found Melody standing in the doorway. "Hi, honey. Thanks for watching the boys earlier. Did you enjoy your day with the horses?"

The girl nodded, even came close to smiling. "Jessie's son is going to teach us to ride tomorrow. He's super nice, and he knows just about everything there is to know about horses. Why don't you lie down in my room for a while?" she suggested once more. "It's quiet up there."

They managed to convince her. Savannah went upstairs, checked on Riley, then crossed the hall to her daughter's room. Melody was already inside pulling the covers down for her. Savannah sat on the edge of the bed, kicked her shoes off and mumbled a word of thanks when she was covered by a thick quilt.

The room was pitch-black when Savannah opened her eyes again, and she automatically glanced at the alarm clock on the night table. It was after midnight; she'd slept five hours uninterrupted. Why hadn't Jessie wakened her? She bolted from the bed and hurried across to where Riley slept, stubbing her toe once in the dark. Luckily, someone had left the bathroom light on and the door cracked. Jessie, no doubt. Savannah placed her hand on Riley's forehead and found it cool.

He opened his eyes. "Hi."

"Hi, yourself."

"What time is it?"

"Few minutes after twelve. Midnight," she added when she noted how disoriented he looked. "How do you feel?"

"Not too bad. A bit woozy. I was just dreaming about you."

"Me?" She didn't try to hide her surprise.

"I dreamed you were giving me a bath."

"Actually, I did sort of give you a bath earlier. To break your fever."

"I remember now. It wasn't a dream. Why aren't you in bed?"

There was something decidedly intimate about holding a conversation with a man in a darkened bedroom. Especially since that man had discarded his pajama top and kicked the covers aside again.

"I just took a long nap," she said, determined to start paying more attention to his health than his body. "You're due your medicine." She reached for the prescription bottle on a nearby dresser and poured him fresh water. "Do you think you could eat something?"

"I'll eat tomorrow. Just give me the medicine so you can go back to bed."

When Savannah arrived downstairs a moment later, she found the twins asleep and Melody snuggled beneath the covers in the room beside theirs. She smiled. Jessie had obviously decided to let Melody sleep in the room next to the nursery so Savannah could rest uninterrupted. Instead of waking her daughter, Savannah very quietly slipped into her gown, grabbed a blanket, and headed for the den and the overstuffed couch.

Savannah was awakened the next morning by a gentle nudging.

"Mom?"

She resisted, sinking deeper beneath the covers. The nudging persisted.

"Mom, please wake up!" Melody cried.

Savannah opened her eyes. Two facts were readily apparent: It was late, and her daughter was in a panic. She bolted upright on the sofa, coming wide awake in the process. "What is it, Mel?" she demanded.

"The twins. I'm afraid I—"

Savannah was off the couch and running. Her shoulder slammed against the doorframe on her way out; pain radiated along that side of her body. She didn't have time to worry about it. In the kitchen, she found the twins dragging Tupperware from a cabinet. They grinned when they saw her. Other than the fact that their noses were running, they looked perfectly fine.

She turned to her daughter, mouth gaping, arms akimbo. "What's wrong?" she all but shouted. "They look okay to me."

Melody gave her a funny look. "They're not hurt. Is that what you thought?"

Savannah went weak with relief. "It crossed my mind, Melody."

"It's even worse than that."

She was ready to shake the girl. "What is it?"

Melody suddenly burst into tears. "Well, I saw you sleeping in there, and you looked so comfortable, and I didn't want to wake you—"

"Go on, go on," Savannah said frantically.

"So I decided to feed and bathe the boys. I was very careful with them in the tub the way you showed me."

"Melody, get to the point, please."

"I took off their bracelets when I put them in the tub, and I forgot which bracelet went with what boy."

"Oh, jeez, is that all?"

The girl looked confused. "Don't you realize what this means? We can't tell them apart. I called them each by name but they both just looked at me."

"I'm sure there are one or two differences between the boys. Riley will know."

Melody grabbed her mother's sleeve. "Please don't tell him, Mom. He'll think I'm a retard. I don't even think he likes me."

Savannah ruffled her daughter's hair. "Of course he likes you, honey. He's just not feeling well. Give him time."

"Please don't tell him." Her tears stopped, and she perked suddenly. "I'll bet Aunt Jessie knows which twin is which. Call her."

They heard a noise overhead and decided it was coming from the bedroom where Riley slept. "Where are the bracelets now?" Savannah asked.

"Still in the bathroom."

"Okay, go get them and put them on the boys. It

doesn't matter if they're mixed up for a little while. I'll try to contact Jessie."

Melody hurried away. She was gone less than a minute. She handed one of the bracelets to her mother. Footsteps on the stairs made them look up. "We have to hurry," Savannah whispered, going to one of the twins and reaching for a chubby arm. Neither boy was in the mood to stand still, but they managed to get the colored bands on their wrists, just as Riley walked through the door. Mother and daughter stared at him silently for a moment, looking at him as though he were something that had just crawled out of a black hole.

"What's the matter?" he asked.

"Why aren't you in bed?" Savannah demanded, thinking he still looked like he belonged in ICU. Riley spoke to both boys and tousled their hair. The twins grinned up at him, then continued with their play. Savannah and Melody held their breaths.

Without a second look at the boys, he said, "I had to get up and see what the rest of the world was up to."

"What do you take in your coffee, Mr. Locke?" Melody asked anxiously.

"Call me Riley," he said. "Just black on the coffee, thanks." He glanced at Savannah. "Do we have any aspirin down here?"

Before Savannah could make a move, Melody grabbed a small bottle from the windowsill and filled a glass with water. She carried it to him, and he thanked her. Then, she carried two steaming mugs to the table. "Drink your coffee, Mom," she said. "I'll just take the boys into their room so you and Riley can have some peace." The girl gave her mother a conspiratorial wink as she ushered them out. It was obvious she wanted to get the boys away before Riley discovered the mix-up.

Riley swallowed the aspirin and sat quietly for a moment, willing it to take effect. He was already beginning to wish he'd never gotten out of bed; the thought of climbing the stairs made him tired.

"What's wrong with Melody?" he asked after a moment. "She seems awfully nervous this morning."

Savannah set her coffee cup down gently. "Oh, just typical teenage girl stuff," she said lightly. "No need to worry. But I *am* worried about you," she said. "You'd better get back into bed before you get worse." Not only was she worried about his health, she was anxious to call Jessie. She couldn't very well do it with him sitting there.

Riley was about to tell her he couldn't get any worse, but a noise in the hall made him pause. He glanced up as David slinked into the room looking at odds with the world. "Is breakfast ready?" he said, without bothering to wish anybody a good morning.

"Not yet," Savannah told him. "Make a cup of cocoa. I'll cook once I've had my coffee." She noted his look of displeasure. "If you're too hungry to wait, there's always cold cereal. Riley bought several boxes at the store." She pointed to a cabinet, and David went to it.

He moaned when he saw what the choices were. "Oh, man, didn't he buy any *good* cereal?"

It irritated Riley the way the boy talked as though he wasn't even in the room. "I bought three different kinds," he said calmly. "I figured that would offer enough of a selection."

David closed the cabinet hard enough to make Savannah jump. "I'm going back to bed," he said. "Wake me when there's something good to eat."

Savannah kept her gaze fixed on her coffee cup. She could feel the color in her cheeks and didn't want Riley to see how embarrassed she was.

"Are you just going to let him get away with that?" he said.

She could feel his gaze on her, but she refused to meet it. "David's always been moody in the morning. I try to ignore it."

"Gee, I don't see how that's possible, what with all that stomping and slamming."

She finally looked at him. "He didn't actually slam the cabinet," she said. "It probably just sounded that way because of your headache. Your sons will slam a few doors one day, Riley. Mark my word."

He felt too bad to argue with her at the moment so he let it drop. Nevertheless, he knew he would never tolerate such behavior from his twins. Instead of saying as much, though, he stood and ventured over to the window. He saw his brother outside talking to several workers. He could see the tractors at the far end of the field, pulling the tomato setters. It was a slow process, planting two hundred acres of tomatoes. He felt guilty as hell for not being out there. He heard Savannah scoot her chair from the table and join him.

"Riley, you really should be in bed," she said. "Everything's under control. Maybe in a few days—"

"A few days!" he almost shouted, and it sent an ache through his head that made him grimace. "I can't lie in bed that long. Do you realize what's involved here?"

"No, but I do realize you could come down with something worse if you're not careful."

They argued for several minutes before Riley reluctantly agreed to return to his sickbed. Savannah promised to check on him later. He was still grumbling under his breath when he reached the top of the stairs where music was blaring from one of the bedrooms. He entered the room he was presently using and closed the door behind him, but it did little to block out the sound.

Savannah knocked on the door a few minutes later, carrying a glass of juice. "Is that music bothering you?" she asked.

He stared at her a full minute before answering. How could it not bother someone? Unless the person was dead and past hearing. Still, he didn't want to put more stress on her than she already had. It was bad enough she was having to play nurse to him and his twins. "It's fine," he said at last.

She looked relieved as she came farther into the room. "I'm so used to it, I just tune it out. If it gets to be too much for you, let me know."

He took his medicine, then watched as she moved around the bedroom, straightening this and that. She had already combed her hair and put on a little makeup. He wondered how she'd managed to do it so quickly when some women spent hours making up their faces. Could be those women didn't have as many responsibilities as she did. Despite all that, she always managed to look fresh and put together. Like now, for instance, in her white jeans and a navy blouse that emphasized her perfectly proportioned body and defined the smallness of her waist.

"Is something wrong?" Savannah asked, noting with growing discomfort those brown eyes were following her every move.

Riley blinked, embarrassed to have been caught staring. Truth was, he felt like a big oaf next to her. "I was just wondering how someone as little as you manages to get so much done in one day."

She laughed softly and sat on the edge of the bed, and she realized how natural it felt to do so. "I like staying busy," she said. "I've always been that way. And it feels good to be back in the country; perhaps that explains my sudden spurt of energy." She regretted the words instantly. Riley might think she was trying to convince him to let her and her children stay. It was important he come to that decision alone. Despite the fact that she had fallen in love with the area already. Despite her growing attraction to him.

"You wrote in your letter you were born and raised in a small town," he said, suddenly more curious about her now that they were face-to-face. Until recently, he had only known her as the nice-sounding lady with pretty eyes whose eloquent letters were penned on scented stationery. He'd found himself wondering what kind of woman wrote letters on flower-scented paper. Now he knew. "What made you leave?"

Savannah glanced toward the window. The shade had been raised. Sunlight streamed in and painted gold designs on the wood floor. "I met a man in my senior year of high school who dreamed of being a country-western star. He heard me sing in the choir at church and asked if I'd audition with his band. I did, and I guess they liked me because they hired me on the spot."

"So you moved to Nashville?"

"As soon as I graduated high school and turned eighteen. In the meantime, I guess I sort of fell in love with the lead singer. We eloped."

"What do you mean you *guess* you fell in love with him?" Riley asked. "Didn't you know?"

She shrugged. "I'd never been in love before. Actually, I'd never even dated that much. My parents were strict, especially my daddy. He only allowed my sister and me to date boys from the church, and only if they knew the family well. Unfortunately, there weren't very many cute boys in our church." She paused. "I remember there was one boy that my sister was allowed to go to the movies with a couple of times, but his parents got a divorce so that was that. My poor sister was brokenhearted. She ended up marrying a minister, and I'd be willing to bet my best coat she doesn't love him."

"Is she happy?"

"I don't hear from her often; she's not supposed to correspond with me since I did what I did. My parents sort of disowned me over the whole incident." Savannah looked at her watch. "Oh my, I can't believe I'm just sitting here yapping away when there's so much to do downstairs." She started to get up, then paused. "Before I forget, Ben suggested having Sam teach David and Melody to ride the horses. I realize we're sort of taking one day at a time here, but even if my kids only managed to get in a couple of lessons, it would give them something to do." She decided it wasn't the time to tell him they needed to make a decision by next Monday. Spring break was officially over at that time, and her children would have to be enrolled in school somewhere. But she knew Riley didn't feel well enough to discuss it, and, besides, they still had four days to decide. She was determined to be patient for the time being.

Riley looked thoughtful. "I suppose it's okay," he said. "No sense hanging on to those horses if nobody's going to ride them. And Sam's very responsible for his age. You tell him I said it was okay as long as everybody's careful and nobody gets hurt." Riley paused and reached for the phone. "Never mind, I'll call Sam myself and tell him what's going to happen if I have to take somebody to the hospital with a broken arm."

"Sam's not home right now," Savannah blurted out. "He's in town with his mother."

Riley put the phone down. "Oh?"

"Yes, I called a little while ago. To ask Jessie about a recipe," she added quickly, deciding the little white lie was better than admitting they'd gotten the boys mixed up and had needed her assistance. "She's supposed to call me the minute she gets home."

Riley shifted on the pillow, trying to get comfortable.

"What recipe are you wanting to ask about?" he said curiously. Actually, it was just a way to keep her there longer.

Savannah gave him a blank look. "What recipe?" she said dully, then frantically tried to come up with something that sounded fancy enough. She couldn't very well admit needing help for something as simple as meat loaf and mashed potatoes.

"I was . . . uh . . . thinking of preparing a nice . . . uh—" she paused. "A nice beef bordelaise," she said, remembering what she'd ordered once on a rare date that hadn't consisted of dinner under the golden arches.

"No kidding?" Riley looked impressed. "I'm not sure I've ever eaten it, but it sounds great." His look softened. "I certainly appreciate the fact you're going to so much trouble, Savannah."

She almost shivered at the way he said her name, and for a brief instant she wanted to confess she didn't even know the ingredients for beef bordelaise. But then he smiled, leaving her instantly fluttery and weak-kneed, and she decided she would find the ingredients even if one of them was camel meat and she had to drive to the nearest desert to find it.

"I need to go," she said, knowing she had to find Jessie right away.

"I feel guilty lying around doing nothing," Riley told her.

"Well, you shouldn't be getting up and down. You'll only end up with a fever. You don't want me to have to bathe you again, do you?"

Riley suddenly had an image of her gentle hands on his body. Something stirred low in his belly, and when he spoke his voice was unnaturally husky. "Only if you use warm water this time."

She felt her pulse skitter to a halt. "Don't count on it," she said, tossing the words over her shoulder in such a way one would never have guessed her stomach had dipped lower than a gopher hole. The only giveaway was the fact that she almost missed the doorway on her way out, slamming her already sore shoulder against the frame once again, causing Riley to wince.

"Are you okay?" he asked, sitting up in bed.

She was more worried about looking stupid than dislocating her collarbone. "I'm fine," she mumbled, cursing vilely under her breath as she made her way downstairs.

Why had Riley said what he had, she wondered to herself once she reached the bottom. Had he enjoyed having her bathe him, despite the cold water? Had his nipples contracted because he'd been cold, or had he actually been aroused? She felt her face grow hot.

She couldn't think about that now. She had to find Jessie so she could identify the twins and figure out what the heck went into that beef dish. Lord, poor Jessie was probably going to rue the day she convinced Riley to take out that ad.

Savannah found David at the kitchen table eating cold cereal. She hurried into the nursery where Melody was on her hands and knees studying the twins as a scientist might study new cell development under a microscope. The boys stared back at her much the same way.

Finally, one boy offered Melody a stuffed dog and said, "Muh."

"Melody, what are you doing?" Savannah asked, giving her daughter a bemused look.

"Trying to see if there's a difference," the girl replied. She sighed. "It's hopeless. They're like reflections of each other."

"Have you tried to reach Jessie lately."

The girl nodded. "Not ten minutes ago. Uncle Ben said she'd just called to let him know she'd finished her errands and to ask him what he wanted for dinner tonight."

Savannah perked up. "She's at the grocery store."

"Yeah, but which grocery store?" Melody said without taking her eyes off the boys.

"How many can there be in a town the size of Pinckney?" Savannah replied, and made her way to the kitchen for a phone book.

"You are so lucky you caught me when you did," Jessie said, walking through the door sometime later, carrying a grocery sack. "I was in the checkout line when they paged me."

"Can you tell the difference between the twins?" Melody almost whispered.

"Why heavens yes," the woman replied matter-of-factly. "Trevor's bracelet is blue, and Travis's is red."

"Is there any other way?"

"Well, let me think," Jessie replied as she knitted her eyebrows. "Yes, Trevor has a little kidney-shaped birthmark on his outer left thigh, and Travis has a tiny mole next to his navel." She paused, looking suddenly perplexed. "Or does Trevor have the mole and Travis the birthmark?"

As Savannah and Melody began to look more anxious by the moment, Jessie laughed, "No, honestly, Trevor has the birthmark, and Travis has the mole." She paused suddenly. "Sounds like someone removed their bracelets."

Melody tossed her a sheepish grin as she started for the nursery. "I'll go straighten it out."

Jessie put the sack on the table and faced Savannah, one hand on her hip. "I can't turn my back on you for a minute, can I?"

Savannah tried not to smile. "Not for a minute," she agreed, trying to look remorseful. She chuckled despite her best efforts.

"Did you make coffee?"

"Fresh and hot."

"Okay, find me that recipe you read to me over the phone, and I'll pour us both a cup."

Five minutes later they were sitting at the kitchen table reading through a recipe for beef bordelaise.

"This looks simple enough," Jessie said.

"Nothing is ever as simple as it looks."

Jessie raised curious eyes to her. "Oh, that sounds interesting. Are we still talking about this recipe or something entirely different?"

"Forget I said anything," Savannah replied, not ready to share her concerns about her and Riley just yet.

Jessie let it pass. "Didn't you tell me you grew up in the country?" she asked. When Savannah nodded, she went on. "And you never learned to cook?"

"My mother and my older sister did the cooking. I was the tomboy. I couldn't spend ten minutes in a dress without tearing a hole in it, and my mother learned it was easier to keep my hair cut short because it stayed dirty all the time."

Jessie smiled. "You must've been young when you married."

"I'd just turned eighteen. My children came quickly, one right after the other."

"Where's your ex-husband now?"

"California, last I heard. He didn't make it in music, so he decided to try acting. I haven't seen him in years."

"He doesn't try to help you with the children? Financially, I mean?"

"No. It would be easier if he had, but I didn't want him around David and Melody. I don't think he would have been a good influence."

"Riley would make a good father to your children, Savannah," Jessie said. "He's honest and hardworking. And he'd be a loving husband to you."

Savannah nodded. "I'm sure he'd make an excellent father," she said. "If he decides he wants to tackle a couple of teenagers." She sighed, knowing she had to share her worries with Jessie or burst. "As far as our relationship is concerned, he appears more interested in finding a good mother for his boys than anything else."

"Are you interested in more?" Jessie asked.

Savannah was thoughtful. Of course she was interested in more. She'd taken one look at Riley and knew she wanted to be more than just a mother to his children. But it wasn't that simple. "It's not up to me," she said at last. "Riley has to make the final decision. He has to make up his own mind what he wants. Besides, it's only been a few days, and he's been sick. I'm sure he hasn't given much thought to romance."

"I can't believe you're willing to be so accommodating," Jessie said, then glanced at the doorway to make certain they were alone. "Sometimes men don't even know what they want, honey. They have to be shown. And if you want a man to think about romance, you've got to set the stage."

Savannah paused in the midst of snapping a bean. "What do you mean?"

"Stand up."

"I beg your pardon?"

"Stand up so I can get a better look at you."

Shaking her head and sighing, Savannah put her coffee cup down and stood.

"Hmmm. Turn around."

Savannah made a full turn. "Okay, what?"

"We've got our work cut out for us."

"Thanks a lot."

"That's not what I meant. You've got the body and the looks; I just think you're afraid to show them off. Tell you what, I'm hiring a sitter for you Saturday, and we're going shopping."

Savannah thought of what little cash she had. "I can't afford much."

"This one's on me, honey. We've got to make Riley Locke sit up and take notice. Once I'm finished with you, he won't be able to take his mind off romance."

"I feel ridiculous," Savannah announced several days later as she followed Jessie out of the department store. She tugged at the hem of her short skirt, then the back of her hair. "Lord, how much did they cut off?"

Jessie laughed as she unlocked the door to her station wagon. "They didn't cut that much, they shaped it. It was a mess, girl. When's the last time you had a haircut?"

"I always cut it myself."

"Oh, well . . ." She rolled her eyes.

Savannah waited until Jessie unlocked her door, then opened it and tossed her bags in the backseat. She started to sit, then hesitated.

"What is it?" Jessie asked.

"Darn skirt's too tight," she muttered. "I can't sit down."

"Tug it up some, then try."

Savannah glanced around the parking lot to make sure nobody was standing nearby. She pulled the skirt up several inches, then, sitting on the edge of the seat, pulled her legs in and closed the door. "Oh, this is going to go over real well when I have to bend over to pick up a baby," she mumbled.

Jessie laughed. "Just make sure Riley's standing behind you when you do it."

Savannah reached for her seat belt. "I don't know, Jessie. It feels like I'm trying to trick Riley into something. First, I don't mention having children of my own, then I pretend I can cook when I can't, now I'm supposed to strut about the house like a sex kitten."

"Women have been doing that sort of thing since the beginning of time, honey," Jessie said.

It was close to dinnertime when Jessie pulled into the driveway. "I can't come in," she said. "I've got to get home and put supper on the table. Be sure to call me later and let me know how it went." She pulled away as soon as Savannah collected her bags from the backseat.

Savannah felt shy as she entered the house a moment later. Leona Cookson, a neighbor, met her at the back door. "Oh, my," she said breathlessly, her eyes automatically going to Savannah's hemline. "Don't you look . . . pretty."

Ignoring the woman's stunned remark as she stepped inside the door and put her bags on the table, Savannah asked, "How'd everything go?"

"Just fine," Mrs. Cookson said. "Ben's boy, Sam, was here all afternoon teaching your son and daughter how to ride. The twins played quietly. I changed them a little while ago and put them in their cribs, and they fell fast asleep. I just checked them, and they're fine." She turned toward the door, then faced Savannah once more, whispering the rest. "Mr. Locke has been pacing the floor since he came in from the fields, asking if I've heard from you. He's in his office now. He's been coughing a bit; I guess he's still trying to kick that flu bug." She glanced around the kitchen. "I thought about starting supper, but I wasn't sure—"

"That's fine, Mrs. Cookson," Savannah said. "I've got enough leftovers for a small army. I'll just pop them in the oven."

"Well, then, if it's all the same to you, I'll call my husband to come get me."

Savannah began pulling leftover chicken and pot roast from the refrigerator as the other woman made the call.

She waited until Mrs. Cookson hung up before speaking. "How much do I owe you for baby-sitting?" she asked.

The woman looked shocked that she would even ask such a thing. "Oh, dear, I didn't do it for money. I was just being neighborly. My children live so far away, I seldom get to see my grandchildren; it was a treat for me to sit with these youngsters. I've offered to sit before, but Mr. Locke never calls. I reckon he thinks I'm too old." She looked sad.

"I'm sure that's not it," Savannah said quickly. "Riley's just afraid he'll intrude."

"I just have one question before I go," the woman said. "And you're more than welcome to tell me to mind my own business, but did Mr. Locke really find you by running an advertisement for a wife?"

Savannah hesitated. "Uh, yes, as a matter of fact he did," she said, wondering if Riley would appreciate people knowing. "He was very selective, of course, because of the twins."

"Yes, he would have to be. And you plan to marry right away, of course?" she asked. When Savannah didn't answer, she went on quickly. "I would never say anything unkind about Mr. Locke, especially with all he's been through, but some folks might not be so generous. They'd frown on two adults living under the same roof without benefit of marriage. Especially with four helpless children involved."

Savannah took the woman's hand and led her to the door. She was so involved in the conversation, she didn't hear Riley come downstairs or see him pause in the doorway to stare at her short skirt. "Then I know I can trust you to set the record straight with the townsfolk, Mrs. Cookson, that absolutely no hanky-panky is going on under this roof. In fact, you might mention to them how sick Mr. Locke has been."

"Of course I will, dear," the woman said.

They were on the porch now. As though acting on cue, a battered pickup truck pulled into the driveway. "Oh, that must be your husband," Savannah said. "Please come back soon. You can imagine how eager I am to get to know all my new neighbors."

Savannah opened the door to the truck and helped the woman inside, speaking briefly to the skinny bald man at the steering wheel. She waved as they pulled away, then hurried inside to put dinner in the oven. Were folks really talking about them? she wondered. Riley was sitting at the kitchen table, wearing a frown.

"Have you got a headache?" she asked.

He turned to her. Once again, his eyes zoomed in on the skirt. "I'm hurting all right, but the pain is nowhere near my head."

Savannah, in the process of putting dinner together, paused. "I beg your pardon?"

He stood and crossed the room, coming to a halt only inches from her. Savannah felt something quicken inside her. She could literally feel the heat from his body. He stepped even closer, backing her against the cabinet. Every fiber in her body snapped alive. The front of his thighs touched hers.

"We need to talk about that poor excuse for a skirt," he said.

FIVE

Savannah stood there for a moment, not knowing what to say or do. "You don't like it?" she asked.

He put his hands on the counter on either side of her. "Could be I like it too much. Could be I'm wondering what you've got on underneath."

The underlying sensuality of his words held her rapt attention. His face was so close, she could see the pores in his skin and the individual whiskers along his jaw. He had still not taken to shaving on a regular basis. What would he think if she told him she wore simple cotton panties that had been mended more times than she could remember? No, she couldn't do that to him.

"Who says I'm wearing anything?" she asked, lowering her voice so she wouldn't risk being overheard by two curious teenagers. She had the distinct pleasure of watching his jaw go slack.

Riley put a finger beneath her chin and tilted her head back so she was forced to meet his gaze. His look was galvanizing, causing her insides to jangle.

"I'd say you just bought yourself a whole lot of trouble."

As though looking to seal his promise, he captured her lips with his. The kiss was slow and thoughtful, more a caress, and it sent shivery sensations to the pit of her stomach. He encircled her small waist and pulled her against him. Savannah could clearly feel his arousal.

Riley knew it was happening too fast as he crushed her to him and prodded her mouth open with his tongue. Already, he could feel the heat in his body spreading, the fires of passion fanned by the fact that he'd gone so long without a woman's touch. It hadn't mattered, though, despite Ben's good-natured teasing that he needed to get laid. He'd convinced himself he didn't need a woman and had fought Jessie every step of the way over that ad.

But now, he realized how mistaken he'd been.

Finally, he was forced to break the kiss, and they both gasped for breath. Riley realized he was trembling, and he cursed himself for feeling eighteen years old again. He could see the kiss had affected Savannah as well. Her cheeks were flushed, and she wore a dreamy-eyed expression.

"I wish there was somewhere we could go," he said huskily.

"Go?" Savannah realized she wasn't thinking straight.

Riley rubbed his lower body against hers. "So we don't have to stop at kissing," he said.

His meaning was suddenly very clear. Savannah tried to back away, but the cabinet blocked her attempt. "Riley, I don't think I'm ready for something like that."

He felt his hopes fall.

He released her abruptly. "What the hell is going on, Savannah?" he said, his voice edged with anger. Actually, he was trying to hide his frustration and embarrassment. "Why'd you come home wearing that skirt in the first place, if you weren't trying to get my attention?"

Savannah could hardly speak for being mortified. "Of

course I wanted your attention, Riley, but that doesn't mean I'm ready to jump in the sack with you."

"You're waiting for me to make good on my original offer of marriage, aren't you?"

Her cheeks flamed. "No. I was only trying to see if we're compatible in a physical sort of way."

"So now that it's obvious we are . . . uh . . . compatible, where do we go from here?"

"I'm not sure. Maybe we should spend more time together without the children." She took a deep, shaky breath. "After all, we're allowed to have a little fun, too, aren't we?"

Riley had finally calmed down enough to see she was making sense. He wasn't really sure why she'd worn that skirt, only that he liked it. "You're right. You and I haven't had any time alone together. Seems all you've done is cook and clean and care for sick people. We can go out to dinner tomorrow, just the two of us."

Savannah couldn't have been more pleased with the suggestion, and she only hoped he was offering because he truly wanted to spend time with her instead of feeling obligated for all the work she'd done.

"That would be nice," she said. "We'll need to get a sitter for the twins. I wouldn't feel comfortable leaving them with Melody just yet."

"I'll ask Jessie to look after them. It's only for a couple of hours."

Jessie was only too happy to watch the twins, then insisted David and Melody come, and they would grill hamburgers and watch videos. Neither teenager looked happy to be spending the evening with their "corny" cousins as David referred to them, but they were polite when Jessie offered them a soft drink and told them to join everybody on the deck. The twins were thrilled to be there, of course, although Jessie shooed Riley and Savannah out quietly when they weren't looking so neither boy would cry.

Savannah was still worried about the children as they made the long drive into town in a late-model Ford Explorer that Riley used when he wasn't driving his pickup. He hadn't wanted to take her out in his pickup with her all gussied up, and Savannah was glad he'd noticed the trouble she'd gone to. Her rust-and-navy sarong-style dress had come straight off a clearance rack some years back, but still looked new since she'd only worn it a few times. Riley had dressed up as well; neat slacks, a dress shirt, and a camel-colored sport jacket. He smelled heavenly, Savannah thought, and remembered the kiss the day before. That same kiss had kept her awake part of the night and had her gazing out the window that morning when she was supposed to be cooking breakfast. As he pulled into Pinckney's historic district, he pointed out various sights.

"We always fill our prescriptions at Gray's Pharmacy," he said. "Willie Gray has done more for this community than anyone else except for Jessie. And, of course, we do our banking at Low Country Federal. You'll like Theodore Bedlow, the president. He and I played hookey from school a couple times when we were kids. Went fishing. And that over there is Mabel Todd's bakery. I can't think of another person who can make sticky cinnamon rolls like Mabel."

He made it sound as if she'd be around long enough to meet these people. Savannah chuckled. "Sounds like you know just about everybody in town," she said.

He shrugged. "That's how it is in small towns. You should know."

She watched him parallel park in front of a restaurant called Abigail's. "We weren't really allowed to associate with anyone unless they belonged to our church," she said. "Oh, it was okay to smile and speak to strangers in passing, but, unless the people were part of our congregation, we just didn't include them. Our pastor was afraid they'd lead us into a life of sin," she said.

Savannah suddenly realized they'd stopped moving, and Riley was staring at her curiously. "I can't believe I told you all that," she said.

"What kind of church did you belong to?" he asked.

"We were Baptists. It's just the minister, Reverend Peabody, was about the strictest preacher I've ever met. As far as he was concerned, you could spit your gum out on the sidewalk and burn in hell for it."

"Sounds like a tough guy."

"And my parents clung to every word of it. Seemed like everything we did was a sin, and we were bound for torment because of it. I don't teach that sort of thing to my children. I don't want them to live in fear and tremble at the thought of meeting their Maker."

"I don't blame you," he said. "Is that why you aren't close to your parents today?" She glanced away quickly, and he had a feeling he'd touched a nerve.

"That was their choice, not mine. But I'm sure the good Reverend Peabody had something to do with it."

Riley didn't know what to say, and he was determined to avoid any painful topics. She deserved a break after the week she'd put in. "You ready to go in? Stay where you are, I'll come around."

Savannah did as he said. He opened her door a minute later and helped her out. The night was cool and breezy, she caught the sweet scent of some flowering bush and decided it had to be a camellia. Riley opened the door to Abigail's and ushered her in. Savannah found herself in a dimly lit rectangular-shaped room with small tables draped in white cloths. Candles flickered like blinking stars in cut-glass containers. A hostess asked about reservations, then seated them in the back and promised to have a waiter there right away.

The waiter appeared, an unsmiling sort who looked bored to be there. Riley, noting how stiffly he stood, couldn't help but wonder if he had too much starch in his underwear. "May I have a wine list?" he asked.

The man nodded and turned around with military precision before he stalked away. Riley rolled his eyes at Savannah. "I don't think Lurch likes us," he whispered. The waiter returned with the list. "Do you have a preference?" Riley asked.

Savannah shook her head. What she knew about wine could be engraved on the head of a sewing pin. "I'm sure I'll like whatever you order."

Riley selected a wine, and the waiter left without a word to collect it. "They must've been desperate when they hired this guy," he said.

"Pretty nice restaurant," Savannah said, glancing around at the oil paintings on the wall and the delicate china and crystal placed in precise locations on the tables. She was glad she'd dressed up when she saw what the other customers were wearing.

"They serve the best filet mignon you'll ever taste," Riley said. "It comes with a bernaise sauce that's out of this world. Of course, everything's good here."

The waiter returned a few minutes later bearing a wine bottle and two glasses. He made a production of opening it, then poured enough for Riley to taste. Offering Savannah a conspiratorial wink, Riley made a big show of smelling it first, sloshing the wine around the glass, and holding it close to the candle as though looking for sediment. "I just want to make sure there's no grape seeds in it," he told the waiter, who watched curiously.

"Yes sir," the man said.

"The stuff I buy at the convenience store is full of 'em."

"I don't doubt it."

Riley drained the glass, then smacked his lips loudly.

"This is pretty good, though. Why don't you pour the lady a glass. I'll let you know when we're ready to order."

"Gladly, sir." The waiter looked relieved to be going. He filled each glass, then placed the wine in an ice bucket and hurried away.

"To new beginnings," Riley said, holding up his glass. "I know it's corny, but it really does apply here."

Savannah didn't lift her glass. "Riley, why are you giving that man such a hard time?"

"Because he's a snob, and I dislike snobs."

"Maybe he's supposed to act like that. In order to keep his job," she added. "Did you ever consider that?"

"Okay, I'll be nice," he promised with a boyish grin.

Savannah raised her glass to his. "To new beginnings," she said, echoing his sentiment. She took a tentative sip. "It's good," she said, allowing herself to lean back in her chair and relax a bit. She was so used to running these days, it felt good to sit and do nothing.

Riley smiled. "You look very pretty tonight," he said, "but I barely recognize you without a twin on your hip. I'm afraid I've put too much on you."

"I'm okay," she said. "Really. Besides, I'm doing something I like for a change, and that makes all the difference."

"I want you to leave your Saturday nights open for me." His voice was smooth but insistent.

She smiled and took another sip of her wine. "That can probably be arranged."

Riley leaned back in his chair as well. "You know, once the planting is over, I'll have a little more time on my hands. I'll be able to help you with the twins and the house."

Again, he talked as if she was going to be around for a while. "Have you started planting the cotton yet?" she asked.

"I'm holding off for another week. Just to make sure the

temperature doesn't dip too low at night." He shrugged. "Ben thinks I'm crazy for messing with it; nobody grows Sea Island Cotton anymore, although at one time this area produced massive quantities. Now, it has little commercial value."

"Why is that?"

"It's more difficult to grow than regular cotton, and it's susceptible to bacterial blight. But I've been talking to the staff at the agricultural department at the university, and I found a guy whose great-grandparents used to grow it north of here. He's just as eager as I am to see it make a comeback. You'll notice him at the farm from time to time, he drives a red pickup that's almost completely covered with rust. He collects soil samples and takes plant measurements. I just leave him about his business since he looks like he knows what he's doing."

"It sounds exciting," she said.

"Well, Ben wasn't excited about it when I first approached him with the idea, but he grudgingly agreed to let me have a hundred acres. We didn't lose money on the deal, but we didn't make a whole lot either because there wasn't much of a market. Sea Island Cotton is used for finer, smoother fabrics. Now that I've found a buyer, I hope to do better this year. I'm still managing with my hundred acres, but next year I'm going to convince Ben to let me have more. Actually, all I have to do is convince Jessie; she's got my brother wrapped around her little finger." He grinned. "And Jessie's easy 'cause she's crazy about me."

Savannah chuckled. "I'm beginning to think you're somewhat of a con man, Riley Locke."

"You do what you have to do. Especially when it's a family business and everybody has to get along. That's not to say Ben and I always agree on everything, but every time we come close to knocking heads, Jessie's there to smooth out the differences."

"She's a wonderful person."

His look sobered. "I don't know what I would have done without her when . . . you know." He paused. "The twins were so small, and I didn't have the first clue how to care for them. My mother had gone into a nursing home several years before so I couldn't very well ask her to help me. Thankfully, Jessie was there to give me a crash course in parenting. She even offered to take them during the day while I worked, but I couldn't burden her with them. She's very active in the church and community. I didn't want her to have to give that up." Riley glanced at his wristwatch. "I suppose we should order." He motioned for the waiter, who brought menus. "I already know what I want," he said, "but you might prefer something else."

She glanced over the menu, then decided to go with his suggestion of the filet mignon. Once the waiter took their order, he left them abruptly and without a word. This time Riley looked amused. "So your family has always farmed?" Savannah asked.

Riley nodded. "That's all we've ever known. Fortunately, we've done fairly well with it, this is a super area for growing tomatoes, and we've built up a good reputation with our buyers. We usually plant about three hundred acres each year and harvest in June."

"Who does the picking?"

"We employ migrant workers. We have a packing house on the property where we get the tomatoes ready for shipping."

"How many migrant workers do you usually employ?"

"A couple of hundred."

"That many? Where on earth do you stay?"

"We have a camp. It sort of resembles army barracks. It's not the Hilton, but it's dry and cleaner than most. Jessie's good about seeing that the plumbing works and that it's free of lice and other parasites. She also sends the rever-

end to visit on Sunday. I'll drive you by there sometime so
you can see where it is. Don't worry, the men pretty much
keep to themselves. Some of them have been coming for
years so we don't have any trouble."

Their salads arrived, and they chatted easily through
dinner. Savannah was surprised how comfortable she felt
with him, but then she realized they'd been living under the
same roof for a week now so it should come as no surprise
that they should be able to find something to talk about. By
the time she'd finished her filet—she'd absolutely refused
to leave even a sliver of it—she was stuffed.

Riley chuckled at the sight of her near empty plate,
wondering where such a small person had put so much
food. He made a production of looking under the table to
see if her feet were any bigger from what she'd consumed.
The waiter came over and asked, in what Riley considered a
haughty tone, if there was a problem.

Riley crooked his finger, and the waiter leaned closer.
"The lady thinks a mouse just ran across her foot," he said
softly, and had the pleasure of seeing the smug look wiped
from the man's face. "She's in a bit of a hurry to leave as
you can imagine. Just bring us the check."

Savannah barely made it out of the building before she
erupted into a series of giggles that soon had Riley chuckling along with her. "I can't believe you did that, Riley
Locke."

He tried to look contrite. "I'm sorry, Savannah, but the
guy deserved it. What he didn't deserve was the fifteen
percent tip I left him, and if I didn't have such a generous
spirit, I'd go right back in there and get it.

"I'll bet he's called the manager and they're both trying
to check under the table discreetly right now." She laughed
harder at the thought of the stuffy-looking waiter scram-
bling beneath the table in search of a nonexistent mouse.

"They'll probably go out and buy traps tomorrow," Riley said.

Fresh peals of laughter overtook her, and she hiccuped so loudly, Riley arched both brows at her. Before he knew it, he was laughing right along with her, loud hearty guffaws that had them bending over in the parking lot. Then, just as it looked as though they'd exhausted themselves and were in control, Savannah hiccuped again, and it set them off once more.

Riley grabbed her hand and pulled her toward the Explorer, though it wasn't easy with her doubled over laughing like a wild hyena. "Let's get out of here before we get arrested for disorderly conduct," he said.

He helped her in the car, then joined her on the other side. They were still laughing as they pulled out of the parking lot onto the main road. It reminded her of a time she got tickled over something her sister whispered to her in church. No matter how hard she'd tried she hadn't been able to stop snickering. Finally, her mother had yanked her up and literally dragged her outside, then paddled her bottom with her bare hand. Savannah had been more humiliated than anything, and she hadn't so much as cracked a smile during the rest of the sermon.

She was in control of her faculties by the time they left the mainland and made the drive on the narrow highway that led to Gull Island. Exhausted, she leaned her head back against the seat and sighed. "I can't remember when I've had such a good time. Thank you, Riley."

He reached over and squeezed her hand. "You're a lot of fun." He meant it sincerely. How many times had he happened on her while she was cleaning or washing dishes, only to find her singing along with the radio as though she hadn't a problem in the world. And just two days earlier, when Melody had come across an old hula hoop, Savannah wouldn't give up until she'd mastered it. In the beginning, he'd had as much fun watching her as the rest of them, but after a while, all those gyrating hips had stirred up his juices and convinced him he'd be better off checking the battery on his pickup truck.

"I hadn't realized how much I'd missed having a good time myself," he replied honestly.

"I'd like to go back to Abigail's again," she said.

"We can. It'll be our place."

Savannah liked the sound of it; it had a permanent ring to it. She was also thankful for the fact she and Riley genuinely liked each other. At least it seemed that way. And that kiss. Her stomach got all quivery every time she remembered how he'd tasted. She was still pondering their relationship when Riley pulled into the driveway leading to his brother's house.

"Look at that; every room in the house lit up. No wonder Ben complains about his power bill." Riley climbed out and came around to her side. He helped her out, then held her hand while he closed the door. "Come here," he said, pulling her close.

Savannah's stomach took a nosedive as he gazed down at her. "Is something wrong?" she asked.

He was smiling as he shook his head. "Only thing wrong is I've been trying to figure out how to kiss you again since yesterday. I can't seem to think of any clever way to go about it . . . you know, something that'll sweep you off your feet."

She could feel his breath on her cheek. "You already have," she said softly. "The first time I saw you standing there in that silly-looking apron trying to take care of two sick babies. I knew right then I was a goner."

Riley was genuinely touched by the confession. His eyes seemed to darken as he cupped her face in his hands and kissed her deeply. His tongue slipped past her lips as he stepped closer, so close, he pressed her back against the door of the Explorer.

She could feel the warmth and power in his body, the sheer strength, and she marveled that he could be so gentle. She opened her mouth wider as he continued to explore each dark corner. He was the first to break the kiss. They merely stared at each other for a moment.

Riley wondered if she had enjoyed the kiss.

Savannah wondered if he was going to kiss her again.

"You taste good," he said at last.

"You're a good kisser," she replied, then wondered if she'd been forward in saying so. What *did* couples talk about during these awkward moments?

"I'm out of practice. We might have to kiss more often."

She liked the sound of it. "That sounds good to me, but frankly, I think you've got it down to an art."

Linking his fingers with hers, a grinning Riley led Savannah toward the house. He couldn't remember when he'd felt so carefree, so content, and he knew it was due to the woman beside him. She'd not only lessened his burdens considerably, she made him feel more optimistic about his life than he had in a long time. Telling him he was a good kisser had put a bounce in his step.

They'd just reached the porch when the light came on and Ben stepped out. "Well, now, looks like you two had a nice evening," he said, offering them a smile that didn't quite hide the worried look in his eyes.

Savannah felt her heart leap in her chest at his expression. "What's wrong, Ben? Is it the children—?"

He closed the door. "Calm down, Savannah, it's nothing serious. David and Sam got into a little scuffle tonight, that's all."

"What happened?" Riley asked.

"Oh, they were playing pool. Sam accused David of

cheating. One thing led to another and before I could get up there they had a bona fide fistfight going on. Somebody swung a pool stick, though neither one will admit to it. Anyway, the stained-glass light over the pool table got broken. Jessie paid over two hundred dollars for that light. I told the boys they were both going to pay for it, but I wanted to clear it with you two first."

"Of course," Savannah said, determined to see that her son did whatever necessary to make up for the damage.

"David can work for me after school and on Saturdays to earn the money," Riley told his brother, then glanced at Savannah. "You know school starts back next Monday."

She glanced at him. He didn't have a clue how she'd worried about getting her children enrolled.

"I'm so sorry," she told Ben. "How's Melody?"

Ben shrugged. "I don't reckon the girl has said two words since she got here. Just asked Jessie if she could sit out in the gazebo by herself. Been there since dinner, although Jessie tried to get her interested in playing cards or watching TV with us." He glanced at Riley. "The twins did fine. They whimpered in the beginning, of course, but we got them interested in Josh's old toys."

They entered the house a moment later and found David sitting in the kitchen by himself and Melody still in the gazebo. The twins were on the carpet in the den and, Sara, Ben and Jessie's daughter, was entertaining them. Jessie was sitting at a desk in the corner of the room working on church business.

"I'm sorry you had problems," Savannah told her. "I wish you had called us."

Jessie waved it aside. "I wasn't going to ruin your evening just because our children forgot their manners. Besides, both boys know they're each responsible for paying for that broken light."

"I can get you the money right away," Savannah said, thinking of the small savings she had.

"Absolutely not," Jessie said. "I expect David and Sam to earn the money themselves. It's up to you whether you punish David, but I've told Sam he's grounded until he pays me back."

"Melody didn't spend time with Sara?" Riley asked.

Jessie shook her head. "She said she wanted to be alone. I asked her if she was feeling all right, and she assured me she was fine. I figure it's best to give them their space when they get like that. Especially girls." She patted Savannah on the back. "Don't let it worry you too much. They need time to adjust, that's all."

With the exception of the twins, everybody was quiet on the ride back. Once home, Savannah asked Melody to assist Riley in getting Trevor and Travis ready for bed, then told David to join her in his bedroom.

"What happened?" she asked her son the moment they were alone.

"Sam accused me of cheating."

"Were you?"

"No. I'm just better at pool than he is. He couldn't take it, started running his mouth—"

"And you feel that was reason enough to get into a fistfight and break Aunt Jessie's light?"

"She's not my aunt," he said loudly. "I'm not related to any of these people. I don't even know what the hell we're doing here."

Savannah felt a surge of anger rush through her. "Don't use that language with me, young man, and stop yelling in my face. I'm still your mother."

In the nursery across the hall, Riley could hear every word. Melody shot him an apologetic look. "Try to ignore my brother. I don't think he means half of what he says. He's just mad."

"I don't know you anymore," David told his mother, voice still raised. "I thought I did, but you've changed. Look at you, you just up and move in with some man you don't know, and not once do you stop and consider our feelings. What's the matter, Mom, did you just get lazy? Are you sleeping with him so you can get your bills paid? There's a word for that, you know."

David had barely gotten the last sentence out of his mouth before the bedroom door flew open and Riley stood there, a dark scowl on his face. He crossed the room in two steps and grabbed the boy up by his shirt collar. "Listen to me carefully," he said, talking through gritted teeth. "You are in my house. I don't ever, *ever* want to hear you speak to your mother like that again."

David swallowed. "Take your hands off me!"

Savannah stepped closer to Riley and put her hand on his shoulder. "Riley, please—"

He didn't so much as budge. "I'm going to teach this boy some manners, Savannah. If he wants to be treated like a man, then he's going to have to grow up and stop acting like a sniveling brat."

"You can't tell me what to do," David said.

"Wanna bet?" He let him go. David took a step back and rubbed his neck. "Starting Monday, you're coming to work for me," Riley said. "The minute I see that yellow school bus turn down the road, I'm going to start looking for you. You'll work till dark. On Saturday, you'll work from eight o'clock in the morning till quitting time."

"In your dreams, man. The agreement is between you and my mother and has nothing to do with me."

"You're involved whether you like it or not," Riley replied. "As long as you're under my roof."

"Maybe I don't want to live under your damn roof."

Riley shrugged. "That's up to you, but those are my terms."

Tossing his mother an angry look, David grabbed his jacket and started for the door. Savannah, who'd stood and listened to the whole thing in mixed disbelief and horror, reached for her son. "David, where are you going?"

"Didn't you hear?" the boy said angrily. "Your lover just gave me a choice, and I choose to get the hell out of here."

"You can't leave!" she cried, then started to follow.

Riley grabbed her and closed the bedroom door, then barricaded it with his body. Even in her state of shock, Savannah tried to get by. "Let me out, Riley. I have to—"

He grabbed her by both arms and shook her. "Listen to me, Savannah, you can't give in to him."

She was beside herself. "He's fourteen years old, I can't just let him walk out."

"He won't go far, trust me. But he has to learn, once and for all, that he can't run roughshod over his family." Riley shook his head. "I'm not going to let him talk to you the way he did tonight, ever again."

"He didn't mean it, he was just angry." Her eyes glistened with tears. "What's he supposed to do, sleep out in the cold?"

"He's got his jacket with him. Do him good to get a little cold, make him think all the harder about how he's been acting."

Tears fell in rivulets down her face. "Oh, I don't know what I'll do if—"

"Do you trust me, Savannah?" he said softly.

She met his gaze, and found his look deeply concerned. "Yes."

"Then trust me now," he said simply.

She didn't say anything at first. Riley was right, of course. She couldn't allow David to treat her as he had if she hoped to gain his respect. When had she lost control of her son? She thought about his bad grades and the gang he'd joined for a brief period, and she wondered if she'd ever had control. "I don't know where I went wrong," she said at last. "I tried so hard."

"Stop blaming yourself for everything bad that happens in this world," he said. "David's a troubled teenager, just like the millions of troubled teenagers all over the world. Nothing you did made him that way. Odds are, he'll snap out of it, but we're going to have to be patient."

"How do you know so much about teenagers?"

"I was a real pain in the butt growing up. Put my parents through the ringer, so to speak. But I eventually grew out of it."

"How old were you when you finally did?" Savannah asked, feeling hopeful.

"Thirty." Her look of horror made him laugh. He reached for her. "Just kidding." He held her close for a long moment. "I'll leave the house unlocked tonight. David is free to come back in whenever he feels like it, but he has to be ready to follow the rules."

Melody had finished putting the twins in their pajamas by the time Riley and Savannah came into the nursery. Although it was after ten o'clock, both boys were wound up tight and ready to play. "I think the brief nap they took at Aunt Jessie's gave them a spurt of energy," Melody said.

They played with the boys for a while longer, until both started rubbing their eyes. Finally, they put them in their cribs, covered them with their blankets, and turned the light low. Savannah paused outside their door. "I'll be down in a minute," she told Riley, who'd already started for the stairs. She glanced at Melody. "Could we talk for a minute?"

The girl shrugged. "Sure."

Once inside, Savannah sat on a chair in front of a dressing table and watched Melody get ready for bed. "Honey, how come you wanted to sit in the gazebo by yourself at Aunt Jessie's?"

Melody rolled her eyes. "You're doing it again, Mom. You're making a big deal over nothing."

"I don't mean to make it a big deal, I just want to understand what's going on with you."

Melody was thoughtful for a moment. "I guess I'm trying to get used to all the changes going on around me. It's like one minute it's just the three of us; you, me, and David. Then, the next thing I know we belong to a whole new family, but it's not really our family because you and Riley aren't even married. Then, there's Uncle Ben and Aunt Jessie and Sam and Sara and—" She paused. "What's that youngest kid's name who always sits in the corner reading?"

"Joshua."

"And we're not really related to them because—"

Savannah nodded. "Because Riley and I aren't married yet. I know, honey, but it's going to take a little more time."

"How much time?"

Savannah thought about the signed contract. She knew it was both legal and binding because she'd paid a lawyer almost one hundred dollars to look at it. But what woman wanted to force a man into marriage when his heart wasn't in it? She strongly suspected the problems in Riley's first marriage made him reluctant to repeat the act.

"You're going to have to be patient, Melody," she told the girl after a moment. "And trust me to do the right thing."

SIX

Dawn came, and with it no sign of David. The house remained ominously silent, with the exception of Savannah's quiet weeping as she lay fully dressed on the sofa in the den while Riley paced the floor in front of her. He felt each sob deep in his gut, but when he reached out for her she became as stiff and unyielding as quarter-inch plywood.

"You're not being fair to me, Savannah," he said softly. "You came here expecting me to take your children in and raise them as my own, but the first time I try to discipline your son—"

"You threw him out of the house."

"I gave him a choice."

"You don't understand," she said, her throat catching on another sob. "He's never had a father."

"You can't continue to make excuses for the boy, Savannah."

She sniffed. "What if it were Trevor or Travis you were dealing with? Would you do the same?"

"Yes. I expect all of them to show us respect. One day it might come to this with the twins as well."

"David could be lying on the side of the road murdered," she said miserably.

"That's not likely and you know it." He frowned as he said it. He wasn't worried about the boy being accosted. What did worry him was the thought of David wandering off into a swamp full of alligators and snakes. How would he ever live with the guilt? All he could do was hope and pray the boy would have enough sense to stay away from the wetlands.

"What if he falls in the swamp?" Savannah said, as though reading his mind. She sat up. "I think it's time I look for him."

"Okay," Riley said, his frustration evident in his voice. "If that's what you want. Maybe next time he gets mad he'll raise his hand to you?"

He sighed. "This is the reason I hesitated to take on a couple of teenagers in the first place," he said. "But I decided to give it a try since I was asking you to raise my children."

"Explain to me how you've tried," she shot back. "You were willing to marry me sight unseen once I agreed to keep your house and raise your children. But when I show up with kids of my own, you back off like—"

"So that's what this is about," he interrupted. "You expect me to marry you despite my reservations?"

She glared at him with burning, reproachful eyes. No doubt he thought she would jump at the suggestion. Her temper flared. "Wrong, Buster," she said contemptuously. She came off the sofa in one leap. "I wouldn't marry you now if you got down on your knees and begged." She started past him. She would grab a flashlight and look for David herself.

Riley reached out and grasped her arm, pulling her to an abrupt halt. His profile was rigid, his mouth set in a grim line. "If you're going to look for him, I'm going with you."

The look in her eyes was stubborn and unyielding. "Why would you do that?" she asked.

"Because it's dark, and I don't want you to step in a hole and hurt yourself. Grab that afghan off the couch while I go for a flashlight."

They stepped out the back door a moment later. With the exception of a tall utility pole near the detached garage, everything was black. The night air was crisp, smelling of dark rich soil and freshly cut grass. Overhead, the sky glittered with a million stars. Riley switched on the flashlight and grazed a path of light in front of them.

"Let's check the barn first," he said.

The big door squeaked when Riley pulled it open a few minutes later. He stepped through first, then motioned for Savannah to follow. About halfway across they spied the mama cat and her kittens. She mewed and licked a nursing baby.

"It's okay, girl," Riley said soothingly, and Savannah was comforted by his reassuring tone, as well.

They found David at the other end of the barn, his jacket rolled pillowlike beneath his head, his body stretched out on fresh straw. Savannah saw no noticeable injuries.

"He looks perfectly fine to me," Riley said in a voice that told her he'd known that fact all along. "Go ahead and cover him."

Savannah was tempted to wake the boy and invite him into the house, but she knew she couldn't. After all, he *had* been wrong to talk to her so badly, and Riley *had* given him a choice. It was much clearer to her now that she knew he was safe. She very gently placed the afghan on him and turned to go. David didn't so much as stir.

Inside the house, Riley locked up and turned off lights while Savannah checked the twins. She almost ran into him in the hall.

"Riley, I'm sorry for spouting off the way I did. I was afraid and—" The look on his face stopped her cold.

"It's been a long day," he said. "Let's just go to bed."

The following morning dragged for Savannah. She prepared breakfast, fed the twins, and went about the business of straightening the house, along with Riley and Melody's help. Everybody was quiet, as though holding their breath for something to happen. Savannah didn't let herself cry until she was in the shower.

She and Riley had been making progress on their relationship; now it looked as though it was all lost because they couldn't agree on her son.

Melody came in after lunch and pulled her mother aside. Riley had put the twins in their sweaters and taken them out for some fresh air. "I just checked on David. He's still asleep," she whispered.

Savannah had debated about checking on the boy all day, and she was thankful Melody had gone into the barn for her. She noted how late it was. "Are you sure he's really asleep and not hurt?"

"Believe me, Mom. The guy is snoring like a grizzly bear. I went out to check on the kittens and there he was, sprawled out on fresh hay, covered with that blanket." She paused. "You and Riley need to make up. He looks miserable."

"Does he?" Savannah had been so tied up in knots, she hadn't noticed.

"He's got bags under his eyes. Looks like he hasn't slept in a week."

Savannah found him and the twins on the front porch, with Riley in the swing and the boys trying to push him. They gave Savannah a sloppy smile when she stepped out, and her heart turned over in her chest. She wondered if Riley noticed how much they resembled him.

"You want me to take over for a while?" she asked.

"I'm fine." He smiled stiffly. "Why don't you go relax. Take a nap or read a magazine. I heard you up a couple of times during the night, you must be tired."

Savannah thought he sounded like an employer giving her the afternoon off. What she would have preferred doing was joining him in the swing, but pride kept her from suggesting it. While he didn't appear angry exactly, his coolness toward her did not invite conversation or anything else.

Her lips thinned in irritation. "Are you going to stay annoyed with me forever?" she asked, placing a hand on her hip. He didn't answer. The rangy-looking mutt that wandered up from time to time or when he was hungry, climbed the front steps and fell in an exhausted heap at the front door.

"Daw!" Trevor exclaimed, and both boys hurried over to pet the animal. Riley grinned as the boys stroked and petted the dog until he finally rolled over and offered his stomach.

"Aren't you afraid he'll bite?" Savannah asked Riley.

He shook his head. "Not Bo. He's been coming around for months now. The boys love him."

"He needs a bath," Savannah said. "And a trip to the vet's office if you plan on keeping him."

"I'm not sure we have much say in the matter. He's pretty well made himself at home."

Travis rubbed the dog's belly and his back leg went wild. Both boys' mouths formed a perfect O of surprise.

Riley chuckled, as did Savannah. Their gazes met and locked. Riley's face softened.

"Sometimes when I look at my boys . . . and I see how cute they are . . . it almost breaks my heart."

She was thoughtful. "And then they grow up and become teenagers, and they break it all over again."

She disappeared inside the house a moment later, leaving Riley to ponder her words.

Jessie showed up a little later, still wearing her church clothes, having been detained by a couple of meetings. She kicked off her high heel shoes, poured a cup of coffee, and regarded Savannah. "Why didn't you tell me you used to sing in the church choir?" she demanded.

Savannah paused in making a vegetable dish, one of Jessie's recipes. "Who told you?"

"Melody told me Saturday while I was sitting with her in the gazebo. After I told her that our choir director had quit after the Easter celebration the last week in March. She was offered a job at the big church in Pinckney." She paused. "Melody also told me you used to sing professionally."

"That was a long time ago," Savannah said.

"Some things stay with you forever. Your daughter says you have a beautiful voice. She says she still remembers the lullabies you sang when she was little."

Savannah looked up from her work. "What are you getting at, Jessie?"

"I want you to be our new choir director."

Savannah simply stared at her for a moment. "And where would I find time for that?"

"You only have to practice one night a week, and be there on Sunday. It would get you out of the house and you could meet people."

Savannah explained to Jessie what it was like for her attending church as a child. "The minister brainwashed my parents," she said. "After a while, they stopped smiling. It was as if they were afraid to be happy in case that was a sin too."

"I'm sorry you had to go through something like that,"

Jessie said. "Reverend Hilby is nothing like that. But don't take my word for it, why don't you and Riley and the kids join us next Sunday? Judge for yourselves."

"Do you think Riley will go?" she asked, although part of her worried if she and her children would still be there.

"I don't see why not. He grew up in that church."

"Let me think about it."

Savannah was still thinking about it long after Jessie left. Although she'd taken her children to church plenty over the years, she'd never felt comfortable enough to join one. She'd had no desire to become the fanatic her parents had been, but she did want her children to believe in a higher power. People needed to believe in something, she'd decided long ago, and it was wrong of her to let her bad experiences stand in the way of her children's spiritual well-being.

Dusk was hovering over the newly planted fields when David knocked on the back door. Standing at the stove stirring a pot of mashed turnips, it was all Savannah could do to keep from racing to the door when she spotted him through the window. Instead, she waited, heart in her throat, as Riley calmly made his way to the back porch and opened it. She strained to hear.

"Yes?" His voice sounded tight and constricted. Savannah knew he'd spent an anxious day as well.

David looked up at the man. "I'd like to talk to you."

"I'm listening," Riley said evenly.

"I know I was wrong about what I said to my mother."

"Perhaps you should be saying this to her instead of me," Riley said.

"I will. But I want to get a few things straight between us first."

"I'm still listening."

"I didn't want to come here, and I don't want my mother to have to marry a complete stranger just because things got bad in Nashville. If she remarries, it should be to someone she loves."

"And you don't think your mother could ever love me?"

"Not if you expect her to act like a hired hand."

Riley was offended by the remark, but he refused to let it show. "I've offered to hire someone to do the cooking and cleaning, but your mother likes staying busy. I try to help all I can. Maybe you could help out if you're so worried." He paused. "Surely you don't believe you were all better off living in Nashville where your mother was working two jobs and you and your sister never saw her."

David didn't say anything for a while. "So where do I fit in?"

"Wherever you like. You can live here or you can go to a place where you'll be more comfortable. There are plenty of good boarding schools. But if you do decide to stay, I expect you to treat everybody with a certain degree of respect."

"What about this business of me working for you?" the boy asked.

"Three hours a day after school, all day on Saturday."

"Until I earn the money to fix that broken light?"

"We'll talk some more after you've paid Jessie. I don't agree with you lying around all day hooked up to a pair of earphones. Your free time would be better spent on your artwork. I've seen your drawings. You have remarkable talent. Of course, it's up to you if you want to do anything with it."

It was obvious David was pleased with the compliment, although he did his best not to show it. "What's my mother say about this?" David said. "Or is she allowed to have a say?"

Riley wondered if the boy would ever come around. "It's a free country. Your mother is entitled to her own opinion."

Savannah, who'd heard the whole exchange, joined Riley on the steps. "I've thought about this long and hard, David," she said. "I love you and I want you to be a part of this family, but I stand behind Riley one hundred percent. You're going to have to change your attitude if you expect to live with this family." She realized, even as she said it, they weren't a true family yet. She and Riley, although they'd tried to present a unified front to the children, had not committed themselves to each other.

At first the boy looked surprised that his mother would take sides with Riley. After a moment, the look turned to resignation. He took a deep breath. "Okay," he said after a moment. "I guess it won't hurt for me to try a little harder to get along with everyone."

Riley was relieved. He wasn't quite sure what he would have done had the boy refused to meet them halfway. He sniffed the air. "What's that smell?"

David looked embarrassed. "It's probably me. I guess I could use a shower."

Riley nodded. "Good idea. Otherwise, we'll have to call you Trigger."

David laughed and made his way upstairs.

Dinner was more relaxed now that David and Riley had come to an understanding. The teenager didn't glare at the noisy twins in their high chairs as he usually did, nor did he comment on how messy they ate. Instead, he amused everyone with tales of how he'd spent the night. He even offered to help Melody do the dishes afterward so Savannah and Riley could bathe the little ones. As Riley watched her interact with the twins, he couldn't help but feel a twinge of anxiety. Both boys had grown attached to Savannah in an amazingly short period of time. He worried how they'd take it if things didn't work out.

As usual, Trevor and Travis splashed so much in the tub that Savannah found herself soaked to the skin by the time she pulled the first one out and handed him to Riley. She didn't mind. It made her think of when her own children were babies.

Riley chuckled at the sight of her, then stilled when he noted her blouse was damp in front and plastered to her skin. He could clearly make out the bra beneath it, not to mention her nipples, which had hardened considerably. He swallowed; actually, it was more like a gulp.

"Is something wrong?" Savannah asked, half afraid he might be suffering a relapse from the flu.

Riley turned away quickly and tried to concentrate on the wet and wiggly boy he held. "No, I'm fine." He carried Travis to the nursery and lay him on the changing table, where he finished drying him and gave him a light dusting of baby powder. He'd diapered the boy and was struggling to get him into pajamas when Savannah walked into the room with Trevor.

"Okay, wiggle-worm," Riley mumbled. "Hold still." Travis giggled in response and kicked all that much harder.

"Do you want me to dress him?" Savannah asked, knowing how the twins liked to play at the most inopportune moments.

"Naw, I can handle it," Riley told her. "It's just a game between us guys, right, Trav?"

"Well, would you guys mind snapping it up a bit?" she said wearily. "Trevor's got chill bumps on his arms."

Riley glanced over at the sound of her voice. "You okay?"

She nodded. "Just tired, that's all."

"I guess neither of us got much sleep last night." He pulled the boy off the changing table and finished dressing him in his crib so she could use the table for Trevor. "Why don't we call it an early night?"

"Sounds good to me."

By the time Savannah trudged up the stairs twenty minutes later, her back was killing her, and she could think of nothing else but a hot shower. The aspirin she'd taken earlier hadn't stopped the pain. Thankfully, Riley had seen to helping Melody and David finish the kitchen, and she could only hope they would remember to lay out their school clothes before bed and get their books together. The bus came early to Gull Island.

In the shower, Savannah turned the water on full blast, then adjusted the temperature, hot as she could stand it against the small of her back. She'd had problems with her back for years. It had started when she was pregnant with David. Her labor, it seemed, had been directed in that area. By the time she'd arrived home with her new son, she'd barely been able to lean over the crib without bringing tears to her eyes. It had disappeared for a time, until she'd found herself pregnant with Melody.

She knew she was hurting from picking up the twins. Every time she walked into their room they reached for her, chubby little arms thrust out in such a way it was obvious they craved affection. She couldn't have denied them that any more than she could have denied them a drink of water. She carried one or the other everywhere she went, and now she was paying. That made her anxious. What would Riley think if she told him she was unable to lift them? Although he would probably never say it aloud, he might think she wasn't living up to her part of the bargain.

Savannah stepped out of the shower and dried herself, then slipped into a gown. The hot water had helped somewhat, but she could still feel the ache deep within her muscles. She saw her panties draped over the towel rack and winced at the thought of bending over to step into them. Instead, she made her way to the bed and, moving gingerly, climbed in. It was then that she realized she hadn't brushed her teeth, but the thought of getting up again almost made her cry.

Savannah sighed and kicked the covers aside. The only thing worse than a backache was getting a cavity and having a dentist drill holes in her teeth. She swung her legs over the side of the bed.

Okay, that wasn't so bad, she told herself. Getting up was the killer. Maybe if she did it fast. No, she wasn't that brave. Slowly, she pushed up from the bed. She moaned. The pain came from way down deep. She clasped her hands to her back.

"Savannah?"

She glanced up and found Riley standing in the doorway, wearing a funny look. She started to raise up but couldn't. "Yeah?"

"Is something the matter?"

He looked so concerned, she was certain he was over his mad spell. "I was just going to brush my teeth."

He stepped into the room, still wearing that puzzled look. "Why are you standing that way? Did you hurt your back?"

Her secret was out. "Well, yeah—"

"From carrying the twins, right? I knew something like this was bound to happen. Why didn't you tell me?"

"I was afraid you'd be—" She paused and tried to straighten, then winced.

"You were afraid I'd be what?" He came closer. His forehead was bunched into a frown. Still, he didn't look angry; he looked more concerned than anything. "What can I do to help?" he asked gently, his voice so tender, it almost brought tears to her already weary eyes.

"Do you have something I can rub on my back?"

"If I do, I'll find it. Can I help you into the bathroom?"

"No, it's best if I just go at my own speed."

"Have you taken anything for the pain?"

"A couple of aspirin. They've probably worn off by now."

"I'll see if I can find something stronger." He started for the door, then paused. "Are you sure you don't want me to—" She had already disappeared into the bathroom and closed the door.

Riley hurried down the stairs and began a thorough search for the deep heating rub. He found it at the very back of the medicine cabinet. Next he checked the cabinet for a painkiller, found something, then called Jessie to make sure he could give it to Savannah. He raced up the stairs with his discoveries. Savannah was just coming out of the bathroom.

"Don't lie down just yet," he said, rushing into the bathroom for a glass of water. He took one of the pills from the bottle and handed it to her. "You're not allergic to codeine, are you?" She shook her head. "Jessie said this is standard pain medication. You shouldn't have any trouble."

Savannah was really hurting. "At this point I'd take it even if it put hair on my chest." She popped the pill in her mouth and swallowed water.

Riley took the glass and set it on the night table. "Go ahead and get into bed. I want to rub some of this deep heating ointment on you before you go to sleep."

Savannah was only half listening as she went about getting into bed without causing herself excruciating pain. When his words sunk in, she felt her eyes widen. "Uh, that's not really necessary," she said in a brisk tone. "The pain pill will help."

"Jessie told me to put this stuff on you, and that's what I intend to do," Riley said, reading the instructions on the tube. "Can you turn over and scoot the back of your gown up?"

"No, I can't," she sputtered, reaching for the covers.

Riley pulled them away. "Don't do that. I have to—"

"I'm not wearing panties," she said, almost under her breath.

"What?"

She gritted her teeth. "I'm not wearing panties."

A strained silence followed. Riley felt the heat rush to his lower body. He stood there several seconds, trying to compose his thoughts. He cleared his throat, and the voice that came out sounded more like that of his father. "Well, that can't be helped, Savannah. You need this medicine if you hope to get better. You do want to get better?" He paused. "Besides, you didn't let modesty get in the way when you were trying to bring my fever down."

Savannah sighed heavily, turned over on her side, and offered her back to him. Then, without warning, she gave a little wiggle and pulled her nightgown to her waist. "Okay, there," she said.

Riley felt the color drain from his face at the sight of her pert behind. Her knees were slightly tucked, probably to ease the pain, but it caused her hips to flare slightly. He dropped the tube on the floor, and it rolled beneath the night table.

"Well?" Savannah said impatiently. She was thankful he couldn't see her face, she was certain she had enough heat in her cheeks to keep the furnace going for a week.

Riley was already on his knees. "I, uh, dropped the tube while taking the cap off," he said, feeling like a clumsy adolescent as he scrambled for it. "Just take a minute."

"Are you doing this to embarrass me?" she asked, resisting the impulse to dive beneath the covers and deal with the discomfort.

He found the tube, grabbed it, and took his place on the edge of the bed. "Don't be silly," he said. He removed the cap, tucked it in his shirt pocket, and squeezed a generous amount of the mentholated rub on one finger. "Okay, here goes," he said, swiping it across her lower back. She stiffened, and he didn't know if it was from his touch or because the ointment was cold. He began to slowly massage the medicine into her skin. "Tell me where it hurts the most," he said.

She hesitated. "A little lower down."

He closed his eyes, felt sweat pop out on his forehead. He moved his hand lower. "Am I rubbing too hard?"

She sighed her pleasure as the knot of pain seemed to unfurl inside. "No, it's just right. Oh, that feels great, Riley. I can't believe I acted the way I did."

He felt tiny rivulets of sweat trickle down his temples. His upper lip was damp. He tried not to look at her, tried not to think of what was tucked between her perfect thighs, of the warm breasts snuggled beneath the gown. He'd tried to convince himself he didn't need this. Now he realized what a liar he'd been.

The pain medication and massage was obviously working; Savannah could barely hold her eyes open as Riley pulled the gown in place. "Better?" he asked.

"Mmmm." She was drowsy.

He backed away from the bed. "I'm going to check the kids once more, then jump in the shower."

"I thought you took a shower before dinner," she said sleepily.

"Yeah, well, I could probably use another one." A cold one, he added silently.

Riley raced down the stairs as though the hounds of hell were after him. He'd made a mistake thinking he could administer to her needs and remain as detached as she'd been when he was the one in need. Instead, he'd reacted like a horny schoolboy, sweating and trembling and doing everything but drooling on himself.

He checked the twins first. They were sleeping soundly. As he gazed down on their peaceful faces, he promised himself he would sit them down one day and warn them just how dangerous women were. Sure, he'd give them the speech about drugs and drunk driving and safe sex, but he'd make damn certain they knew what happened to a man once he let a woman get under his skin. He suddenly realized that was *exactly* what'd happened to him. In just a brief period of time, he'd let Savannah Day get under his skin in a big way.

He climbed the stairs once more and knocked on Melody's door. He waited until she said come in before opening the door. She was sitting at her desk studying a biology book, and he wondered, as he had many times over the past few days, how brother and sister could be so different. The only book he'd seen David crack was a *TV Guide*. And David didn't share her fascination with the twins. At best he found them a nuisance.

"Lights out at nine-thirty, right?"

She nodded. "Is Mom okay?"

"Yeah. She just pulled a muscle in her back. From lifting the twins, I'm sure. She's sleeping now."

"G'night, Riley."

He found David sitting on the edge of his bed, wearing earphones. The boy looked startled to see him as he pulled them off. "I knocked, but I guess you didn't hear me," Riley said. "Don't forget, bedtime's at nine-thirty."

"Don't you think that's kinda early for someone who's almost fifteen?" David asked.

"Not when you've got to get up at five to catch a six o'clock bus."

"Yeah, but Mom's driving us in so we can register. We'll be able to sleep later."

"Look," Riley said patiently. "You've still got an hour to go. You can listen to music or spend it arguing with me."

"So what time am I supposed to report to work tomorrow?" the boy asked.

"I figure you can change clothes and grab a snack first."

"Where will I find you?"

"I'll find you."

❖――――――❖

Riley was already up when Savannah came down the next morning. Although her back felt much better, her head was groggy from the medication she'd taken the night before. A cup of coffee would do the trick. Riley was in the kitchen supervising the twins, who were doing a sloppy job of feeding themselves scrambled eggs. "How're you feeling?" he asked the minute she stepped into the kitchen.

"Much better. Are David and Melody—?"

"Been up about an hour now. Already had their morning soft drink. You want me to register them in school for you?"

She saw that he'd already shaved and showered and put on fresh clothes, jeans and a navy shirt. He looked wonderful and probably smelled that way too. She remembered how his hands had felt on her body the night before, and she almost shivered. "No, I'd better take them," she said at last, mentally scolding herself for thinking of Riley's body when she should be getting her kids to school. "I'm sure it's not easy starting a new school, especially with less than eight weeks left in the school year."

"You want a cup of coffee?"

Savannah couldn't think of anything she wanted more. "I'll get it." She stumbled to the coffeepot and poured a cup, then went about stirring cream and sugar into it. "I appreciate you taking over for me last night," she told Riley.

He shrugged. "That's what it's all about, isn't it? You took over for me when I was sick." He studied her as though trying to decide if she was truly better. "I figured I'd call this chiropractor friend of mine this morning, see if he can work you in today or tomorrow."

She shook her head. "That's not necessary." When he

started to protest, she went on. "I've had this problem before, and I know what to do."

"Stop lifting the twins?"

"I can't stop lifting them," she said. "They're babies, they need to be picked up. But there's a right way and a wrong way to go about it, and I need to start paying attention to that. Also, there are exercises I can do to strengthen my back muscles. Believe me, I went through this when David and Melody were born. Like I said, I know what to do. It's just a matter of doing it."

"I really don't mind making the appointment," Riley said, wetting a paper towel and wiping Trevor's face. "Maybe there's some kind of brace—"

"I'm not wearing a back brace," she said emphatically. "Just let me do it my way first. If it doesn't work, I'll visit your chiropractor." When he didn't look convinced, she went on. "I'm a big girl, Riley. I know what's best for me." She carried her coffee cup upstairs so she could sip it while she dressed for the trip to town.

The tension was thick as Savannah drove her solemn-faced son and daughter into Pinckney in Riley's Explorer. Her children obviously didn't want to have to start in a new school; that much was evident in the way David scowled fiercely out the window and Melody dabbed her moist eyes with a tissue.

"Lighten up," she told them. "You have less than two months left. After that, you're free all summer."

"Free to do what?" David shot back. "To shovel manure? Sit on the front porch and pick my teeth? Wow, I can hardly wait."

"Perhaps you'd rather be back in Nashville in that crummy apartment," Savannah said sharply. "Where your sister was in danger."

"Riley's place isn't exactly the White House," he muttered.

"It could use some sprucing up," she agreed. "But all that takes time. It's warm and safe, and there's plenty of room for everybody. That's what counts."

Savannah drove on, determined not to let her son make her feel guilty. She thought of the years she'd spent working sixteen hours a day and told herself she had made the right decision by coming. She could actually be a mother to her children now. She could cook healthy meals. Once she learned to cook, that is. She could make clever little snacks for them when they came home from school. She could help them with their homework and have long talks with them. The twins would have a mother as well. What was wrong with wanting those things? she asked herself for the umpteenth time.

"This really stinks," David said, as they parked beside the school.

Savannah shot him a dark look as she turned off the engine. "If you're going to take that attitude, then you're going to be pretty miserable," she said.

"How do you expect me to feel?" he shot back at her. "Don't I have anything to say about my life? Where I live or how I spend it?"

Savannah sighed heavily. In the backseat, Melody had reverted to her withdrawn self.

"I'm not going to argue with you this morning, David," Savannah said at last. "I made the decision to come here and that's all there is to it. Do yourself and everybody else a favor, and try to deal with it in a mature way. Melody, are you okay back there?"

"Everybody's going to think I'm a geek with my hair like this," the girl replied.

"It happens to be very flattering," Savannah told her. "If you look in the new *Spiegel* catalog, you'll see most of the models are wearing their hair very short these days." She saw Melody didn't look convinced. She sighed and checked her watch. "Okay, let's pull ourselves together and go inside."

Registration didn't take long once Savannah filled out the necessary forms. A secretary offered to escort David and Melody to their classes. Savannah followed them out into the musty-smelling hall. "Don't forget which bus you're supposed to take," she said as they walked away. "I'll see you later." They didn't respond; they didn't even look back. She felt like crying.

Savannah found Riley pacing the floor in the den when she returned home, and she assumed he was anxious to get out in the fields. A *Barney* video held the twins' attention. "Thanks for looking after the boys," she said, shrugging out of her lightweight jacket. "I can take over from here."

Riley studied her briefly in her dove-gray pleated slacks and cranberry blouse. A narrow belt emphasized her small waist and full hips. "We need to talk," he said.

"Sounds serious," she told him, draping her jacket over the back of a chair. "Is something wrong?"

He smiled gently. "You always expect the worst, don't you, Savannah? You're always waiting for the other shoe to drop. Maybe one day you won't have to feel so insecure."

"What is it, Riley?" she asked, wondering where the conversation was leading.

"Sit down, please."

She did as he said and waited to find out what was going on. She watched him take a throw pillow from the sofa and drop it at her feet. Her confusion grew to new heights.

"You said you wouldn't marry me even if I got down on my knees," he said, making a production of kneeling before her and putting one knee on the cushion. The twins, forgetting their show for a moment, obviously thought they were playing a game and hurried over to climb on their daddy's back. Riley was not deterred. "But I'm going to ask you anyway." He chuckled when her jaw dropped. He took her hand in his. "Savannah Day, would you please do me the honor of becoming my wife?"

SEVEN

Savannah was thankful she was sitting, otherwise her knees would have buckled beneath her and she would have fallen facedown on the rug. "Your fever must be back," she said, remembering how he'd teased her when it had shot up so high. But when she placed her hand against his cheek she found it cool.

"I don't have a fever. Actually, I feel pretty good. But don't you see, getting married is the right thing to do, the *only* thing to do in our case. What do you say?"

"You're serious about this?"

"Of course I'm serious."

She continued to sit there. "Is it because of what Mrs. Cookson said?"

"I don't like to think of people talking bad about you, but that's not the only reason. We planned from the beginning to get married; that's what we agreed on. It's just—" He paused. "I guess we got sidetracked. But it's time we make a commitment."

"What about David and Melody?"

"We'll just have to take it one day at a time. But I

promise I'll try to be a good influence in their lives. So what do you think?"

It was all she could do to keep from bursting at the seams, grinning from ear to ear. She finally had all the things she wanted; a decent man who could provide a stable home for her children and possibly fill that vacant spot within herself. She was tempted to throw her arms around Riley and kiss that handsome face to pieces. On the other hand, she didn't want to seem too eager. She had walked on pins and needles for a week wondering if he was going to want her to stay, maybe it was time she gave him a dose of his own medicine.

Riley couldn't imagine what was taking her so long to answer. Maybe she was in shock. "Savannah?"

She looked up. "I'm sorry," she said at last. "I guess I wasn't prepared for this. I mean, it bothers me to think people might be talking about us, but that's not reason enough to get married." What she'd really wanted to hear instead of him wanting to put an end to the gossip or make a commitment for their children's sake, was for him to say he cared for her just a little. She didn't expect him to feel passionate, undying love after only a week, but she'd hoped he would have some feelings for her. She certainly had feelings for him, and although she had been willing to enter into a loveless marriage for security reasons, she knew in her heart she wanted more. She deserved more and so did her children.

"I suppose what I'm saying is I need a little more time," she said at last.

If Savannah had been stunned by the proposal, it was nothing compared with how Riley felt when she told him she wasn't ready. He had expected her to embrace his marriage proposal wholeheartedly. After all, they had already agreed on it; they had a contract. Could it be she was having second thoughts? He knew, contract or not, he would never push her into something she didn't want.

"Savannah?"

She didn't budge. "Yes?"

"I guess I'm a little rusty at this sort of thing, but I'm willing to do everything I can to make you happy." When she didn't respond, he went on. "That's how much I want you to stay, not just because my twins need a mother but because . . . well, I need you too. That's all I'm going to say about the subject for now."

Savannah didn't start breathing normally again until he left to check on the work going on outside.

The next day, Savannah and Melody were on the floor playing with the boys when the doorbell rang. "I'll get it," Melody said, leaving her mother in charge of building a tower out of wooden blocks. Trevor hit it with his fist, and it came crashing down. Both boys squealed with laughter.

"That's it, mister," Savannah said, poking him playfully. "I'm not going to sit here building towers if you're going to knock them all down." Still smiling, she glanced up and found Melody standing in the doorway holding a vase of yellow roses. "What in heaven's name—?"

"They're for you, Mom," the girl said. "Have you ever seen anything so beautiful?"

Savannah couldn't imagine who would be sending her flowers, much less roses. "Is there a card?"

Melody handed her a miniature envelope, and Savannah opened it. The card simply said Riley. She handed it to her daughter, who was bursting with curiosity.

"Why do you suppose Riley is sending you flowers?" Melody asked.

Savannah pondered it. She hoped it meant he was eager to receive her reply to his marriage proposal, but she decided not to share that information with Melody at the moment. She reached for the card and tucked it inside the envelope once more. "Maybe he just wants to thank me for taking care of him while he was sick," she said. "Would you please take them upstairs to my room so the twins don't get their hands on them?" Now that Riley had recovered from the flu, he was back in the room off the nursery.

Savannah could feel Riley's eyes on her at dinner. Afterward, he helped Melody and David clean the kitchen so Savannah could bathe the boys. He was sitting at the kitchen table when Savannah returned, followed by a couple of blond, pajama-clad toddlers demanding their 'nak, which stood for snack. Now that they had recovered from the flu they couldn't seem to get enough in their bellies. Riley put the boys in their high chairs while Savannah prepared milk and cookies.

"Have you . . . uh . . . thought about our conversation from yesterday at all?" he asked.

Savannah gazed at him and remembered how he'd looked that first day wearing a frilly apron and trying to nurse two babies back to health. He'd appeared vulnerable and unsure of himself. He appeared that way now. She felt a tinge of sympathy for him because she'd made him wait for her answer when she already knew in her heart she wanted to be his wife. She only hoped he wasn't doing it out of some sense of obligation and that one day they would have more in common than raising a houseful of children. She longed for love.

She stepped closer. "I've thought of little else, Riley," she said at last. "And I would very much like to marry you."

His relief was palpable. He reached for her and pulled her into his arms, then kissed her softly on the lips. "I'll try very hard to be a good husband," he said, "and a good father to your children." He chuckled after a moment as though he needed to ease the tension. "Lord, I can't believe I'm marrying such a shrimp."

She punched him playfully. His stomach was hard and firm, but she already knew that from having bathed him. "I only look small because you're so big," she said.

"You're a shrimp, Savannah, face it." He released her after a moment. "If it's all the same to you, we can apply for our marriage license tomorrow and be married by a justice of the peace as soon as the waiting period is over."

She nodded, but she wished he'd spent more time teasing her or talking about his feelings than making plans. And, even though she would like to have been married in a church, she knew Riley would prefer a less complicated wedding. That was the difference between men and women, she reasoned. "That's fine," she replied.

"Do you want me to be with you when you give David and Melody the news?"

"I think I'd better do it alone."

Riley saw that she didn't look eager to face her children. "I'll look after the twins," he said. "Why don't you go tell them."

The light was fading as Savannah made her way to the barn. David and Melody were putting fresh hay in one of the stalls. She was thankful they had the horses to keep them occupied these past few days. "What's up, guys?" she said.

Melody almost smiled at her. To any other person, she might look like a normal girl, but Savannah saw the difference, the look of sadness that still lingered in her eyes. "Sam says we need to start putting the horses up at night instead of letting them run loose in the pasture all the time. So we're trying to clean up a bit."

"I helped some," David said, stretched out on several bales of hay, hands tucked beneath his head.

"He thinks he's too good to shovel manure," Melody

said, tossing a look at her brother. "I told him with his poor grades he'd better get used to hard labor."

"So what'd you think of Sam?" Savannah asked.

"Aw, he's a real know-it-all," David grumbled. "Don't do this, don't do that. A geek if you ask me."

"You think everybody is a geek," Melody replied. "Sam's nice, Mom. He's not—" She paused. "He's not like most boys; he has manners. And he was real careful about teaching us all the safety rules of horseback riding."

"That's good." Savannah had only met the teenager briefly, but she'd been impressed with his respectful attitude toward adults.

"I need to talk to you about something important," she said, taking a seat on a bale of hay next to her son. Melody set the pitchfork aside and waited.

"You're going to marry him," David said dully.

Savannah jerked her head around. "How'd you know?"

"I figured it was just a matter of time. That's why we came in the first place, right? So you could find a father figure for us."

"You don't act thrilled about it."

He leveled his gaze at her. "How do you expect me to feel? I don't even know this guy, and you think I should be ecstatic that he's going to be my stepfather. Do you realize he and I haven't exchanged a dozen words between us? Except for him telling me what work to do."

"You brought that on yourself," Savannah pointed out.

"Besides, you haven't exactly gone out of your way to be friendly to him," Melody said.

David shot her a dark look. "Hey, what's your problem, Sis? You want to spend the rest of your life stepping in cow dung and going to school with hicks?"

"It's better than where we just came from," she said. "At least I can feel safe if I decide to go outside. And I don't have to watch Mom work herself to death the way she was

before. Don't you care about anybody besides yourself?"
she asked.

"Let's not argue," Savannah said tiredly. "I wanted this
to be a new beginning for us all. This is not such a bad
place to grow up. Maybe it will seem a little backward at
first, David, but you'll make new friends and, before you
know it, you'll be going off to art school in Charleston. I'm
going to write to them right away and ask for information
on their program." She paused and gazed at her children a
moment. "You know how important your education is to
me. I want to see you both go as far as you can in this
world."

"Are you prepared to go through it all over again with
Riley's brats?" David said. "They're still in diapers, for
Pete's sake."

"Don't call them that. Those babies deserve a chance
like anybody else," Savannah said softly. "It's bad enough
they lost their mother. They shouldn't have to be raised by
baby-sitters."

"That's not your problem, Mom," he said.

"I don't see it as a problem. I see it as an opportunity to
give them the love and affection they need and deserve. I
missed out on a lot of that when you and Mel were babies
because I had to work so much."

David's jaw hardened. "Sounds like you've already
made up your mind. Why bother discussing it with us?"

"Because I want you both to be happy for me. I want
your blessing. But either way, I'm going to marry Riley
Locke."

Riley found Savannah on the front porch later that evening, hands on the banister, gazing off into the distance.
The twins were asleep, and the older children in their
rooms doing homework.

"Mind if I join you?" he asked, hesitating at the door.

She smiled. "Please do. I was watching the lightning."

He closed the door and joined her. "It's beautiful, isn't it?" he said. "I saw on the Weather Channel we're going to get rain."

"What's it sound like under this tin roof?"

"Nice," he said, remembering the many nights as a boy and a man that he'd been lulled to sleep by the sound. "You should get a good night's sleep." He thought of her in that big bed alone and wished he could join her.

"Look, I was thinking. We can go to the courthouse as soon as it opens tomorrow and apply for that license, then drive over to the jewelry store and select our rings. Afterward, we'll run by the furniture store and pick out a new bedroom suite. If you don't see something in the store you like, you can always order from their catalog."

"You've got a busy morning planned for us," she said, although she was secretly pleased he didn't expect her to sleep in the same bed he'd shared with his wife.

"If you're nice, I'll even spring for lunch."

"Big spender, huh? What should we do about the twins?"

"Why don't we take them with us; we can handle them. There's two of us against two of them. We shouldn't have any problems. Besides, we're smarter than they are."

They were quiet for a moment, each of them caught up in their own thoughts.

"Well," Riley said. "I guess there's no way to find out unless I ask. How did David and Melody take it?"

"David was the only one to voice an objection. Melody didn't say much of anything."

Riley put his hands on her shoulders and turned her so that she was facing him. "Do you want me to talk to him?" he asked, noting the concern in her eyes.

She shook her head. "I think it's best if we leave him alone. Hopefully, he'll come around in time."

Riley raised his hand to her cheek, noting the petallike softness. "I want this to work, Savannah," he said. He kissed her lightly on the lips. "I think you'll agree it's in everybody's best interest."

She nodded, but it wasn't exactly what she'd wanted to hear. She wanted him to tell her how much he cared for her, that he might very well be falling in love with her if he let himself believe it. She wanted him to tell her he needed her, as a wife first and a mother to his children second.

Their gazes locked, as Riley opened his mouth to speak the porch light flashed on and Melody pushed the door open.

"Mom? Aunt Jessie's on the phone, she wants to speak with you."

Savannah tried not to look disappointed as she made her way inside.

The whole thing would've been funny had Savannah not been so nervous about applying for the marriage license. They left the house bright and early, with the twins dressed in their nicest outfits, when all of a sudden they smelled a dirty diaper and were forced to turn back for home.

"As soon as we get settled, I'm going to begin potty training these boys," Savannah announced once they were on the road again.

The courthouse was an antiquated two-story building that smelled of mold and floor wax. Riley held the front door open while Savannah herded in both boys. Travis, obviously becoming tired from climbing the many steps outside, sat down in the middle of the floor and held his arms out to Savannah.

"Let me carry him," Riley said. "I don't want you to hurt your back again."

They went inside the first door marked Marriage, Fishing, and Hunting Licenses. Riley chuckled. "That's convenient. I can renew my fishing license while I'm here."

"How romantic," Savannah muttered.

A prune-faced woman greeted them from a front desk and inquired about their needs.

"We want to get married," Riley said, giving her a big grin as Travis struggled in his arms to get down once more.

The woman arched both brows at the sight of the twins, and Savannah forgot her nervousness long enough to be amused. "I see."

"Will it take long?" Riley asked. "We've got to buy rings and a bedroom suite, then go to lunch before these guys get fussy for their naps."

"I'll hurry as fast as I can," the woman promised.

True to her word, they were out of there in half an hour, a feat considering the fact that Trevor managed to sneak the lady's ink pad right out from under the adults. Savannah spent the next ten minutes in the ladies' room, scrubbing his face and hands.

"Let's walk to the jewelry store," Riley suggested to Savannah.

Once there, they selected simple gold bands while Trevor and Travis made games of pressing their faces against the glass display case and leaving fingerprints, smudges, and traces of runny noses wherever they went. The store manager looked relieved to see them go as he grabbed his glass cleaner and went to work.

They selected a mahogany rice bed and matching night tables, highboy, and triple dresser for their bedroom furniture, while Trevor chewed on a fake rubber tree plant. "I guess we'll take that plant too," Riley told the salesman, noting the damage.

"As well as the silk dogwood," Savannah said as she pulled delicate white petals from Travis's tight fist.

They were exhausted by the time they strapped the boys into high chairs and ordered lunch at a casual restaurant overlooking the water.

"I thought you said it would be easy," Savannah said, frazzled from having taken the twins with them. "I thought you said we were smarter than they were."

Travis reached for the cracker basket, and Riley tried to intercept. The basket slid off the table and onto the floor, strewing crackers in a dozen different directions. He sighed as he left his chair to clean them up. "Yes, but they're faster," he said. "Next time we hire a sitter."

They were married three days later at Ben and Jessie's house by a justice of the peace with all of the children in attendance, including the twins, who insisted on being held by the bride and groom for much of the ceremony. Although it was obvious Riley didn't approve of Savannah holding Trevor, there was little he could say while they were exchanging their vows. As he handed Travis to Ben so he could place the ring on Savannah's finger, he noticed the other twin had drooled on her new white suit with navy piping. Most women would have been annoyed. Savannah took it in stride, just as she did her sullen-faced son, who stood at the very back of the group as though he didn't wish to be associated with any of them.

Riley realized how lucky he was to have found such a woman. He supposed he owed Jessie a debt of gratitude for pushing him into placing that ad.

Savannah handed Trevor to a waiting Jessie when it was her turn to put the ring on Riley's finger. She was trembling so badly, she was certain she'd never get it on, but she took one look at his gentle, understanding smile and felt better. He had never looked so handsome as he did now in his new navy suit and silk handkerchief. But then, she had been attracted to him the moment she'd laid eyes on him in that silly apron. She was doing the right thing, she assured herself. Everyone, including her own children, would adjust in time.

". . . I now pronounce you man and wife," the justice of the peace said. "You may kiss your bride, Mr. Locke."

Sighs erupted from around them as Riley pulled Savannah into his arms for a kiss that, while proper enough, left her pink-cheeked and breathless. She didn't have long to dwell on the kiss; a tearful Jessie threw one arm around Savannah and hugged her until Trevor protested being squeezed between the two women. They laughed. "Welcome to the family," Jessie said.

All at once, Savannah had tears in her own eyes. "Thank you, Jessie. You've treated me like a sister."

"Congratulations, Savannah," Ben said, giving her a brotherly peck on the cheek. "I hope you and Riley will be very happy." He took Trevor from his wife so that he had a boy riding either hip. "Ya'll need to stop spoiling these young'uns and make them stand on their own two feet." Nevertheless, he didn't make a move to put the twins down as he mingled about the room.

Savannah turned to Melody, who seemed to be trying desperately to keep a brave face, despite the tears that glistened in her eyes and gave her away. She literally threw herself in her mother's arms. "I'm so happy for you, Mom. I'm going to do everything I can to help you with my new little brothers."

David stood right behind his sister. "Congratulations, Mom," he said stiffly. He shook Riley's hand and mumbled the same thing before excusing himself.

Once Riley had paid the justice for marrying them, the man wished them luck and left. Ben popped the cork on a champagne bottle, filled four glasses, and toasted the new couple while Jessie took pictures. Her daughter and Melody herded the twins out of the room so the adults could be alone. Sam and David were in the den watching TV since the pool table was off limits for the time being, and Joshua was in his room playing Nintendo.

Finally, Jessie pulled hors d'oeuvres from the refrigerator and made mint juleps and suggested they move to the deck so Ben could put chicken and ribs on the barbecue grill. With her permission, he shrugged out of his coat and tie and rolled up his shirtsleeves, but she cautioned Riley to stay as he was. "I want to take a few more pictures," she informed him.

It was a perfect Saturday afternoon, warm and cloudless. As they exited the house, Jessie readied her camera. "Savannah, you and Riley go sit in the gazebo so I can get a picture," she said. "By the way, I'll make sure you get copies."

"Jessie, would you lay off the picture-taking, for Pete's sake," Ben said.

"I don't have a picture of them in the gazebo," she protested.

"I don't have a picture of them in the gazebo," Ben mimicked in a high-pitched voice, then winked at his brother and his new wife. "Okay, if you two will just put up with it a little longer, we can all get out of these monkey suits and put on real clothes. I'll throw the camera in the pond if she keeps this up."

Jessie shot her husband a dark look. "You and what posse, Benjamin Locke?"

Inside the gazebo, Jessie instructed the newlyweds where to sit. "Scoot closer," she urged. "You're married now, remember?"

Savannah did as she was told, despite the fact that she

was still in a daze. Was this striking man next to her really her husband? "Is this okay?" she asked.

"Perfect." Jessie snapped a picture. "Now, Savannah, sit on Riley's lap and put your arms around his neck."

Husband and wife looked at each other. "Jessie sometimes gets carried away," Riley said.

"I wish somebody *would* carry her away," Ben muttered. "And send that camera with her."

"I heard that," Jessie said. "Just keep quiet and cook. Riley and Savannah will thank me one day for taking these pictures. After all, they'll want something to show their children and grandchildren."

Savannah tried to hide her startled reaction. Children and grandchildren? Who said anything about more children? She glanced up and found Riley watching her, a speculative look on his handsome face, the same face she'd bathed when he'd been feverish. Would she ever feel comfortable enough to reach up and stroke that strong jaw lovingly? She wondered what he was thinking, wondered whether a baby was in their future. She was only thirty-three, they still had plenty of time.

The next thing she knew she was being hoisted onto his lap.

"How's this, Jessie?" Riley called out, grinning like a schoolboy when Savannah gasped in surprise.

She was so flustered, it was all she could do to remember to keep her legs together. She had an impression of strong thighs and a massive chest. She felt giddy. Was she losing her balance or was the champagne going to her head?

"Okay, now, give her a big kiss," Jessie said, obviously enjoying the whole thing.

Without having to be further prompted, Riley lowered his head and kissed Savannah squarely on the mouth. She was not prepared. Not for the kiss or Riley's tongue, push-

ing past her lips and dipping deep inside her mouth. She
felt her insides melt like chocolate on a warm windowsill.

"Perfect!" Jessie declared, snapping frantically. "Okay,
Riley, you can stop kissing her now."

Riley went on doing what he was doing. Savannah, head
swimming, grasped his lapels to keep from falling as the
kiss deepened.

"I don't think he wants to stop," Ben said, having come
up beside his wife to watch.

By the time Riley lifted his face, Savannah was one big
shivery glob of mush. Her skirt, the same one that had
looked so demure on the rack when she bought it, had
crawled high on her thighs and several buttons on her
blouse had come undone.

Her cheeks flamed when she looked up and found both
Jessie and Ben watching, and she instantly struggled to get
off Riley's lap. She stood, took a deep breath to compose
herself, then started down the gazebo steps, only to trip.
Riley's strong arms prevented her from falling facefirst in
the dirt.

"You okay?" he asked.

"Fine," she said in a crisp, matter-of-fact tone that was
meant to hide her embarrassment. She had made an absolute fool of herself in front of her new family. "Jessie, could
you please show me where I can change into more comfortable clothing."

"Sure, honey." As though sensing her discomfort, Jessie
grabbed her hand and ushered her away quickly. "Don't
worry," she whispered. "If Ben kissed me like that I'd be
coming apart at the seams too." They disappeared inside
the house.

Riley, wearing a frown, picked up his drink and made
his way to the grill. "Need any help?" he asked his brother.

Ben shook his head. "Why don't you change into something comfortable?" He looked up. "Hey, why the long face?"

Riley shrugged. "I think Savannah's mad at me for kissing her."

Ben looked bewildered. "She's your wife. Didn't you warn her you might lose your head and do that sort of thing once in a while?"

"You don't understand. We don't exactly have that kind of relationship. Know what I mean?"

Ben nodded as though he did know. Finally, he shook his head. "No, I don't know what you mean."

"Well, hell, Ben, she hasn't been here but a couple of weeks, and there's kids all over the place. What kind of relationship would you expect us to have?" He set his drink down and shoved his hands deep in his pockets. "You saw for yourself how upset her son is over us getting married."

Ben put his arm around his shoulder. "Give it time, little brother. Just give it time."

It was late by the time they arrived home, and the twins were fussy and ready for bed. As Savannah put Travis into pajamas, Riley did the same with the other boy. They tiptoed out of the room and went into the kitchen. From the den they could hear the television set.

"I've been thinking," Riley said. "Why don't you take the Explorer, and I'll use my pickup truck. I'll worry about you in that old car of yours."

Savannah smiled from the sink as she went about straightening the kitchen. "You mean my clunker?"

"You might as well get rid of it, you know."

"Get rid of it? I was saving that car for David."

Riley tried not to show his amusement. "David will run away from home if you give him that car."

She looked hurt. "I've had that car for a long time, Riley, and I plan to keep it. Just in case—"

He frowned. "In case of what?" When she didn't answer, he stood. "In case it doesn't work out between us?" he said.

"That's not what I meant."

"Isn't it?" It was his turn to look hurt. "If we both try, there's no reason it won't work."

"I haven't had much success with relationships," she said, thinking of the parents who'd disowned her and the first husband who'd left her for another woman.

"Maybe your luck is about to change," he told her, then grew serious. "Look, I thought maybe it would be a good idea for us to stick to our regular sleeping arrangements for the time being. I don't expect anything to change right away just because we're married."

Savannah had mixed emotions at first, then decided he was probably right. She didn't want to rush into anything they weren't prepared for.

"I want to move the twins upstairs now that they're older and have the new bedroom furniture put down here in the master suite once it's delivered," he said. "We can keep the monitor on at night in case they wake up. You can do what you wish with that little sitting room."

"Maybe I'll turn it into a sewing room," Savannah told him. "I've always loved to sew. I could make clothes for the twins."

"I can afford store-bought," he said.

She wondered if she'd offended him. "I wasn't trying to insinuate you couldn't. I thought it would be fun."

"I want you to know you don't have to worry about money. My brother and I aren't exactly millionaires, and we live frugally for the most part, but you and the children will always have more than you need. I know how important that is to you."

"Thank you, Riley," Savannah said, then curiosity made her ask, "Are we going to share the same bed when the new furniture arrives?"

He looked at her. "It's up to you. But don't worry, I'm not going to push you into anything until I'm sure you're ready."

He meant sex of course. She tilted her head back and regarded him. "And how will you know when I'm ready?" she asked coyly.

He allowed himself one brief smile. "I haven't spent my whole life planting tomatoes. I'll know."

The bedroom furniture was delivered the following week after the nursery was moved upstairs and the master bedroom painted and the wood floors sanded and varnished. They'd also selected furniture for the sitting room, a green-and-mauve sofa and chair and a ladies' writing desk. Since Riley was involved in the last of the planting, Savannah organized the workmen and tried to keep the twins out the paint cans.

"Very nice," Riley said that evening as he surveyed the rooms. "It's been so long since anything was done to the place."

Savannah was in the process of basting the hen Jessie had helped her cook, and Riley was playing with the twins when he had an idea. "You know what we should do?" he said. "We should redecorate the whole place."

Savannah paused in her work. "Redecorate?" she said, suspecting she'd go crazy if she spent another week like the one she'd had.

"Uh-huh. We'll let David and Melody choose their own colors and furnishings. It'll seem more like their own room that way. Anyway, we need to have all the floors redone and order new drapes; I'll get the name of that woman Jessie used to make hers. We'll have to paint, of course. I can pick up a couple of color charts when I go into town tomorrow."

"Whoa, there, boy," Savannah said, laughing when the twins started to clap at Riley's excitement. Even David and Melody ventured into the room, looking curious. "Aren't you getting a bit carried away?"

"You obviously have no idea how long it has been since this place was fixed up," he replied. "Not since—" He paused and tried to remember but couldn't.

"You'll have to admit it has held up well," she told him.

"We definitely need a dishwasher," he said, as though he hadn't heard.

David and Melody did a high five and said in unison, "Yes!"

The twins started clamoring for attention. Melody picked up one, Riley grabbed the other. Both of them sat at the kitchen table. David, giving a shrug, joined them.

"We need to think of a color scheme," Riley said.

"How about black?" David offered.

"Black!" all three cried.

He held his hands up as if surrendering. "Sorry, it was just a thought. Is it okay if I do my room black? Riley said we could decorate them the way we wanted."

"We'll talk about it," Savannah told him.

"Yeah, right," he said, getting up from the table. "Which means no. I think I'll get back to my homework. Mom, you can just pick out something nice and boring for me. I don't care what it looks like." He disappeared into the dining room once again.

"Maybe I'll surprise you," she called out but received no reply.

Savannah and Riley spent their first night in their new bedroom. With the monitor next to her, she felt confident she would hear the twins if they woke in the middle of the night. She felt shy as she climbed into bed, wearing the shimmering night dress Jessie had chosen for her. The scalloped lace-trimmed neckline and full sleeves gave it a romantic air. She didn't want Riley thinking she was looking for romance unless he was looking for it as well. Nevertheless, she felt a thrill inside when she found him staring at her. She had caught him watching her several times the past few days, and each time she'd wondered what he was thinking. Did he wish she was taller? Did he still think she was too skinny? She had put on five pounds in the almost three weeks she'd been there, and the added weight had softened her face. She didn't look so gaunt and weary when she gazed at herself in the bathroom mirror each morning.

"That's very pretty," he said, as he climbed into bed beside her.

She smiled. "Thank you. I was saving it for our first night in our room. To sort of celebrate."

He leaned on one elbow and regarded her quizzically. His hair was still wet from his shower, and he smelled of soap. He wore navy thermal running shorts and a white, loose-fitting undershirt, and she knew he did it strictly for her benefit. "Oh, and I thought you were wearing it for me."

She felt her cheeks grow warm under his gaze. She didn't have an answer for him. As long as they were talking about the children or the crop or what they were doing to the house next, conversation flowed like corn liquor at a barn dance. But the minute things got personal, her tongue tied itself in one great knot. "Do you think I should check on the boys?" she asked, knowing it was a safe topic.

He looked amused. "You've already checked twice.

You'll only end up waking them, and then they'll want to play all night."

She nodded. There didn't seem to be anything else to say.

"How are David and Melody adjusting to school?" he asked.

"It could be better," she said, knowing her children hadn't discussed their feelings with him. "It's going to take time. I thought once we finish decorating we might encourage them to invite friends over. That should help."

"Fine with me," he said. He set the alarm clock, then leaned over and offered her a chaste kiss on the lips. As he raised his head, he thought he saw disappointment in her eyes. He turned off the lamp, lay back on his pillow, and wondered at it as he stared into the darkness.

Had she not wanted him to kiss her or had she expected it to be a little more passionate? Did she need more time or was she waiting for him to make the first move? He sighed. Damned if he understood women at all. Maybe he *had* spent too much time in the tomato fields.

Savannah heard Riley's sigh of frustration and wondered if it was directed at her. Had he grown tired of their platonic relationship? Was he waiting for her to give him the signal now that they had moved into their own bedroom?

Legally, he had every right to expect more, but Savannah was terrified at the prospect. She had only been with one man in her life, and that man had obviously grown bored with her because he'd looked elsewhere for his affections as soon as their second child was born. Or maybe he'd been cheating all along. Perhaps he'd found her lack of experience dull and worrisome and had found someone more exciting right away.

What if Riley found her equally boring? What if he

took a lover in Pinckney? Would he still keep her as a wife and mother?

Savannah turned on her side. She was being ridiculous comparing Riley to that louse of an ex-husband of hers. And like Riley had said: Just because she'd had a little bad luck in the past didn't mean she was destined for more in the future.

Somehow, some way, she was going to have to show Riley she was ready to take another chance with love.

"Have you thought anymore about signing on as our choir director?" Jessie asked the following Sunday as she showed Savannah how to bake a ham.

It was a beautiful afternoon and Riley and Melody were taking full advantage of it, tossing a large plastic ball to the twins in the backyard and trying to teach them to catch it. Unfortunately, the boys were a bit slow to grasp the ball. By the time they clasped their chubby arms together the ball was long gone. Savannah and Jessie stood at the kitchen window and shared a good laugh over their attempts.

Savannah watched Riley scoop a boy up and toss him in the air. It was obvious the man was crazy about his sons. He also had a genuine affection for Melody, and the girl seemed to be warming up to him as well. He and David, on the other hand, were no closer to becoming friends. David simply performed the work Riley gave him, then spent the rest of the time in his room. Savannah was worried.

She suddenly realized Jessie had asked her the same question twice regarding the choir director's job.

"I don't know, Jessie. I really do have to think about it some more." Savannah had pondered it for days. It would be nice to have her own income, no matter how small, just something she could tuck away for emergencies. Nevertheless, she didn't want anything to interfere with her time spent with the children. Not only did the twins need a mother, her own children needed to be able to count on her being there after the years she'd spent working so many hours.

"You'll get a salary, you know," Jessie said as though reading her thoughts. "Nothing big, but enough to make it worthwhile. Try not to take too long," she added. "I'm getting a lot of pressure to hire someone. I have other candidates, but I'd rather see you get the job. Besides, you'd have plenty of time for the children."

"I won't make you wait very long for my answer," Savannah said. They went back to discussing the menu. "Do you think Riley suspects you've been cooking most of the meals?" Savannah asked.

"I haven't been cooking the meals, you have," Jessie told her. "I was just there for moral support. As for your question, it wouldn't surprise me if Riley has already figured out what we were doing. I mean, it's kind of obvious the way I run over every time you start dinner. The man's not blind."

"Well, he certainly hasn't said anything to me," Savannah replied.

"Maybe he doesn't care if you can cook or not," Jessie told her. "Have you ever considered that?"

"He has to care a little bit," Savannah told her. "It's not like we can send for takeout whenever the mood hits."

"Maybe it's just not his top priority," Jessie replied. "There are more important things."

"The twins, of course."

"And the relationship the two of you have."

"We don't really . . . um . . . have a relationship."

Jessie sighed heavily. "Have you worn that gown yet? The special one?"

"Yes, and he thought it was very pretty. You know what

I think, Jess?" Savannah whispered. "I think he still loves his first wife."

"You're wrong. That relationship was over long before Kara's death. If Riley feels anything, it's guilt." When Savannah didn't look convinced, she went on. "He married you; he has to feel something. I know what the problem is. Too many children running around. Are the two of you planning to go out again this Saturday night?"

"As far as I know. We'll have to get a baby-sitter, of course."

"I'll help. Maybe you should get someone who can spend the night," she added, then laughed at Savannah's shocked expression. "In the meantime, I'm going to loan you this book I bought a few years back when it looked as if Ben and I were getting into something of a rut."

"What kind of book?"

Jessie didn't hesitate. "It teaches you everything you need to know about seducing your man."

EIGHT

Savannah could not remember when she'd been so nervous. Jessie had arrived bright and early Monday morning and slipped a thin book in between the various cookbooks she'd loaned her. "Riley'll never think to look here," she said.

Savannah peeked at the book in her free time, then tucked it between a bath towel in the evening and locked herself in the bathroom under the pretense of taking a long bubble bath. Riley, in the midst of his remodeling project, didn't seem to suspect anything unusual. His only comment was the fact that her fingers and toes were beginning to look like prunes. She couldn't help but wonder what he would think if he knew what she was reading behind the locked door or what he'd do if she pulled some of the stunts suggested in the book.

As if she didn't have enough on her mind, he was driving her crazy with wallpaper samples and paint colors. Now that his cotton was planted, he couldn't seem to think of anything else. He'd borrowed a catalog from the furniture store in Pinckney and showed her a modern black-lacquered bedroom suite he thought David would like. Mel-

ody selected her own furniture, a dark green Shaker-style
bedroom suite with added desk and bookshelves.

The painters attacked David's room first, feather-paint-
ing his walls in two shades of gray. Next, an artist friend of
Jessie's came in and added a number of bold red and black
brush strokes to sort of tie in the color scheme. In the end
it resembled a mural. Although David had grumbled when
he was forced to move out of his room temporarily, it was
obvious he was curious about what was going on in there.
Savannah told him it was off limits until the decorating was
finished.

On Friday, the decorator arrived from Charleston, driving a van loaded with accessories. He was a tall, skinny man
with kinky hair who never stopped moving.

"Where's the rug?" he demanded the minute he saw
the room. "And the furniture? I have nothing to work with
here."

Riley tried to calm him. "The rug man got a late start;
he should be here any minute. But the furniture won't be
here until around lunchtime."

The decorator looked stressed and frazzled. "I'm due
back in Charleston, I can't wait till midday."

Riley sounded weary when he spoke. "Look, the bedroom suite is a shiny black lacquer, and all the colors we're
using are on the wall. Can't you just use your imagination
or something? It's for a teenager. Just pull out anything in
your van that looks weird and different."

As though acting on cue, a truck bearing the name Kit's
Carpets pulled into the back, and two men jumped out
carrying a long roll of carpet. A red Chinese rug was rolled
out in David's room and a soft cream plush placed in Melody's.

Savannah couldn't have been more thankful to have the
workers. Between the painters and the carpenters roaming
through the house, making the twins anxious and fretful,

she would never have been able to pull it all together. Riley was already discussing what they would do with the den and living room and how they would update the kitchen and baths once they put the final touches on the teenagers' rooms.

She should have been excited, she told herself. She would have been excited if she hadn't just read a chapter on erogenous zones. She couldn't help but wonder what Riley would do if she walked up to him and started drawing circles with her tongue on his inner wrist and elbow. Probably send her back to Nashville in a straight jacket.

By lunchtime she could stand the commotion no longer. She took Jessie up on her invitation to her and the twins for lunch. Savannah scribbled a note to Riley, who was upstairs in the midst of all the chaos, then strapped the boys into their car seats in the Explorer and left.

"The place is an absolute zoo," she told Jessie as they ate chef salads and fed the twins leftover shredded barbecue and mashed potatoes. "It must be costing Riley a fortune."

Jessie waved the statement aside. "He can afford it. Besides, he should have done something to that place years ago. I think he would have but—" Jessie paused, her face grew pink.

"What?" Savannah insisted.

"Kara never wanted to live there. She wanted to build this monstrosity in town, and Riley simply couldn't do it. Or wouldn't." She took a bite of her salad. "The Locke family has always been a strange bunch," she said. "They could have afforded to tear that house down and start over, but they were simple people who appreciated what they had. Ben and Riley are the same way. You wouldn't believe what I went through when we had this house built," she said, chuckling. "Ben kept saying, 'Do we need to get this fancy?'" She rolled her eyes. "Our house is big and comfortable enough, but it's certainly not fancy."

Savannah shook her head. "Now Riley's discussing what to do with the rest of the place."

"Good. Make him put in new appliances, including a dishwasher. And tell him to enclose that back porch so you don't have to brave the elements to get to the laundry room."

They ate their salads in silence for a moment, each of them coaxing food into a twin's mouth. The boys weren't interested in lunch; they wanted to play. As Jessie cleared the table and put the dishes away, Savannah ushered the boys into the backyard, where Josh's old swing set sat like an abandoned friend.

"Are you ready for Saturday night?" Jessie asked, joining her a few minutes later. "It's tomorrow, you know."

Savannah felt her stomach take a dip. Of course she knew it was tomorrow. She was as nervous as a treed coon over the whole thing, and couldn't believe she was actually going through with it. "As ready as I'll ever be, I suppose. I figure Riley will either laugh in my face or drag me home and lock me away until I've come to my senses."

Jessie chuckled. "Just remember, no matter how anxious you feel, you're doing it for a good cause. It's obvious you and Riley are crazy about each other; falling in love is just a matter of time."

Savannah remained thoughtful for a moment. As far as she could tell, she was already in love.

The noise and clutter had miraculously disappeared by the time the yellow school bus wheezed to a stop out front and David and Melody stepped out. The furniture had arrived shortly after lunch, was set up and dusted and waiting final approval from the teenagers. A plump, middle-aged woman arrived with bed spreads and window treatments and was in and out of the rooms in no time. All the noise and confusion was well worth it, though, when Savannah saw the look on David's face as he opened the door and stepped inside his room.

"Oh, man," he said, checking out the prints on his wall which were of snazzy sports cars and motorcycles. The decorator had also put out ultramodern chrome lamps and a black marble sculpture of a man playing an electric guitar. Savannah and Riley stood in the doorway waiting for the verdict. "I thought you guys were going to do something hokey," he said, looking genuinely awed and touched at the same time. "But this is . . . wow!" It was obvious, for the first time in his life, the boy couldn't think of anything to say.

Melody was pleased as well, the eyelet bedspread and dust ruffle and matching pillow shams had been made in a soft ivory. The decorator had chosen dainty Tiffany lamps for her and a huge basket of silk and dried flowers for her dresser.

Riley grinned, but Savannah could only feel relieved. She hadn't meant for Riley to be so extravagant, but she was thankful her children felt more at home now. She went downstairs, checked on the twins who were taking a late nap, and started dinner.

Once Riley proclaimed the grill was hot enough, Savannah carried the hamburger patties out. She set the tray on a table beside the grill, brushing past him as she did so. She caught a whiff of his woodsy-scented aftershave. He always smelled so good, even when he came in sweaty from working. There was something wholesome, even sexy about a man who'd worked up a sweat. As usual, his clothes seemed to be a part of him. His jeans, soft and faded from so many washings, fit him nicely and emphasized his strong body. He'd rolled his shirtsleeves to his elbows, exposing slightly muscular arms feathered with black hair.

"Are we still on for tomorrow night?" he asked.

"Huh?" Savannah looked up quickly. "Oh, yes, of course." She paused. "Actually, I was hoping I could just meet you somewhere. I plan to do some shopping beforehand. How about I meet you in the lounge of that cute little motel?"

"The General Lee?" He looked puzzled. "You know, that place doesn't draw a lot of couples, Savannah. It's mostly men stopping by for a quick one after work."

She shrugged. She wanted other men to be there, watching her. At least the book said she did, and Jessie, who'd helped mastermind the plan, considered them geniuses for coming up with the idea in the first place. "No problem," she said at last. "We can have a cocktail together before we go to dinner. Is six-thirty okay?" Of course she planned to arrive a few minutes late, but he didn't have to know that.

Riley saw that she was serious and decided to let her have it her way. Once she saw the sort of crowd the General Lee lounge drew, she'd never want to go back. "Whatever you want to do is fine with me," he told her. "Is Mrs. Cookson baby-sitting?"

"No, I have someone who can stay later if we need her to. She goes to Jessie's church, she'll be good with the kids."

When she started back inside, Riley stopped her, reaching out to grasp her small hand. "Why don't you sit with me for a minute?"

His touch sent tingles up her arm, clear to her elbow. "Just let me check to make sure Melody will listen for the twins," she said, hurrying inside. When she came out a few minutes later she was carrying two soft drinks. She handed one to Riley. "That girl is crazy about those babies," she said, handing him one and taking a seat in one of the metal yard chairs.

"She's very good with them," Riley said, closing the lid

on the grill and sitting beside her. He popped open his soda and handed it to her, then took the other one and opened it as well.

Savannah was touched by the simple but courteous gesture. "I think the twins could prove therapeutic for Melody," she said.

"When are you going to tell me what happened to her?"

Savannah took a sip of her drink. "She was attacked by a gang of boys."

All the light went out of his eyes. "Was she—?"

"No, she wasn't raped. They bruised her up a bit and chopped her hair off. She's a different person from what she was. I decided I wasn't going to hang around Nashville in case the boys decided to come back."

"How's she doing in school?"

Savannah sighed. "Not as well as I'd like. She was a straight A student before the attack, and now she gets high C's on most of her test papers. And she always made friends easily. You know as well as I do she hasn't mentioned making a new friend here." She sighed. "I've been thinking I should arrange for her to see somebody."

"A psychologist?" he asked. When she nodded, he scooted forward on his chair. "Listen, you've got one of the best counselors in Pinckney right in the high school. Her name's Ginny Norris. We went to school together; she married a close friend of mine. I could ask her to look out for Melody."

Savannah pondered it. "I don't want to do anything to embarrass her."

"Ginny'll be discreet. And if it doesn't work out, we can always look elsewhere."

She liked the way he said *we*. It made her feel secure, suggested theirs was a long-term relationship. "You'll call her?" Savannah asked.

"First thing Monday morning."

She leaned back in her chair, feeling more relaxed knowing he would look into it for her. She'd never had someone so willing to help her with her children; in fact she'd had no one. She didn't quite know what to say. At the same time, it made her more determined to see their relationship progress even further, to the husband-and-wife stage. She was thankful for Riley's friendship, but she wanted more. She could only hope he felt the same way.

Riley stood and flipped the hamburgers, then adjusted the flame on the gas grill. "You sure are quiet," he said once he'd rejoined her. "Something on your mind?"

If only he knew. Savannah smiled suddenly. "I was just remembering the look on David's face when he saw his room."

Riley chuckled. "He must like it; he hasn't come out. We may have to send dinner up on a tray."

"I appreciate what you've done. My children have never had anything that nice."

"Well, this place has needed sprucing up for a long time."

"You can tell it's been well cared for."

"My grandmother and my mother worked on it all the time."

"Jessie told me your mother was in a nursing home."

He nodded. "Alzheimer's. It got to where I couldn't leave her alone for a minute for fear she'd set the house on fire."

"Do you visit her?"

"Not as often as I did in the beginning. She doesn't know me half the time anyway. It's pretty depressing." He finished his soda and set the can on the ground.

"We should probably visit her together," she said.

He nodded, but he seemed reluctant. "Yeah, I know.

I've sort of dumped that responsibility into Ben's and Jessie's laps."

"Have you always lived in this house?" Savannah said, changing the subject.

He grinned. "You mean, was I a mama's boy?" He shook his head. "After high school I spent three years going to college in Columbia. I dropped out when I realized the only thing I really wanted to do was farm. So I rented a little cottage not far from here and went to work for my father. Ben had already been working for him a while. Then, one day, my father's heart just stopped, and he dropped dead right in the field."

"I'm sorry," Savannah said.

Riley nodded. "He'd had a happy life." He stood once again and checked the burgers.

Savannah watched him for a moment, fascinated by his every move. It was hard to believe a man with his looks had advertised for a wife. "Jessie told me you were a real womanizer at one time," she said, smiling slightly.

He looked up in surprise. "Yeah, well, Jessie has a big mouth. I keep telling Ben he needs to do something about it, but I think he's scared of her."

She could see that he was uncomfortable with the topic, but she pressed on, partly out of fun but mostly out of curiosity. "Is that why you waited so long to get married the first time? So you could be the town Romeo?"

He closed the lid on the grill. "I wasn't a Romeo, I just liked to go out and have a little fun now and then."

"How do I know you'll stay faithful to me?" she asked, a teasing lilt to her voice. "What if, after a few years, you decide you want to sow a few more wild oats?" Although she was, in all honesty, just kidding around, she couldn't help but wonder if he wouldn't grow bored with her after a while when and if they consummated their marriage.

"I wouldn't cheat on my woman," he said. "It's as simple as that."

Savannah felt something quicken inside of her. He'd called her his woman. The notion that she belonged to him made her feel warm and tingly. She shivered.

"Are you cold?" he asked.

"No, I'm fine." She realized it was time to change the subject again. "Jessie has offered me a job as choir director for her church," she blurted out.

"That's nice," he said. "You have a knockout voice." When she looked surprised, he went on. "I've heard you sing."

"It doesn't pay much."

He shrugged. "Yeah, but you wouldn't be doing it for the money anyway, would you?"

"No, I suppose not. I'd only have to work a few hours a week. Practice is on Wednesday night."

He lifted the grill. "The burgers are ready," he said, turning off the gas.

"What do you think?" she asked.

"I think you should do it if that's what you want. It's not Hollywood, but maybe you can derive some sort of satisfaction out of it." He loaded the hamburgers onto a plate. "Besides, I don't like to think of you cooped up in this house all the time. It's not healthy. And I can watch the twins when you're gone. I don't want to give you the impression I'm dumping them on you." He saw that she still didn't look convinced. "What's the problem, Savannah?"

She shrugged. "I just don't want you to think I'm not keeping up my end of the bargain."

He set the plate down and put his hands on her shoulders. "This isn't a job you can be fired from. This is a marriage. Give and take and all that sort of thing." He smiled gently. "Let's try not to take everything so serious, otherwise it won't be any fun."

Savannah stood there, frozen in place as he looked into her eyes. His face was so close, she was certain he was going to kiss her. Instead, he reached up and tweaked her nose. "I don't know about you, but I'm hungry," he said, releasing her. He reached for the plate of hamburgers and started for the house. He didn't see the look of disappointment shadow her face.

Savannah gazed at the petite woman in the mirror and wondered, not for the first time, if she'd lost her mind. She had entered the motel room little more than an hour before and soaked in gardenia-scented bubble bath while Jessie went about turning the simple room into a veritable love nest. There were fresh flowers on the dresser, an ice bucket holding champagne on the table, and satin sheets on the king-size bed.

While Savannah anxiously fidgeted in a chair before the dresser, Jessie reapplied her makeup with a heavy hand, then teased and fluffed her hair so that it looked as though Savannah had twice as much of it as she really did.

But that was nothing compared to the outfit she wore.

Her skirt was leather and cut midthigh, so short, she couldn't sit down without pulling it even higher on her legs. Jessie had pronounced it perfect when Savannah had tried it on that afternoon. The bustier was black as well and cut so low, Savannah found herself unconsciously tugging it up. Topping it all off was a gold-beaded vest, black fishnet stockings, and spiked heels.

"You look like you got naughty on your mind," Jessie had told her before she'd wished her luck and slipped out of the room so that Riley wouldn't see her car when he pulled in.

As Savannah stood there she knew one thing for certain. She was terrified.

What if Riley didn't like it? What if he found it a total turnoff? After all, he was a simple farmer. He might not appreciate a woman in leather and fishnet. What if she embarrassed him?

What if he got up and walked out on her? Her heart skipped a beat at the thought.

Worse, what if he decided she was too brazen, too wild to raise his children? She swallowed.

She checked her wristwatch. Almost six forty-five. Riley was probably wondering what'd happened to her. She sighed. The book had claimed this was a surefire way to get a man's attention and make him fall head over heels in love with you, but she was an absolute wreck just thinking about the part she was to play.

Savannah let herself out a moment later and headed to a discreet door on the side of the motel marked Lounge. She opened it and stepped inside, then blinked several times as she tried to get accustomed to the darkness. It reminded her of the many bars she'd sung in professionally when she'd been too young even to take a drink. She'd wondered, as she did now, why it had to be so dark. If folks weren't ashamed of what they were doing, seems they could at least turn up the lights. Savannah made her way to the bar, careful that she didn't slip on the parquet floor. Finally, she could see. She glanced around the bar, looking for dark hair and wide shoulders, but all she saw were strange men staring back at her as though she'd just stepped off another planet. She suddenly wished she had never come up with this idea.

She took a seat at the end of the bar, and realized as she did so that bar stools were not designed for short people wearing tight leather skirts. She felt the skirt ride way up on her thighs. She looked up and found every eye in the place staring at her, including the unshaved bartender.

"Are you Savannah Locke?" he asked.

"Yes." The word came out on a gush of hot air.

"You had a phone call. Somebody named Wiley."

"Riley?"

He shrugged. "Whatever. Anyway, he says he had a flat tire coming out so he's going to be a little late."

"Oh."

"You want something to drink?"

Savannah glanced around and wondered, dressed as she was, why she thought it odd that strange men were staring at her. Of course, had Riley not been late he would have seen her grand entrance and would have been turned on by all those stares. Husbands and boyfriends like it when other men looked at their women, it *aroused* them. At least that's what the damn book had said in Chapter Three. "Did he say how late he was going to be?" she asked.

"Naw."

She took a deep breath. "Okay, then I'll have a glass of wine." When the bartender didn't make a move to get it, she offered him a baffled look. "What?"

"What kind of wine?"

"Oh, white."

He went for it. When he returned, he set the glass in front of her. "This one's on the house."

She was surprised. "Well, thank you."

"Then I want you to leave."

"I beg your pardon?"

"I don't need any more trouble with the cops, lady."

"But I haven't done any—"

"Is mean ol' Burt giving you trouble, honey?" a male voice said.

Savannah snapped her head around and found herself looking into the face of a chubby redheaded man. Like Burt, he hadn't been near a razor in days. "I'm fine," she said curtly, wanting to get rid of him immediately.

"How come you got to be so mean, Burt?" the guy

went on. "Cain't you see this is the first purty face you've had in here in months?"

"You know why I'm trying to be so careful," Burt mumbled.

The redheaded man climbed onto the stool next to her. "This 'uns on me," he told the bartender, pointing to her drink.

"That's not necessary," Savannah insisted. She grabbed her bag. "As a matter of fact, I was just leaving."

"Now see what you did," the man said to Burt. "You done hurt her feelings. You don't have to leave, honey," he said, putting a restraining hand on her.

"No, I think it's best I just head back to my room," she said, trying to pull free without drawing attention to herself.

"You got a room here?" he asked. "Well, why didn't you say so? I can get us a bottle and . . ." He leaned closer and whispered the rest. Savannah's cheeks flamed a bright crimson. "I'll even reimburse you for the room," he said.

She could only stare back at him in disbelief. The man had just offered to pay for sex with her.

"Excuse me, miss?"

Savannah yanked her head up and found herself looking into the face of a young man in a business suit. "Yes?" she said, noting how clean-cut he appeared and hoping he could intervene if need be.

"Could I speak with you outside?" When she hesitated, he flashed a badge. "I'm Detective Harrison from—"

Oh, thank goodness, Savannah thought, trying to get down from the tall stool without exposing more flesh than she had. "Yes, of course," she replied, thinking she would ask him to walk her back to her room. She could watch out the window for Riley's truck, after she scrubbed off all her makeup and changed into respectable clothes.

"You don't have to go with no cop," the redheaded man said. "Money never exchanged hands."

Savannah offered him a blank look. "What?" It only took a split second for his meaning to sink in. They obviously thought she was a hooker. She glanced at the young man. "Detective, I can explain everything."

"Let's go outside, please."

She followed him and stepped out into the parking lot, glad to leave the dark, smoke-filled room behind. "Detective Harrison, I know what this must look like," she said, indicating her garb and feeling like a first-class idiot for ever letting Jessie talk her into such a fool thing. "It's not . . . I'm not—" She was so embarrassed, she could barely speak. Then, just when she didn't think things could get worse, Riley pulled up.

"Oh my God!" she said.

The detective glanced over his shoulder. "What is it?"

"It's my husband! He can't see me like this."

"You mean you're married? Does he know that you're a—"

"I'm not a hooker!" she yelled. Savannah tried to make herself small behind the young man as Riley climbed out of his truck and made for the lounge door. He opened it, then glanced in their direction, tossing the man an indifferent look. He paused when he caught sight of the petite woman in the leather skirt, trying to hide behind him.

"Savannah, is that you?" he asked. He frowned in bewilderment and stepped closer.

"Sir, is this your wife?" the detective asked, stepping aside so Riley could get a clear look at her.

Riley nodded dumbly. "I think so."

"You mean, you don't know?"

Savannah tried to smooth her hair down. "Hello, Riley," she said shyly.

"Savannah, what in the hell is going on?" he asked. "And who is this man?"

Once again, the young man flashed his badge and introduced himself. "I'm afraid your wife was trying to solicit a customer inside the bar."

"She *what?*"

"It's all a big mistake, Riley," Savannah said quickly. "I was sitting there minding my own business when this man approached me and—"

"Why are you dressed like that?" he interrupted, indicating her clothing.

Embarrassment turned to mortification. "It's a long story."

"You have a choice, ma'am," the detective said. "You can either tell it here or at headquarters."

Savannah looked from one man to the other. Finally, she rested her gaze on Riley. "I did it for you," she said, her eyes stinging with tears. "So you would find me desirable." She looked at the detective. "See, I was afraid my husband only wanted me around for the children. So I planned a romantic evening and dressed like this to . . . to get his attention," she said. "It's not easy for us to find time for each other." She felt a tear slide down her cheek and swiped it away. "I even rented a room so we could be alone for the evening," she said, turning to Riley once more. The look on his face was one of utter amazement.

Both men were quiet. The detective must have believed her because he suddenly looked embarrassed. "Maybe I overreacted," he said. "We've had complaints about solicitation taking place here, so when I saw you dressed like that—" He paused and backed away. "Why don't I just leave the two of you to work this out?"

Riley watched the man climb into an unmarked car and drive away. Finally, he faced Savannah, and they stared wordlessly at each other. "You say you rented a room?" he said, unable to mask his surprise.

She nodded as fresh tears filled her eyes. "Yeah, pretty dumb, huh?" She reached into her purse for a tissue and dabbed at her eyes. "Do I have mascara running all over the place?"

He smiled slightly. "Uh-huh." He took the tissue and mopped the damp areas. "Here, blow."

She blew her nose, wadded up the tissue, and stuffed it into her purse. "I'm sorry if I embarrassed you."

"I don't embarrass easily, Savannah. Let's go back to the room so you can wash your face."

She led him to her door and fumbled in her purse for the key. He took it and unlocked the door. He pushed it open, then motioned for her to enter first. The room was cool and smelled of the gardenia bubble bath she'd used earlier.

Riley closed the door and locked it, then surveyed the room. "Champagne?" he said, arching one brow.

Savannah felt herself blush. "Well, you know. To sort of break the ice."

He walked to the table and reached for the bottle, then untwisted the metal tie. He popped the cork and filled the two plastic glasses that sat nearby. He offered one to Savannah. "You look like you could use a drink." He picked up the other glass and toasted her. "To leather skirts," he said, genuinely touched that she had gone to such lengths to get his attention.

She wondered if he was trying to hide being angry and disappointed. "Don't worry, I'm about to take it off," she said, already heading for the bathroom.

"Leave it on," he said.

NINE

Astonishment lit her pale face; the champagne glass almost slipped from her hand. Leave it on? She raised the glass to her lips and tossed the liquid back in one clean gulp.

Riley saw the surprise on her face, and he almost chuckled. He had laughed and smiled more in the last month since Savannah had come into his life than he had in at least a year. "Too bad we don't have any music," he said, deciding she needed something to help her relax. He took a seat in one of the chairs at the small round table. He let his gaze fall on her shapely legs and the high heel shoes. His stomach muscles tensed; his pulse quickened. He suspected she had no idea what she was doing to him, what she'd *been* doing to him these past few weeks.

"Music?" she said aloud, then remembered Jessie fooling around with the TV earlier and finding a station that played easy-listening. She reached for the power switch on the television set, and the room was suddenly filled with soft classical sounds. When she raised up, she found Riley staring. A flush of heat spread through her body.

"Is something wrong?" she asked.

"No, as a matter of fact, I couldn't be more flattered."

"Flattered?"

"That you'd go to so much trouble for me." He set his glass down and stood. "Would you like to dance?"

"Dance?" She realized she was repeating everything he said. "Of course," she said, then moved to set her glass down. Instead, she gulped the rest of the champagne and placed the glass on the TV set. She heard Riley chuckle. "What?"

"You're nervous."

"Just a little."

He started to reach for her, then hesitated. "Why don't you take that jacket off?" When she hesitated, he went on. "You'll be more comfortable. Here, let me help you." He stepped behind her and reached for the lapels, then, very slowly, pulled the jacket down her shoulders. He heard the material whisper against her bare arms and wished he could follow it with his lips. He folded the jacket once and lay it on the bureau. When he faced Savannah once more, he found her back was still to him.

He wasn't sure what it was she was wearing, but from the back he was awarded a view of lovely sloping shoulders. Her fair skin appeared as soft and unblemished as his boys'. "Turn around," he said softly.

She did so. Slowly. Hesitantly.

He felt his breath catch at the back of his throat when she offered him a frontal view. The garment she wore was fashioned from lace-covered satin. It was hooked tight along the front and dipped low at her breasts. They rose from the lacy cups like ivory mounds. His mouth went dry at the sight. "You're very pretty," he managed, his gaze riveted to the upper most hook and eye. He stepped closer and took her into his arms.

For a moment, they simply stood there, adjusting to each other's touch.

Riley marveled at how small she felt, yet how womanly.

Savannah was impressed, once again, by his size, and the heat flowing from his body.

He caught a whiff of her perfume and wondered where else she'd sprayed it; wondered if he'd know firsthand before the night was over.

She buried her face against his chest and inhaled the scent of cologne and soap and male flesh. She longed to open the buttons of his shirt and nuzzle the black curls that covered him. She knew he had a fantastic body; she'd had plenty of chance to see it when he was sick.

How had they managed to progress to this point in only a matter of weeks? she wondered. She thought of the mornings they spent together drinking coffee, discussing the business of the day, and problems that needed to be solved. Of getting David and Melody up and on the school bus, of playing with the twins and sharing a hundred other small things. Of doing the dinner dishes together and sitting on the front porch afterward. Theirs had not been a normal relationship. They'd had all the responsibility up front, whereas most couples took time to get to know each other before the children came along. Somehow, Savannah suspected they were better for it.

A Johnny Mathis song began, and Riley moved slowly, taking her with him. Despite their differences in height, they fit together nicely, thanks to the high heels she wore. Savannah made a mental note to wear them whenever they went dancing.

Riley slipped both arms around her waist and pulled her tighter against him, so tight, he could clearly make out each perfect curve. He had wondered about that same little body these past weeks and knew he wouldn't rest easy until he made love to her.

"What are you thinking?" he asked her after a moment.

"Thinking?" she said quickly. "Oh, nothing. Just listening to the music. You?"

"Just listening to the music," he replied as well.

The music stopped, catching them off guard. They parted slightly and glanced at the TV set as though holding it totally responsible for their discomfort.

Riley pulled her back into his arms. "Savannah?" His voice was unnaturally low.

She looked up, breathless. "Yes?"

"You're the best thing that's happened to me in a long time."

"You think so?"

"I think about you all the time. It's hell trying to concentrate on work, but if Ben discovers I'm daydreaming about you, I'll never hear the end of it." He paused and gazed down at her for a full moment. "Know what I think?" He didn't give her a chance to reply. "I think, since you've already paid for this room, we ought to make the best of it."

Her knees instantly became rubbery. "You're probably right," she managed.

"Only one problem."

"What?"

"I'm not sure I can figure out how to get you out of that thing you're wearing."

Savannah laughed softly, not an easy feat considering his statement had just short-circuited her nervous system and sent her pulse skyrocketing. "I can do it," she said, but when she reached for the first tiny hook, she found her hands were shaking so badly, she could barely grasp on to it. She told herself to get a grip. Isn't this what she wanted? But even as she acknowledged that fact, her insecurities nagged her.

"Let me help you," Riley said softly, noting how nervous she was and wishing there was something he could do to ease her anxiety. He reached for the top hook. It felt miniscule under his big fingers. "Don't worry," he said. "If

I can't unhook them, I can always cut it off of you with my pocket knife."

She laughed, and he raised his gaze to her face. Something intense passed between them, a meeting of souls perhaps. Savannah felt it in every fiber of her being.

Riley sensed it as well and felt a deeper significance to what they were doing. The implication that maybe he was beginning to fall for her both frightened and cheered him.

He fumbled with the last hook and pulled the garment aside. He only had to gaze at her breasts briefly to know that it had been well worth the effort of undressing her.

"I don't know what this contraption is," he said, tossing the bustier aside, "but if you ever get rid of it, I'm going to take you over my knee." He smiled, but the smile faded as his gaze, soft as a caress, returned to her breasts.

Savannah tried to still the dizzying emotions his stare evoked. "Perhaps I should have a little more champagne," she said, hoping to calm her nerves and buy some time as well. The book had made all this seduction business sound so easy; she hadn't counted on having anxiety attacks along the way. She was so out of practice, it was pathetic. Worse still, Riley probably sensed it.

Riley did sense it and treasured the knowledge even more that she'd done this for him. "Come here," he said, unaware that his voice had become husky. All he could do was stare at the perfect ivory globes and wonder what it would be like to fasten his lips around her nipples.

She walked toward him. He filled his glass and raised it to her lips so she could drink. Some of the liquid dribbled down her chin. Riley leaned forward and lapped it up with his tongue. He raised up and kissed her gently. "It's okay, Savannah. Try to relax."

Much to her surprise, he dipped a finger into the glass and wet it, then drew a wet circle around one coral nipple. It contracted and hardened at his touch. Savannah shivered.

He dipped his finger into the glass and applied the liquid directly on her nipple before doing the same to the other.

He handed her the glass and sat down in the chair again before pulling her between his knees. Once there, he closed his lips around one nipple and tasted the champagne, already made warm by the heat of her body. He feasted, moving from one breast to the other, closing his hands around her softness and gently squeezing until he feared he'd never get enough. He felt his body respond to the touch and taste of her.

Savannah knew she'd never be able to keep from spilling the champagne if she didn't do something fast. For the second time that night, she gulped it and tossed the plastic glass to the floor. Riley paused in what he was doing and grinned up at her, before resuming his kissing, but she paid him no mind. All she could think about was his lips on her breasts, kissing and caressing and doing things to her she had never thought possible. She moaned softly and grasped his head with both hands, plowing her fingers through his thick hair. By the time she felt him reach beneath her skirt for the waistband of her stockings, she knew there was no turning back.

Riley pulled the stockings down, peeling them past her hips and thighs, below her knees and calves. He paused at her ankle long enough to pull off her heels. When he raised up and saw the skimpy see-through panties she wore, he thought his head would explode. "My Lord!"

Savannah bit her bottom lip, wondering if his reaction was good or bad. She didn't have to wait long. He leaned forward and kissed the golden *V*. She shivered as his moist, warm breath seeped through the panties to her flesh.

All at once, Riley stood, pulling his shirt from his slacks as he did so. His eyes never left hers. "Undress me," he urged gently.

Savannah did as she was told, removing each article of

clothing and draping them over the chair as she went. She was thankful she'd drunk the champagne; otherwise, she would never have been bold enough to remove his underwear. She sucked her breath in at the sight of him completely nude; broad-shouldered, powerful and erect. Modesty made her look away; curiosity and desire made her wish she weren't modest.

"It's okay," Riley assured her. He took her hand and placed it against his chest. "I don't want you to be nervous about touching me. You've touched me before."

Savannah felt something inside of her grow warm at the feel of his hair-roughened chest. She splayed her hand, felt the curls grasp her fingers like silken cords. The muscles in his chest were solid and tight. She could feel the steady rhythm of his heartbeat.

"Why are you afraid to look at me, Savannah?" he said. "We're hardly strangers."

"Yes, but this . . . this is different."

"But isn't this what you wanted?" he asked. "Seems you went to a lot of trouble."

Finally, she looked at him. "I suppose. I just wasn't counting on me being so nervous. Our relationship is good as it is. I don't want to jeopardize it."

"You're right, it *is* good," he agreed wholeheartedly. "But you yourself sensed something was missing, or you wouldn't have planned this whole thing."

"Are you sorry I did?"

His look softened, and he pulled her close. "I think there's only one way to answer that." Without warning, he swooped her high in his arms and carried her the short distance to the bed. She felt small and weightless, and he handled her as gently as he would something rare and precious. He lay her on the bed, then gazed at her a moment before stretching out beside her and pulling her back into his arms. Once again, he kissed her.

It started off slow and lazy, lips and tongues meeting and withdrawing as though they had all the time in the world. Savannah felt drugged, no doubt a combination of the champagne and the dizzy, swirly feelings Riley aroused with his kisses. She relaxed against him, her bare breasts pressing against his wiry-haired chest, while he stroked her neck and shoulders and back in a way that made her feel as though she'd melt right into the mattress. Once again, she felt him at her breasts, kissing until her nipples tightened and quivered for more.

She was only vaguely aware of him removing the panties and pulling the comforter aside to expose satin sheets. He glanced at them briefly with a perplexed look on his face before he resumed his lovemaking.

Champagne, satin sheets, and a loving man. Savannah thought she'd died and gone to heaven. But all of that seemed to float away into nothingness as Riley kissed his way across her stomach to the nest of curls between her thighs. She tensed, felt him pause.

"Relax, babe." His voice was a whisper.

"I don't know, Riley." Her own voice trembled. She had not prepared herself for intimacy on this level.

"I'll die if I don't taste you, Savannah. It's all I've thought about lately. If you don't like it, just say the word and I'll stop."

Savannah took a deep, shaky breath. She had been without a man for so long; she'd even adjusted well to that fact. Now, everything seemed to be happening at once. She didn't say yes to his request, but neither did she say no. He must've taken it as her acquiescence because the next thing she felt was his lips on her inner thighs.

She wondered when she had forgotten how good a man's lips could feel. And how gentle and caressing and warm. Riley's lips were all of those things. His breath fanned her as he rained soft kisses along each thigh, once again taking it nice and slow. She felt an ache take hold inside. Her lower body lifted off the mattress slightly.

"Does it feel good?" he asked.

"Yes." It sounded like her throat was clogged up. "Yes."

"Let yourself go, sweetheart. It's just you and me."

As he kissed and stroked, Savannah realized the ache she felt was more of an emptiness, a wanting that left her anxious and restless and eager. Then, before she knew it, she felt a wetness, a firm touch at the very core of her being. This time her hips lifted far off the bed. Riley's tongue was like the answer to a prayer or a great riddle. She moaned aloud and pulled his head closer.

Her need was great, her desire pitched several times before she cried out and clung to Riley. He positioned himself between her legs and entered her, taking great care not to hurt her. Once again, Savannah was swept up, and their movements became quick and frenzied. She climaxed a few seconds before he shuddered in her arms.

The earth was still spinning for her when Savannah opened her eyes a few minutes later, and she didn't know if she was intoxicated or reeling from Riley's lovemaking. Lying in the crook of his arm, she glanced up and found him grinning at her.

"What's so funny?"

"I was just thinking how shocked Detective Harrison would be with your behavior."

Savannah gave a snort. "He's still wet behind the ears. Imagine, thinking I was a hooker."

"Hmm." Riley was thoughtful for a moment. "So, do you want to hang around and order a pizza or just grab your money and go?"

She elbowed him in the ribs, and he decided to reciprocate by tickling her. Savannah was certain they could hear her shrieks of laughter in the front office. Before long, though, they were kissing again, and when they made love this time they took their time.

The pizza arrived only minutes after they stepped out of the shower. Riley was bare-chested and wearing his slacks, and Savannah was wearing his shirt and her panties. They devoured the food, washing it down with champagne they drank straight from the bottle.

"No more," Savannah said, when Riley pushed the bottle toward her. "I'm going to have a tough time driving home as it is."

"We're not going home," he said, chewing the last piece of pizza.

"Beg your pardon?"

"I called the baby-sitter while you were still in the shower washing that gunk out of your hair."

"And?"

"She's staying the night."

Savannah pondered it for a moment. "I don't know, Riley. The kids might not like it."

"Tough. You're my wife, and I refuse to share you with anybody tonight so you might as well get used to it."

The way he said it with such meaning brought butterflies to her stomach. Still, she was unsure. "Did you talk to David and Melody?"

"No. David was in his room, listening to music, and Melody was reading. It's not likely we'll warp their personality by spending the night in town."

"And the twins—"

"Asleep."

"Well . . ."

"You just gotta find something to worry about, don't you?" When she didn't answer, he went on. "Why don't you worry about how you're going to satisfy your man?"

Savannah laughed in spite of her concerns. "That sounds like a country-western song."

Riley's eyes got big. "That's right! You used to be a professional singer. Sing something for me, Savannah."

"What? Forget it, Riley."

He'd finished his pizza. "Come on, babe, sing me a love song."

"You're full of corn, you know that." She stood and walked toward the bed.

He got up and followed, grabbing her up against him. "You have a choice. You either sing me a love song, or I'm going to tickle you again."

She refused, and he tickled her until her eyes teared. "Okay, dammit, I'll sing something!"

He looked pleased with himself. "Climb up on one of those chairs so I'll feel like I'm watching you onstage."

She laughed. "Riley Locke, you're drunk."

She got up on the chair, taking care to balance herself because her head was still swirling. "Okay, I'm only going to do this once," she said sternly. "So tell me what you want to hear."

He thought about it for a long moment. "I want you to sing 'Stand by Your Man,' " he said, fluffing up his pillows so he could lean against the headboard and watch her perform.

Taking a deep breath, Savannah belted out the words to the song, entertaining him as she sang by opening the top two buttons on his shirt and hiking the hem up so he had an enticing view of her thighs. Riley's eyes never left her. As she sang, she realized singing for Riley gave her more satisfaction than singing to a packed house. She finished the song and curtsied prettily for him. He clapped and whistled and whisked her to the bed where he proceeded to show her how much he'd enjoyed her performance. Afterward, they fell into an exhausted sleep.

❦━━━━━━━━━━❦

They were showering together the next morning when somebody broke in and stole Savannah's overnight bag and Riley's wallet, which had not only a fair amount of cash but an impressive number of credit cards in it. Riley called the police, then informed the front desk. "I guess you know you're going to have to call about those credit cards," the responding officer said.

Riley nodded. "I will as soon as I get home."

Once Riley had given all the information he could, he reentered the room and found Savannah still wearing the bedsheet and looking depressed. "Why aren't you dressed?" he asked.

"Because I don't have anything to wear," she said sourly. "My clothes were in that bag."

"All of them?"

She gave him a rueful look. "No, not all of them. I still have my leather skirt and the bustier. Imagine how excited and proud my children would be to see me in that."

"We can drop by a store on the way home."

"It's Sunday. The stores don't open till one o'clock. Five hours from now."

They arrived home forty minutes later. The baby-sitter tried not to stare at Savannah as Riley went into his office and found enough cash to pay her. When Melody came into the kitchen, she didn't say anything about her mother's attire, but she did give her a funny look as she kissed Savannah on the cheek and asked if she'd had a good time.

David, on the other hand, was not as discreet. He came to an abrupt halt in the doorway. Savannah actually feared he might faint. "Oh my God!" he exclaimed. "What the—"

"It's a long story, Son," she managed, feeling her face heat up like a Bunsen burner.

Riley stepped into the room with a wad of cash and

handed it to the sitter. "Your mother's clothes were stolen from our hotel room this morning," he told David matter-of-factly. "She had to borrow this outfit from the desk clerk."

"The desk clerk?" Melody replied in disbelief.

"Oh, my," the baby-sitter said. "You weren't hurt, I hope?"

Riley looked dreadfully serious. "No, thank goodness." He put his arm around Savannah. "Actually, we were very lucky."

"Did you get a look at the creep?" David asked.

"No. Your mother was in the shower, and I was . . . well, I was asleep, if you can believe it. Didn't even hear him come in." He wasn't about to admit he and Savannah had drunk champagne and made love most of the night and had fallen asleep without putting the chain in place.

David went to Savannah and hugged her. "I'm glad you're okay, Mom. Hey, you ought to save that hokey-looking outfit for Halloween. Folks would get a kick out of it."

"Oooh, gross!" Melody said. "Mom wouldn't be caught dead wearing that awful thing."

Riley poured a cup of coffee and leaned against the kitchen counter. He grinned at the sight of her pink cheeks. "I don't know, I kinda like it." He winked at Savannah over her children's heads.

As usual, Riley was waiting for David when he got off the school bus the following day. "Change your clothes and grab a snack," he said. "I'll wait for you."

"Lucky me," the boy muttered, heading for the stairs.

Sitting at the kitchen table, Riley ignored the grumbling as he drank a cup of coffee and watched the twins noisily pull the pots and pans from a cabinet. They seemed to be having the time of their lives. Nearby, Savannah was in the process of making a meat loaf. He knew she wasn't much of a cook, also knew Jessie had been helping, and it amused him that the women thought he didn't suspect a thing.

"You forgot to put an egg in it," he told her.

Savannah looked up. "Beg your pardon?"

"I'm not an expert on meat loaf, but I know you have to put an egg in it."

"Oh, yeah," she said. "It just slipped my mind, that's all." Actually, she had dropped a glob of hamburger meat on the page of her cookbook, which was placed in a discreet location on the other side of her mixing bowl so Riley wouldn't see it. She couldn't clean it off without drawing attention to it. Stepping around the twins, she went to the refrigerator for an egg, cracked it, and dumped the yolk into the meat mixture. A small piece of the shell went in as well, but she chose to ignore it rather than dig around for it and appear even more amateurish.

"Is that a cookbook you got there?" Riley asked, suppressing a grin.

Savannah placed a dish towel over the book. "Cookbook?" she said. "Uh, no." She dug both hands into the meat and began mixing it.

Riley got up and walked over to her, reached around the mixing bowl and lifted the cloth. "Sure looks like a cookbook to me. You haven't forgotten how to make meat loaf, have you?"

"Actually, I was just testing out a new recipe," she said. "I get tired of making it the same old way." He was standing right behind her, so close, she could feel his warm breath on the back of her neck. He chuckled softly, and she glanced up. "What's so funny?"

"I'm on to you, Savannah," he said, leaning forward and

planting a kiss on her neck. "But after last night, your cooking skills don't concern me in the least."

She blushed, remembering how they'd spent a good portion of the night. She was glad their bedroom was on the first floor of the house and not directly across the hall from her children. She was also glad they had a television set in the room; Riley had turned up the volume so that it blocked out all other sounds. And there'd been sounds, mostly from her.

"Know what I was thinking?" he said. "We should get one of those big tubs for our bathroom. I measured it this morning, and I'm sure we could fit one in there. One with the fancy gadgets and water jets. You and I could take baths together." He kissed her on the neck again. "What do you think?"

She was prevented from answering when David walked into the room, wearing his old clothes, although it was hard to tell since everything he wore looked old and ratty. He grabbed a granola bar from the cabinet and a soda from the refrigerator, then glanced at Riley. "Okay, I'm ready."

"See you later," Riley said as they headed out the door.

Once they were gone, Savannah found herself praying they'd get along.

David didn't seem any closer to accepting their marriage than he'd been in the beginning, but he kept quiet about it for the most part and accepted the chores Riley assigned him. The twins had tired of the pots and pans by the time she got dinner on so Savannah coaxed them into helping her put them away. Melody came down, having finished her homework, and both boys scrambled toward her. She laughed and scooped Travis up. Savannah picked up the other boy, taking care to lift him the right way, and they carried them into the den.

"I swear, I think these babies have gained five pounds since we got here," she said, setting Trevor on the rug and handing him a toy. Melody put the other boy down and gave him a plastic horse to play with. He immediately put it to his mouth.

"How was school today, honey?" Savannah asked, once they'd settled themselves on the plump sofa.

"Fine. My teachers are nice. And there's a counselor who seems really concerned about me fitting in. She wants to put me in the honors program next year, and she keeps encouraging me to join clubs. I figured you called her."

"I haven't called anybody," Savannah said, which was the truth. Riley had contacted the counselor on his own. "How about the kids? Are you feeling more comfortable around them?"

Melody shrugged. "They're okay. I sort of miss my friends in Nashville, though."

"Now that you've got a nice new room you might want to have someone spend the night."

Another shrug. "I'll see."

Savannah knew she'd said enough. If she pushed too hard, the girl would back off. "How's your brother doing? Does he seem happy in the new school?"

"He's hanging out with the hoods. Same as always."

Savannah sighed. She'd hoped David would change his taste in his friends and stop running with the troublemakers and underachievers. She knew he was capable of better grades, but he refused to put forth the effort. She and Melody chatted a few more minutes. "I'd like to get your opinion on something," Savannah said at last. The girl looked up, and she went on. "Your aunt Jessie has offered me a job as choir director at her church."

"Are you going to take it?"

"I haven't decided. I thought we could visit her church this Sunday and see how we like it."

"You miss singing, don't you?" Melody asked.

Savannah nodded. "It used to be my whole life."

"You have a beautiful voice. I can still remember how you used to sing to me at bedtime. You shouldn't let that kind of talent go to waste." She looked thoughtful. "If you take the job, how often would you work?"

"Once a week for a couple of hours."

"I could help Riley with the twins if you need me to."

"I'd really appreciate it, Melody."

"No problem. What else have I got to do?"

Savannah was determined she was going to get her daughter involved in something no matter what.

White Oaks Church was a medium-size brick structure surrounded by boxwood hedges and tall white oaks, thus its name. As Savannah and Riley carried the twins to a side door leading to the basement, David and Melody followed. The downstairs area smelled of baby powder, crayons, and paste. A tall woman with frosted hair greeted Riley and motioned them in.

"You must be the new choir director," she said once Savannah had introduced themselves. "My name's Bea Todd."

"I haven't actually taken the job yet," Savannah told her. "I haven't even had a chance to meet the choir members or find out what they're looking for."

"You'll have an opportunity at the picnic," Bea said.

"Picnic?"

"The one we're having after church so everybody can get to know you. Jessie organized the whole thing, bless her heart. Why we've got enough fried chicken to sink a battleship." She didn't see the funny look Savannah gave her as her gaze strayed to the twins. "Oh, what beautiful boys," she exclaimed. "They look like they belong on the front of a baby food jar. Just sit them on that rug where all the toys are."

Savannah saw that the nursery was crowded with fussy infants and toddlers, probably unhappy with the fact their parents had left them behind. "I hope you have help," she told Bea.

"I'll be okay," the woman said, waving the statement aside. "It's that nasty flu still going around if you can believe it. We're a little short on staff, that's all."

"Can I help?" Melody said.

All eyes turned to the girl. Bea looked pleased with the offer. "Why, that's awfully nice of you, young lady, but I'm sure your mother would rather you attend the service."

Savannah saw the hopeful look on her daughter's face. "I don't mind if Melody stays down here," she said quickly. "If you need her."

The woman hesitated. "Well, we do need someone to read Bible stories to the kindergarten class. Do you like to read?" she asked Melody.

The girl shrugged. "Sure."

"Wonderful. Okay, run next door and look for a big woman in a red dress. You can't miss her, she'll be running around like a crazy lady. Tell her you're going to take over the five- and six-year-olds. And be sure to make those youngsters mind you," she added, but Melody was already out the door.

Savannah started to climb the stairs leading from the basement, but Riley stopped her, placing a hand on her arm. "Don't you want to see that Melody gets settled in okay?" he asked.

She shook her head. "She'll be fine. I think I just had one of my prayers answered."

Reverend Hilby was a tall man who looked to be in his late forties. He stood at least six feet four and was as bony as a coatrack. Savannah suspected his wife had a difficult time finding clothes to fit him. He spoke about stress and worry in today's society, told funny stories about his own experiences, then read several verses in the Bible that related to the subject. Savannah thought he was quite good and she told him so as she exited the double doors leading out. She introduced herself, and he nodded.

"Ah, our new choir director," he said.

"Well, not yet."

"I hear you once sang professionally." He turned to Riley whom he already knew. "You're going to have to convince your wife to join us, my good man."

"You know how women are," Riley said. "They take their own sweet time making up their minds, then they're likely to change it three or four times before they come to a final decision."

The minister laughed. "Yes, I'm married to one of those. I believe the Lord sent her to me to teach me patience. Of course, she says the same thing about me." He let go of Savannah's hand. "You're joining us for the picnic, right? It's in your honor."

"We wouldn't miss it for the world," Riley said.

Once they were outside with David lagging behind, Savannah leaned closer to Riley. "Wait till I get my hands on Jessie. She planned this whole thing behind my back." She scanned the crowd, looking for her sister-in-law, who'd been unavailable since they'd arrived. Finally, they started for the basement and the twins.

"Can I sit in the car?" David asked.

Savannah turned to her son. "Why would you want to do that?"

"This isn't really my thing," he said.

"Well, try to make it your thing," Savannah told him. She and Riley went downstairs to the nursery where they found Trevor and Travis playing with a huge dump truck. The boys squealed in delight when they saw them.

"They were very good," Bea said. "Once they got over missing their mom and dad, that is." She opened the baby-gate blocking the door so the boys could toddle out. "Oh, and your daughter did wonderfully with the primary class. She's on the playground with her group now."

Savannah and Riley carried the boys upstairs and out into the pretty spring day. They rounded the church and came upon a parklike setting where women were in the process of draping picnic tables with colorful vinyl-coated cloths. Savannah spotted Melody on the playground with a group of children. As though sensing she was being watched, Melody glanced up, saw her mother, and waved. She looked happy.

"Put Trevor down and make him walk," Riley said, setting Travis on his feet as well. "You'll hurt your back again." He glanced in Melody's direction. "Looks like she's having a good time."

Savannah set Trevor down. "She used to dream of teaching elementary school."

"Used to?"

"She hasn't thought about it much since the attack. Maybe this will pull her out of her shell."

Riley took her hand and squeezed it. "I have a feeling everything is going to turn out okay."

She hoped he was right. "Where's David?" she said.

"Probably in the car. He'll join us when he smells the fried chicken."

Savannah debated on going to get him, then decided if David wanted to sit out in the car and be miserable, she would let him. "There's Jessie," she said. "Wait till I—"

Jessie saw her and hurried over. "I'm so glad you could come."

"I'll just bet you are," Savannah said sweetly, "since the picnic is in my honor. Everybody thinks I've already accepted the job."

Jessie waved the comment aside. "Oh, well, you will accept once you see how nice these people are. Just simple country folk who'd give you the shirt off their back if you asked them." She was talking much too fast; it was obvious she wasn't going to let Savannah get a word in edgewise.

"I told you I needed time to think about it," Savannah managed. She saw Jessie wave and motion someone over. She turned to see who it was, then froze in absolute horror at the sight of Detective Harrison dressed in jeans and a sweatshirt, heading straight for them. What in the world was he doing there, Savannah wondered frantically.

"Paul, come meet my sister-in-law," Jessie called out. She turned to Savannah. "You'll love Paul Harrison. He's our youth director."

"Hello, Mrs. Locke," the young man said, nodding politely. "You sure look different, I mean nice, today."

TEN

Savannah's first thought was to bolt.

Jessie linked arms with the young man. "This is Savannah Locke, our new choir director. Savannah, Paul Harrison."

"Yes, we've met briefly. It's nice to see you again."

Savannah knew her face was scarlet, but she forced herself to smile and shake hands. "Same here," she mumbled.

"Savannah has two teenagers who might be interested in your program," Jessie said. She swung her gaze in Savannah's direction. "David and Melody would enjoy themselves. Paul takes them on field trips, they even go camping from time to time."

"I'll mention it to them," Savannah heard herself mumble.

"Well, I have to go," the man said. "I'm trying to round up enough boys for a softball game."

"Where's David?" Jessie asked Savannah. "He might enjoy playing."

"Right now he's sitting in the car being miserable."

Paul raised both brows. "Oh, yes, that favorite teenage

occupation. Show me where you're parked, and I'll convince him to play."

Savannah pointed to their vehicle, and the man hurried away. She'd been so mortified over seeing him that she hadn't realized Travis was yanking her skirt. She suspected he was hungry. She picked him up. "Do you know who that was?" she asked Jessie.

The other woman gave her a strange look. "Of course I do. I just told you he's—"

"The man who almost busted me for prostitution at the General Lee."

"That was *Paul?*" Jessie said in disbelief. She glanced in his direction as though seeing him in a strange new light.

"I have never been so embarrassed in my life," Savannah muttered under her breath. "He'll probably tell everybody. I should leave."

"Oh, no you don't," Jessie said. "I worked much too hard to put this together. You're staying till the bitter end." She linked arms with Savannah. "Paul is very discreet, which is why the teens feel comfortable with him. Besides, if anybody says anything bad about you, I'll personally beat 'em up. Now, put that baby down and make him walk."

They joined Riley and Ben who were standing under a tall oak chatting. Ben gave Savannah a peck on the cheek and went on about how pretty she looked. She thanked him and gave Riley her attention. "I think we should go ahead and feed the boys. I'm sure there's something up there they can eat."

"Good idea," Riley told her. "Trevor's sucking on his fist. Why don't you go through the line and I'll watch them."

"We'll try to find an empty table," Jessie said. "Ben, would you mind getting our picnic basket out of the van?"

Savannah headed for the serving line. She was able to find a number of things the boys could eat, mashed potatoes, green beans, macaroni and cheese, and cherry gelatin. By the time she returned, Jessie had grabbed a picnic table and draped a red-and-white-checked cloth over it. She sent Ben to the serving line with a platter of fried chicken and another piled high with biscuits and corn muffins.

The women fed the boys while the men went for food. They arrived back, each carrying two very full plates. "I wasn't sure what you liked," Riley told Savannah, "so I got you a little bit of everything."

She noted the plate held more food than she could eat in a week. "Thanks," she said. Travis had started playing with his own food so she decided he'd had enough to eat. She pulled moist wipes from the diaper bag and went about cleaning him up while Jessie did the same to Trevor. Then, she spread a blanket on the grass and put several of their favorite toys on it. Although the boys were distracted by the crowd, they sat quietly for a time so the adults could eat.

Savannah glanced around, trying to catch a glimpse of her children amongst picnic tables and card tables with folding chairs, children chasing other children. She found Melody and Sara sitting on the back steps of the church eating. Paul Harrison had somehow convinced David to get out of the car, and the two were standing in the food line. From the looks of it, Paul was doing all the talking. Now and then, David nodded.

Savannah nudged Riley. "Do you recognize that man standing next to David?"

Riley gazed thoughtfully in the man's direction. "He seems vaguely familiar."

She leaned closer and whispered in his ear. "He almost arrested me at the General Lee for you-know-what."

Riley grinned. "No kidding, that's him?"

"It's not funny, Riley," she muttered. "My heart almost stopped beating when I saw him."

"Hmm. And I thought I was the only one capable of doing that."

She looked up, and their gazes locked for a moment. It was obvious what he was thinking.

"Stop looking at each other like that," Ben teased. "You're at church now, remember?"

The visiting began once everybody had finished eating, and the ladies had gathered their food containers and cleaned up. Savannah suddenly found herself the center of attention, surrounded by members of the choir who were curious to meet their new director.

"We've never had a real professional," one man said.

Savannah blushed. "It's been a long time since I was on a stage." She was fairly certain the performance she'd given Riley at the General Lee didn't count.

"Doesn't matter," an elderly white-headed woman named Sophie said. "Some things stay with you forever. I've been singing in the choir since I was eight years old. I sing soprano, of course."

"And she can't carry a tune in a washtub," another woman named Dorthea replied. Both women burst into laughter.

"You skunk," Sophie accused, nudging Dorthea playfully. "You'll have our new choir director thinking I can't sing." She gave Savannah a wicked grin. "Dorthea spends so much time singing through her nose, she has to carry one of those nasal inhalers everywhere she goes." More laughter. Savannah found herself chuckling along with them.

A large man named Lyle Hobbs introduced himself as one of the choir's tenors. "We'd love to have you join us, Mrs. Locke. Jessie's told us so much about you."

Savannah had met most of the choir members by the time Jessie showed up and put an arm around her. "Well?" she asked. "Think you might want to give it a try? As you know, our former choir director left us weeks ago. Once I told these folks about you, they weren't interested in the church hiring anyone else."

Savannah found herself flanked by hopeful faces. She couldn't help but wonder why one of the old-timers hadn't offered to direct the group, but she knew a lot of people shied away from that kind of responsibility. Her experience had taught her that most churches were successful because a handful of members made it so. People like Jessie. And she owed Jessie more than she could ever hope to repay.

"Okay," she said at last. The group cheered. "On one condition," she added, then waited for them to grow quiet. "You know I have four children. If something comes up or one of them gets sick, I may have to appoint one of you to take over in my absence. I don't expect anything to happen, my husband is more than capable with the kids, but I just want it understood up front."

They nodded as though it made perfect sense. "So when can you start?" a woman named Claudia asked.

"When's your next practice?"

Sophie didn't hesitate. "Next Wednesday. But we were going to meet at four today to discuss the upcoming revival."

"Revival?" Savannah turned to look for Jessie, but her sister-in-law was nowhere in sight.

Lyle nodded. "We hold it the last week in May for four straight nights, which means we have to practice about fifteen songs."

Savannah felt a dull sinking feeling in her stomach. Jessie hadn't mentioned a revival, but then she'd forgotten to mention a number of things. "Okay, I'll be here," she said, and was met with much hand shaking and back slapping.

"Excuse me," Riley whispered in her ear. "I know you're the woman of the hour and all, but I think we'd best get the twins home for their naps. I've been making monkey faces and goo-goo eyes at them for the past twenty minutes, but they're still fussing."

Savannah grinned at him. "Has it crossed your mind that maybe they don't find your monkey faces entertaining?"

He looked sad. "And you swore you'd never let all this popularity go to your head."

Savannah excused herself after promising to see everybody later. Ben and Jessie were trying to entertain the twins, but it was obvious both boys were in no mood. "Thanks for mentioning the revival," she told her sister-in-law.

Jessie slapped an open palm against her forehead. "Oh, yes, the revival. I knew there was something I forgot."

"Right, Jess," Savannah said sweetly. She noted there were family members still missing. "Where's David?"

"Playing softball," Riley told her.

"Playing softball?" She glanced in the direction Riley pointed and saw her son and his cousin, Sam, in the midst of a game.

"Paul Harrison said he'd bring David home after the game," Riley said. "I told him that was fine. I hope it's okay with you."

"Sure. And Melody?"

"She said she was ready when we were." Riley picked her out in the crowd and motioned for her. They said good-bye to Ben and Jessie and carried the twins to the Explorer, then fastened them into their car seats. Melody joined the boys in the backseat.

"I don't believe it," the girl muttered as Riley pulled out of the parking lot a few minutes later. "David finally got off his butt and did something."

Savannah tossed her a smile. "The Lord works in mysterious ways. How about you? Did you have a good time?"

"It was great, Mom," she said in such a way Savannah

knew she meant it. "I felt like a real teacher. I wish I could do it every Sunday."

The twins had fallen asleep by the time they arrived home. Riley and Savannah carried them inside the house, tucked them into their cribs, pulling their shoes off and covering them before they left the room.

"How about a cup of coffee on the porch?" Savannah asked.

"Sounds good to me."

Melody was in the kitchen. "I'm going to my room to study," she announced. "I have a history test tomorrow."

Savannah nodded as she headed for the coffee maker. "That's fine," she said. "I have to be back at the church in a couple of hours. Dinner will be simple tonight."

"You took the choir director's job?"

"I agreed to try it out for a few weeks."

"I'm glad, Mom. Don't worry, Riley and I can hold the fort down while you're gone." She smiled at Riley. "Right?"

"Right." He waited until the girl was gone before speaking again. "You've got yourself one fine daughter, you know that?"

"Melody has never given me a moment's trouble," Savannah told him as she scooped coffee grounds into a fresh filter. "Until the attack. I'm glad she's beginning to act like her old self. Which reminds me, I have to make a quick phone call." She poured water into the coffee maker and turned it on.

Savannah knew Jessie's phone number by heart. She dialed, and Jessie herself answered on the second ring. "Okay, now that I've agreed to take over the job as choir director, I have one request."

"You want new robes, right?" Jessie said. "Look, I've been pushing for them for months, but Reverend Hilby insisted on buying a church van so we're broke. You'll have to try again next year."

"I'm not worried about robes at the moment," Savannah said. "It has to do with Melody. I want you to let her teach one of the Sunday school classes, preferably the kindergarten or first grade class. I know she's only thirteen, but she's a very mature thirteen."

"I know she is," Jessie replied. "I'll see what I can do."

"Looks like I married a wheeler-dealer," Riley said once she hung up.

They carried their coffee cups to the front porch a moment later and sat together on the wooden swing. They gazed across the narrow road at the newly planted fields as they sipped in an easy silence.

"How's your back?" Riley asked.

"Better, I'm being very careful."

"You and the kids should get a physical. And a dental exam too," he added. "I've put all of you on my health plan. No sense letting all that insurance go to waste."

"Looks like you've thought of everything," she said.

"Yeah, I'm real good at taking care of the practicalities. It's the personal stuff I have trouble with. I guess I just don't always understand what another person needs. Emotionally speaking, that is."

Savannah was sure he was referring to his dead wife, and for a moment she hated the woman who'd made him feel so inadequate. "I think you do very well, Riley. You've certainly made me and my children feel at home. And you always seem to know what I need otherwise." She felt her face grow warm even as she said it. It was clear she was referring to the bedroom department.

Riley glanced down at her, and their gazes locked. Slowly and seductively his gaze slid downward and paused at her breasts. "You think so?" he asked.

Her stomach fluttered under his intense stare. "I *know* so."

Riley put his arm around her and pulled her against him. She nuzzled her face against his neck. He smelled of soap and aftershave and male flesh. Even though they'd been together a relatively short time, Savannah knew she'd be able to pick him out blindfolded in a room of men.

"How long before you have to get back to the church?" Riley asked her.

"Couple of hours."

"Hmm. Wonder how we could fill the time?"

The look in his eyes told her the direction his thoughts had taken. "Melody's in her room studying. She might hear."

He pondered their situation. "Wait here," he said, getting out of the swing. "I'll be right back."

Savannah wondered what he was up to as he went inside the house. She didn't have to wait long for her answer. Riley stepped out on the porch a few minutes later carrying an old quilt. "What's that for?" she asked, truly perplexed.

"Come with me." He held out one hand.

Savannah tucked her hand inside his big one and allowed him to lead her down the front steps and around the house. It wasn't until they were near the barn that she became suspicious. "Riley Locke, what are you up to?" she demanded playfully.

Riley unlatched the barn door and pulled her inside. It smelled of horse and fresh hay. Although David's interest in horses had waned somewhat, Melody's had not. The girl spent all her free time seeing to them and keeping the barn clean.

Riley paused before a ladder and made a bowing, sweeping motion. "Ladies first."

Savannah gave him a funny look. "You don't really expect me—"

"Time's a wastin'," he said. "If you expect an afternoon of good loving, you're going to have to climb that ladder, little lady."

"I'm wearing a dress," she pointed out.

"All the better for me."

She blushed but kicked off her heels and started to climb anyway, glancing down as she did. "Stop looking up my skirt," she told Riley.

"What makes you think I'm looking?" he asked innocently, not even bothering to hide the fact he was straining to see.

Once she reached the loft, Riley tossed her the quilt and hurried up the ladder. The whole area was neat, proof that Melody had cleaned there as well. Large bales of hay surrounded them, sweetening the air. Riley pulled a pocket knife from his slacks, cut the cord on one of the bales and spread the hay out. He then covered it with the quilt. "Madam," he said. "Would you care to join me?"

"You're very good at this," Savannah muttered, scooting onto the makeshift bed. "One would think this wasn't your first time."

He grinned. "A guy can only spend so much time in the tomato fields."

Savannah felt a stab of jealousy as he said it, but it was quickly squelched as he kissed her. Without breaking contact, he very gently pushed her back on the quilt and lay down beside her. The kiss seemed to last forever; with Riley coaxing her lips open and dipping his tongue inside her mouth. He kissed her eyes, her chin, her earlobes, all the while stroking and caressing the rest of her body. By the time he removed her clothes, she was burning up.

Savannah's sexual partners were limited to her first husband. They had not had a very satisfying relationship since most of the band members had lived under the same roof. There was little privacy so the act of lovemaking was often rushed, leaving her unfulfilled physically and emotionally. After her divorce, she'd rarely dated. Men shied away from women with children. At least that had been her experience. The few dates she'd had, mostly with men at work, had been lacking. Part of it had been her fault, she knew. Having to work so many hours, she cherished what time she could spend with David and Melody. Finally, she'd decided she was better off alone. Until Riley's ad.

Both were completely naked now. Riley kissed her breasts, her stomach, and finally the tuft of gold between her thighs before he positioned himself over her and entered. Savannah was swept up by the power and strength of him, and her climax was just as powerful and left her shaking afterward. Riley kissed her fully and passionately as he shuddered in her arms.

They lay on the quilt for a long time afterward, each content just to hold the other and relish the moment. Savannah realized she had never been happier. Or more in love. The thought startled her. She wondered if Riley suspected. The fact that they seemed to get on so well together must offer him some indication how she felt, but she wasn't about to make any grand confessions until she knew his feelings. She had tasted enough rejection in her life to know she didn't like it.

Riley cuddled her closer. "Why so quiet?" he asked.

"No reason," she fibbed. "Just relaxing before I have to go. What time is it?"

He checked his watch. "You've got just enough time to get back to the house and shower."

She groaned and reached for her clothes. They dressed quickly and hurried to the house, Riley carrying the quilt. While Savannah showered, Riley checked on the twins, saw they were still sleeping, and made her a cup of coffee. He carried it to the bathroom as Savannah was stepping out of the shower. "I thought you might need this," he said, catching sight of her nakedness as she reached for the towel. His eyes boldly raked her. "Allow me," he said, setting the cup down and taking the towel from her. When she started to protest, he hushed her, placing one finger against her lips. "A husband ought to have a few privileges, you know," he said, then shot her an absolutely charming grin. "Allow me to dry your back."

Blushing profusely, Savannah did as she was told. She tried to convince herself that a husband drying his wife was no big deal, but to her it was unnerving, simply because she was unused to the intimacies that existed between couples.

Riley tried very hard to remain casual about the whole thing, but he felt himself responding to her body all over again; the pink skin, tinged that color from the hot water. The sweetly scented soap she used. "Okay, turn around," he said, noting the tightness in his chest.

Savannah did as he said, feeling her body grow even warmer under his gaze. It was one thing to let a man look at her through passion-dazed eyes under a dim light, but to stand naked before Riley in the bright bathroom was something altogether different. The desire in his eyes made her stomach quiver. "Remember choir practice?" she said, her voice trembling.

"It probably wouldn't do for you to miss your first time, huh?" he said, although his eyes told her he wanted her to stay.

She saw his need, felt it low in her belly. How could she have ever thought the marriage would be in name only? "I'd be setting a bad example for the other members."

They heard noise in another part of the house. "That must be David," he said. "I reckon I'll go see how the game went." He knew if he stayed, he'd make her late. He reluctantly left her to dress and went into the kitchen where he found David pulling a soft drink can out of the fridge. Sweat stains adorned his shirt, and his neck was creased with red dust from the ball field. "So how'd it go?" he asked.

David popped the top on the can and took a long drink, then wiped his mouth on his hand. "How'd what go?"

He couldn't help his amusement. Sometimes it seemed as if the boy lived on a different planet. "The softball game."

He shrugged. "All right, I guess. I can't believe a cool guy like Paul Harrison would waste his time on a bunch of yokels who couldn't hit the ball if it was the size of a melon. I've played a lot of ball, and I have to say, it's the sorriest team I've ever seen." He took another sip of his drink. "And get this. Paul wants me to help train them so the church can have its own team. I mean, is that the most ridiculous thing you've ever heard?"

Riley took a seat at the table. "What's so ridiculous about it?"

"Well, think how much time it'd take," the boy pointed out.

Riley shrugged. "So what else have you got to do?"

The ninety-minute choir session passed quickly for Savannah, who was so intent on her work that she didn't realize their time was up. She had made a few changes after hearing them sing a couple of songs. She'd moved several people around, asked some to sing louder, others to sing softer, including a man who sang slightly off key at times but provided enough enthusiasm for the rest of the group to make it worth it. For the most part it was a good choir. After practice, they stayed and chatted for a moment, and by the time she left, Savannah felt they'd known one another for years.

When she arrived home, she found the twins sitting in booster seats at the table, spooning leftover casserole into their mouths. They wiggled in their seats and reached for her the minute she walked through the door. She kissed each boy on the forehead.

"See, you've already spoiled them," Riley said. When she started to walk by him, he frowned. "Where's *my* kiss?"

"Tell me again who's spoiled," she teased, standing on tiptoe so she could kiss him on the lips.

"How'd it go?" he asked.

"Great. I'll tell you more once I make a quick phone call." She hurried to the phone and dialed Jessie's number. "I think we need to discuss those white robes, after all."

"What white robes?" Jessie said as though the subject had never been broached.

"The ones you're going to order for the revival."

"I can't, Savannah," she said, her tone taking on a whining sound that was uncharacteristic of her. "You're not the first to ask, believe me."

"Have you seen the choir robes up close?"

"I know they're bad."

"You don't have *any* money?"

"Like I said, most of it went toward the down payment on our new van. It enables us to pick up many of our senior citizens who wouldn't be able to come to services otherwise."

"Okay, what if I was able to find a really good deal on cloth? I could visit that big flea market on the other side of Pinckney. And we could make the robes ourselves?"

Dead silence on the other end. "You realize we're talking about twenty robes at least, and the cloth has to be of good quality or they won't hold up."

"I sew pretty well," Savannah said. "My machine is as old as the hills, but it still works. I'll bet there are others in the choir who sew. And how about the Ladies Auxiliary that meets every Wednesday? Surely we can find one or two people who'll agree to help us."

"I can sew," Jessie replied. "As long as you don't give me anything real fancy like pleats or tucks."

"Savannah?" Riley called out softly.

"Just a minute, hon," she said. "No, the robes will have to be very simple. Of course, we'll want something different for the cuffs and collars. Maybe in a forest-green or burgundy."

"I still don't know if the finance committee will give us the money," Jessie said.

"Why wouldn't they give us the money?" Savannah insisted. "We've agreed to make them ourselves. Think how much we're saving."

"Savannah!" Riley called out a bit louder this time.

She blinked at him. Sometimes he could be worse than the kids when she got on the phone. "Hold on, Jessie," she told the woman on the other end. "What is it, Riley?"

"I'll buy the material."

She blinked several times. "You will?"

"Why wouldn't I? You should have come to me in the beginning. Now, tell Jessie your husband wants to spend some time with you so you're going to have to say good night."

Savannah opened her mouth to say just that, but Jessie beat her to it. "I heard," Jessie said. "And you can bet I'm going to let my tightwad husband know his little brother is springing for our new robes."

"Good night, Jessie," Savannah said.

"Night."

By Wednesday night, Savannah was literally bursting at the seams to give the choir her news. She told them about the exquisite white material she'd bought for the new robes, then asked for volunteers to sew them according to a pat-

tern she'd selected. Almost every woman in the group
raised her hand.

"I've decided on a theme for our revival, and Reverend
Hilby says it'll fit perfectly with his sermons." She grinned
as the group waited in expectation. "We're going to call it
the Old Time Religion Revival." At least half the members
nodded their approval. She went on. "I thought what we'd
do is sing all the old, well-loved songs that everybody
knows. There's 'Amazing Grace', 'How Great Thou Art',
'Onward Christian Soldiers', 'Bringing in the Sheaves'—"
She paused. "Can anybody think of anything else?"

"How about 'In the Garden'?" Avery said.

Savannah nodded and wrote it down. "Perfect."

"We can't hold a revival without singing the 'Old Rugged Cross'," Sophie pointed out.

"Oh, yes," Savannah said, jotting it down. "That's one
of my favorites."

"Why don't *you* sing it?" Dorthea said. "We'd love to
have you do a solo."

Savannah hesitated. "Oh, I don't know."

"You expect us to sing like little canaries," a woman
named Alberta teased. "We're not even professionals."

"I'm not a professional," Savannah insisted. "I haven't
been on a stage in almost fifteen years."

"Okay, just sing us one song," Avery Brown said, "and
we'll be the judge."

Savannah was getting flustered. There was a time when
she'd had no problem performing in front of a crowd, but
now the thought unnerved her. Not that she'd completely
given up singing. She sang all day long; religious songs, pop
songs, lullabies. Her voice had not left her, but she was
afraid her nerve had.

"Don't be shy in front of us," Dorthea said. "We're like
family here."

"Sing the 'Old Rugged Cross'," Sophie said. "We'll be

able to judge firsthand if that's the song you need to sing at the revival."

Savannah glanced at the smiling pianist, who was already turning pages in her hymnal. "I don't know if I remember the words," Savannah told the group. A hymnal, opened to that page, was thrust into her hands. Panic seized her; she could feel her heart beating wildly in her chest. She tried to remember what her high school chorus teacher had taught her to avoid stage fright.

Just pretend you're in a garden singing to rows of cabbages.

Savannah took a deep breath and nodded halfheartedly to the woman at the piano. She was so nervous at first, she missed her cue to begin, then had to wait for the pianist to start over again.

The first verse was the toughest to get through, and she could hear her own voice trembling and cracking. She glanced at the group of men and women in front of her and saw the worried looks on their faces. *They don't think I can do it,* she thought. *They're embarrassed for me.* Savannah got through the first verse and realized, much to her relief, she wasn't going to die. *Cabbages. That's all they are, a bunch of cabbages.*

The second verse started off smoothly and somewhere about the middle of it her self-confidence kicked in. All at once, the group before her was smiling and nodding their heads. A few had their eyes closed. It all came rushing back to her, she could still reach the highest notes with no trouble. She felt her eyes mist as she poured her heart into the song, felt it deep within her soul. When she finished, and the last note on the piano died, there was complete and absolute silence. Then, suddenly, the group began to clap.

"That's the most beautiful thing I've ever heard," Sophie said, mopping tears from her eyes.

"Breathtaking, that's what it was," Dorthea replied.

"You're wasting your talent singing for some lil' old church," Avery told her. "You could be a star. A *rich* star."

Savannah was touched. "I never did it for the money," she said. "And in ways, I'm very rich indeed." She thought of her family; four healthy children. Was it selfish of her to want an undying confession of love from her husband when she already had so much?

"I've got an idea," someone said. "Let's let Savannah sing the last song of the evening during the revival. It'll stick with folks on the drive home."

"I don't know; that's going to take a lot of practice," Savannah told them. "We only have a few weeks. I suppose I could use the old piano at home. I haven't played in years, but after all those piano lessons as a kid, I should be able to pick it up easily enough."

"It's settled, then," Sophie said.

When Savannah arrived home she found Riley bathing the twins in the tub in their bathroom. She got down on her knees and washed one boy while Riley washed the other. She told him about the evening and what had been decided.

"I don't know when that piano was played last," Riley told her. "I'll call someone out to tune it first thing tomorrow."

The next several days passed in a blur for Savannah, between caring for the twins, making choir robes, and practicing her songs on the piano. To make matters worse, Riley had chosen that particular time to renovate the kitchen, so there was much sawing and hammering going on, not to mention strange men traipsing through the house. Once or twice Savannah looked up and found the workers standing in the doorway listening to her practice. They quickly vanished once she spied them, as though embarrassed to have been caught.

The twins were perfect during Savannah's sessions. Sitting on the rug beside her with their favorite toys, they listened in rapt attention as she tried to perfect the songs she'd selected to sing at the closing of each revival meeting. Sometimes the boys tinkered with the keys on either side of the piano as she played, other times they clapped and tried to join in. Savannah took it as a good sign.

When the kitchen was finally finished, she almost wept for joy at the sight of the new appliances, including a dishwasher. The cabinets and wood floor, which had dulled with age, had been sanded and varnished until they looked new. The cozy, country-looking wallpaper she had chosen was up, and the trim painted to blend. It was almost worth all the noise and inconvenience they'd all suffered through.

"You like it?" Riley asked for the umpteenth time over dinner one evening.

She chuckled. "I love it. How many times do I have to tell you?"

David came in through the back door and hurried to the sink to wash his hands. "Sorry I'm late," he mumbled.

"Did you finish the chores I gave you?" Riley asked.

"Yeah, I finished." The boy sat down and reached for a bowl of mashed potatoes. "Haven't I earned enough money to pay back Aunt Jessie yet?" he asked, his tone bordering on belligerent.

Riley shrugged as he bit into a corn muffin. "I'll have to look at my records."

"Why don't you do that?" David said, sarcasm slipping into his voice. "I mean, all I do is work around this place. I don't have a life anymore."

"Let's not argue at the table, please," Savannah said, trying to coax the twins into eating their green peas and carrots.

"I just have one more chore for you this evening," Riley said.

"You mean for after dinner?" David asked in disbelief. "What about my homework?"

"This won't take long. I think one of the horses might've stepped on something. I put her in a stall, and I want you to hold her while I check out her hoof."

"Why can't Melody help you? She's the horse freak."

"Melody needs to help clear the kitchen so your mother can go to choir practice."

David ate in silence. It was obvious he was angry with Riley, but he had the good grace to keep quiet. With dinner finished, he grudgingly followed Riley out to the barn. Riley opened the door, then paused just inside.

"I've been thinking," the man said.

"Yeah, well, can you think while we work?" David asked. "I'd kind of like to get this over with so I can do something I enjoy for a change."

"I've been thinking what a good job you've been doing for me," Riley said, "and the fact that you've earned a raise."

"A raise?" The boy almost choked on the word. He obviously hadn't expected that.

"I was just kidding earlier when I said I didn't know if you'd earned enough to pay your aunt Jessie back. You have. I want you to go over there tomorrow and give her the money and tell her how sorry you are for breaking that light. I also want you and Sam to shake hands. What do you think?"

"I think you expect a lot."

"If I didn't care about you, I wouldn't insist."

David didn't have a reply for that. He was so involved in their conversation that he didn't hear his mother slip up to the door.

"I'd like for you to keep on working for me," Riley said.

"A couple of hours after school, a few hours on Saturday. A man needs his own spending money. You're too old to go to your mother for every dime." Riley started for one of the stalls and unlatched the door. "Besides, you're going to need gas money."

David frowned. "Gas money? For what?"

Riley nodded toward the stall. His face masked with uncertainty, David walked toward it and peeked in. A brand-new dirt bike was parked in the center of the stall bearing a bright red bow. The boy didn't say anything at first, merely looked at Riley. "What's this?"

"I saw it the other day and thought you ought to have it," Riley said. "Course, I had to clear it with your mom first, and that wasn't easy."

"You bought this for *me?*" David said in disbelief.

"Consider it an early birthday present. I figured if you were going to be working for me, you ought to have something to work toward."

Savannah stepped into the barn, and David jerked his head around. "You knew about this?" he asked.

"Yes, and I've already written out a contract on the rules and regulations. Riley is going to teach you the proper way to ride it, and I expect you to follow his directions, otherwise, it goes back in the stall until we feel you're mature enough."

"This is the nicest thing I've ever owned, Mom. I'm not going to do anything stupid." He glanced up at a grinning Riley. "You're all right, you know that?"

The man shrugged and draped one arm across Savannah's shoulder. "I do okay in a pinch."

"I can't wait to see you ride it," Savannah told him. It was a bold-faced lie, and she knew it. She'd been terrified at the thought of David taking on so much responsibility, but Riley had convinced her the boy was old enough.

"Well, first I have to teach him all the safety features,"

Riley said. He pulled his arm away and regarded Savannah in a manner that told her she was clearly in the way. "Listen, little lady," he said, giving a poor John Wayne imitation, "you need to get on back in the house where women and small children belong. This here is guy stuff." He glanced at David, then back at her. "You might get hurt."

Savannah couldn't help the laughter that bubbled up. "Riley Locke, you're going to rue the day you ever said that to me."

David laughed, and Riley nudged him. "See that, boy? You gotta know how to talk to a woman. Put them in their place."

"I don't know, Riley," the boy said as his mother left the barn in a mock huff. "I think you just borrowed yourself a whole lot of trouble."

ELEVEN

The bathtub arrived two days later, a marble monstrosity that Savannah declared had enough gadgets on it to allow a person to perform open-heart surgery. There was much snickering among the older children as to why the adults required such a fancy tub. Although Riley had already pulled the old tub out, it took half the day for the workers to install the new one. Riley immediately drove to the store for a bottle of champagne.

"We'll want to christen it," he explained, putting the bottle in the refrigerator to chill.

"You're going to break that bottle over an expensive marble tub?" she asked in horror.

"No, we're going to drink it. I remember what happened last time I plied you with champagne."

That evening, as they leaned back in the tub, face-to-face and sipping champagne, Savannah confessed to Riley that she had never been so happy. "Everything is just sort of falling into place," she said. "I just wish—" She paused and shrugged.

Riley, who was in the process of washing her toes, paused. "What?"

"I wish my parents hadn't disowned me. I can't imagine them not wanting to see their grandchildren. One day it's going to be too late."

"They never once tried to contact you in all these years?"

Savannah shook her head. "No. And my older sister hasn't spoken to me since my children were babies." She sighed. "But I'm not going to let it stop me from being happy. They made their decision, and they're the ones having to live with it. I just think it's sad."

Riley wondered if her parents regretted cutting their daughter out of their lives. He decided there was only one way to find out.

They made love afterward, and Savannah drifted off in Riley's arms. When he was certain she was sound asleep, he slipped from the bed and quietly made his way to his small office. A brass banker's lamp on the desk provided the only light. He knew Savannah's maiden name, and he knew the name of the town where she'd grown up. As he started to write, he could only hope her parents had not moved.

Dear Mr. and Mrs. Day:

My name is Riley Locke, and I recently married your daughter, Savannah. She is safe and well cared for, as are her children, David and Melody, who are now teenagers. I believe you would be proud of your grandchildren. The reason I am writing is to let you know Savannah, who is now the choir director for our church, will be singing a number of solos during our four-day revival to be held the last week in May. If you think you'd like to attend, you are welcome to stay with us. I am enclosing the address of our church and the dates and times of the revival.

Sincerely,
Riley Locke.

He folded the letter, stuffed it into an envelope, and addressed it. He would mail it first thing tomorrow. He only hoped he wasn't making a mistake.

It was another hectic week. Savannah was just certain they wouldn't have all the robes made in time. Not only was she a wreck over that, the workmen had descended on the living and dining room like demolitionists, and she couldn't hear herself think much less practice her singing. Finally, she packed the twins in the car and drove to Jessie's, where she was able to practice in a little peace and quiet.

"I don't know why you're so worried," Jessie told her. "You sing beautifully." The phone rang, and she hurried to answer it. "It's Riley. He says the truck carrying your new living room furniture got hijacked."

"What does he expect *me* to do about it?" Savannah said testily. She went to the phone. "How could something like that happen?" she asked her husband.

"I don't know. But I talked to that decorating place in town, and they're going to sell us the set out of their showroom window. You remember that sofa and love seat you liked so well? The one they said would take eight to twelve weeks to ship because it had to be built? They don't usually do that sort of thing. Most folks have to order it, but they were willing to make an exception this time." He had to stop to catch his breath.

"In other words, you're paying an arm and a leg for it," she said. After the hardships she'd known, she didn't like to see money squandered.

"No. The owner is an old friend of mine."

Savannah stiffened, and she knew she was just tense. Why did they have to worry about decorating and buying furniture when she had so much else on her mind? "Is there anything else you can do to make life more stressful for me right now?" she asked. "I've got it, why don't we just tear the damn house down and start over from scratch." She saw Jessie give her a funny look, but that didn't stop her. "Just think of the confusion *that* would cause." When he didn't answer, she went on. "Don't you have work to do in the fields?" She regretted it the moment she said it. Her only excuse was that she was frazzled.

He was silent for a moment. "I was just trying to make it nice for you, Savannah." Another pause. "I guess I should have waited until after the revival."

Her heart sank. She realized a lot of what he did was done out of guilt over his first wife. That was the only excuse she could find for the manic episodes he went through over the house. "I'm sorry," she told him wearily. "I didn't mean to snap. And believe me, I appreciate all you're doing. The house looks gorgeous, and I can't even imagine how much it's costing you. It's just this revival is weighing so heavily on me."

"There is one other thing," Riley said, then hesitated. "One of David's teachers called. She's like the team leader or something. She said David's not doing his work, and if he doesn't ace a couple of tests, he's going to fail some classes, and that either means summer school or he has to repeat the grade."

"Oh, that's great," Savannah muttered. "Just great."

"I asked the school if they could recommend a tutor, and they gave me a couple of names. One woman, an ex-teacher, lives a couple of miles from here. I'll call her if you like."

"That would be a big help," Savannah said, knowing she couldn't spare the time to work with him herself. Besides, she was a poor mathematician.

"I thought I'd clean up my office a bit and let them use

that. With those thick paneled walls, it's almost sound-proof."

"Okay, find out when she can start and how many nights she can work with him. Or would you rather I do it myself?" Savannah asked.

"No, I'll call her. But I want one thing understood," he said. "I'm taking the dirt bike away from David until he pulls these grades up. I don't expect him to work for me while he's being tutored, but he still needs to keep up with his household chores."

"He's going to be mad," Savannah said.

"He'll just have to get over it."

As expected, David did not take it well when Riley and Savannah took the dirt bike away and informed him of the tutor who would start the next day, but in the end he decided he would do anything to keep from going to summer school or repeating ninth grade. At the last minute, the tutor they'd hired, who'd somehow escaped the dreaded flu bug until now, came down with it. She sent her granddaughter in her place, a bright, energetic Cindy Crawford look-alike who'd exempted all her high school exams because of her high grades and was basically finished for the year.

"My name's Mandy Frazier," she said. "I hope it was okay to come in my grandma's place."

David stared at her for a full minute before saying anything, then tripped all over himself leading her to Riley's office.

Savannah exchanged nervous looks with her husband. "What do you think?"

Riley scratched his head. "I think he'll either be so lovestruck nothing will sink in, or he'll try to impress her with how smart he is."

Two hours later, neither of them had come out. "Do you think they're okay?" Savannah asked, once they'd put the twins down for the night. Riley shrugged. Finally, she grabbed two sodas from the refrigerator and put several cookies on a plate. She hurried to the office door and tapped briefly before opening it. Mandy and David were poring over a math book.

"Hi, I thought you two might like a little snack," Savannah said.

Mandy smiled. "Thank you, Mrs. Locke. We're almost finished here, once Dave solves this last equation."

Dave? Savannah arched one brow at her son as she set down the tray but said nothing.

He handed Mandy the legal pad he'd been working on, and she smiled beautifully.

"That's it," she said, then reached across the desk and tousled his hair. "See, that wasn't so tough. Once you learn the formula, you're almost there." Mandy refused the soda or cookies. "I'm a strict vegetarian," she said, "and I avoid junk food at all costs."

David, who'd already reached for a cookie, put it back. "I don't care for the stuff either."

Savannah tried to hide her amusement. "So you attend Pinckney High?"

"That's right. I'm a senior. I've been offered a full scholarship to Duke University, so I'll be attending there in the fall."

"I'll bet your parents are pleased, what with college costs and all."

The girl nodded. "They were so happy, they went out and bought me a new car."

"A Mustang with a convertible top," David said, his tone one of awe.

"Sounds like you're doing very well for yourself," Savannah said.

"Thank you, Mrs. Locke. When do you want me to come back?"

"Is tomorrow too soon?"

"I can be here. I'm staying with my grandma right now, since she's sick, so it's no problem."

Savannah waited for Mandy to gather her things, then walked her to the back door. "You'll keep up with your hours, won't you?" she said. "We'll just pay you once you've finished, if it's all the same to you."

Another brilliant smile that showed teeth that belonged in a toothpaste commercial. "That's fine, Mrs. Locke. However you want to work it."

Savannah wondered when the words Mrs. Locke had begun to sound so old. She glanced toward Riley and found him and David staring at Mandy as if in a daze. She suppressed an urge to throw cold water on them.

"I'll walk you out, Mandy," David said. "I want to see your car. Here, give me your things."

"Why, thank you, Dave," she said, heading through the door. "Good night, Mr. and Mrs. Locke. See you tomorrow."

Savannah turned to her husband, who was still staring at the door Mandy had exited. "If you keep that up, you're going to be taking a bath by yourself tonight."

A starry-eyed David stepped through the door a moment later. "Wow, did you see that car?"

Savannah shot Riley a dark look. "I don't think your stepfather was looking at the car."

David rubbed his hands together. "What a babe."

"The girl or the car?" Riley asked.

"Both," David said. He glanced from his mother to Riley. "So how long can I have her?"

"The girl or the car?" Riley repeated, this time wearing a grin. He'd never seen Savannah jealous before.

David grinned as well. "You know, you two were right about me needing a tutor. And guess what? I'm going to pay for it out of my own money."

"Check his forehead and see if he's got a fever," Savannah told Riley.

David wasn't listening. "It never occurred to me that a person could be bright *and* cool. Most of the really smart kids at my school are nerds. Sort of like Melody," he added with a chuckle as his sister walked into the kitchen. She stuck her tongue out at him and went on about her business.

Savannah chuckled. It did her heart good to hear the friendly banter between her children. Melody had obviously forgiven her brother for the attack by his ex-gang members; they often played cards and watched TV together these days. She was even attempting to teach him how to play chess. A couple of times David had even helped her in the barn. There was hope.

The afternoon of the revival Savannah was still working on the robes. She'd gotten up at dawn and sewed until it was time for church, then afterward, with Melody's help, she put together a lunch of leftovers while Riley watched the twins.

David and Mandy had spent much of the afternoon holed up in Riley's office building a replica of the White House out of Styrofoam so he could receive extra credit in history. He'd also made several terrariums out of gallon-size jars, into which he'd put a swamp, a forest, and a desert. This was to improve his science grade, and Mandy swore that, while she oversaw the projects, he did all the work. All he needed to do now was to ace the math test, which counted as two grades, and that would keep him from failing that class as well.

When Mandy left, after promising to be at the revival to hear her sing, Savannah was frantically trying to put buttonholes on the back of a robe, and Riley had just put the

wins down for their nap. David said good-bye to the girl,
then turned hopeful eyes to Riley.

"I've been working like crazy to bring my grades up,"
he said. "Think I could take a spin on my dirt bike?"

Riley's grin faded. "We had a deal," he said. "After the
report card comes in."

"So what am I supposed to do in the meantime?"

"I can find something for you to do," Riley replied
evenly.

"I know what your idea of a good time is," the boy
muttered sarcastically, causing Savannah to look up from
her sewing at the kitchen table. "I'm sick of working all the
time. Can't you for once cut me some slack?"

"Who is going to cut me slack if I don't do my job?"
Riley asked. "How am I going to pay bills if I don't bring in
crop?"

"Why don't you stop trying to pretend you're this
down-and-out farm boy?" David said, suddenly sounding
bitter. "Everybody in town knows you've got money coming out your—"

"David!" Savannah half stood. "Don't you dare talk to
Riley like that."

"It's true, Mom," he said, swinging his gaze in her direction. "The Locke family has always been one of the
richest in town. But to hear Riley talk, it's like he doesn't
know where our next meal is coming from."

"I think you must be confused, Son," Savannah said.
"Riley has been more than generous since we've come here.
Why, just look what he's done with the house."

"You know why he did it, don't you? Out of guilt over
his first wife. She hated it, hated this hokey island too—"

"That's enough!" Savannah said.

"She was leaving him the night she got killed."

Savannah sucked in her breath sharply; all the color
seemed to drain from Riley's face. When she spoke, her

voice was low but lethal. "If you choose to listen to gossip that's your business. But don't bring it home with you Now, go to your room and don't come out until you're ready to apologize."

David glared at her a moment before turning an angry look on Riley. He opened his mouth to say something, then seemed to think better of it and stalked angrily from the room.

Riley sat there quietly, big hands folded together on the table, not knowing what to say or do.

"I'm sorry," Savannah said. "David doesn't always think before he talks."

"I guess it's all over town, the problems Kara and I had They probably hold me responsible for her death. They're probably right."

Savannah went to him. "You can't hold yourself responsible—"

"I shouldn't have let her go out in that weather with her being so mad and all. I should have taken her car keys." He paused, and a shudder rippled through his body. "They said she went off that bridge doing seventy."

Savannah closed her eyes briefly as she imagined the devastation. "Just be thankful the twins weren't in the car with her," she said.

He nodded and pulled her into his arms. "You don't know how many times I've thought that very thing." They were quiet for a moment as they clung to each other, taking comfort from each other's touch.

"I guess it's true I'm doing these renovations out of guilt," he said.

Savannah felt his words pierce her heart. She had wanted to believe he was revamping the place for them when, in fact, it sounded as if he was trying to erect a shrine for his dead wife's memory. Was he still actively grieving for the woman? she wondered. Is that why it'd been so hard for Jessie to convince him to place that ad? Maybe he'd seen that ad as a way to get what he needed—a good mother—without investing himself personally. And maybe he'd succeeded. He'd never once said he loved her, not even during their most intimate moments.

"Maybe I am too hard on David," Riley said, going back to what had led to this conversation in the first place. "Maybe I should have let him take a little spin on that dirt bike."

Savannah was thankful for the change of subject. She was not ready to deal with the ramifications of Riley's confession. "You can't start second-guessing yourself every time you make a rule. Isn't that what you keep telling me?" He didn't even look up. She felt like crying, but not for David. She wanted to cry for herself, for falling in love with a man who might not be capable of loving her in return. But she couldn't cry or feel sorry for herself; she had to finish the damn robes.

Savannah was too nervous to eat dinner, and she knew the revival was only part of the reason. Riley sent her into the bathroom to bathe while he and the older kids cleaned up the kitchen. Everybody was dressed and ready to walk out the door when Mr. and Mrs. Cookson arrived to baby-sit the twins. Riley carried the robes and laid them across the backseat of the Explorer so they wouldn't get wrinkled.

Everything looked the same as always when they pulled up in front of the church, children running across the lawn in their best clothes, ladies standing in small groups sharing gossip and recipes, men clustered together near the parking area, some grabbing a last-minute smoke. Savannah climbed out of the Explorer and immediately went around back to retrieve the robes. Her mind was on the revival and nothing else. She had told herself she would put everything else out of her mind until it was over. Only then did she notice a strange older model car parked across the street.

"We must be having visitors tonight," she said to Riley. She didn't notice the anxious look cross his face as she turned for the sidewalk leading to the back of the church.

He reached for her arm and gave a light tug. She looked up. "Something the matter?" she asked, checking the robes to make sure they weren't dragging along the ground. Of course something was the matter, a small voice said. Everything was the matter, including the fact that her husband was still in love with his dead wife.

"Could we talk for a minute?" he said.

"Talk?" She blinked several times, then checked her wristwatch. "Now?"

"I know my timing isn't right, but I just want you to know I would never do anything to hurt you intentionally."

She frowned at him, feeling almost panicky with worry. Was he having serious doubts about their relationship? Had their earlier conversation about his wife made him question his decision to bring another woman into his home?

Savannah glanced around to make sure they couldn't be overheard. People brushed past them, but didn't seem the least bit interested in their conversation. "Riley, are you sorry you met me?" she asked.

He stared at her as though unsure he'd heard right. "Sorry I met you?" He could only presume she was referring to the problems concerning her son. Also, he knew she was nervous about the revival. "Heavens no," he said.

"Savannah! Sa-vann-ah!"

Savannah turned at the sound of Dorthea's voice. "Yes?" She knew she sounded dazed, but she didn't quite know what to make of Riley's conversation or at least his attempt at it.

"Thank goodness you're here with the robes. We've got six half-naked people standing back there." It was obvious the woman was as nervous about the revival as Savannah was. "Well, don't just stand there like a bump on a log, girl!" Dorthea took the robes from Riley, grabbed Savannah's arm, and started pulling her in the direction of the building. "You two newlyweds will just have to wait until after the service to do your sparking." Savannah was still wearing a funny look on her face when she entered the building.

She was still pondering Riley's strange behavior when she led the choir through the front door singing "Onward Christian Soldiers." The church was packed, folding chairs sat along the aisle because they'd run out of space. She spotted Riley first, handsome as ever, sitting close to the front with David and Melody and a white-haired couple. Riley still wore that worried look, but she couldn't think about that now. They'd have a long talk later, and she would find out exactly what he wanted. Perhaps he would consider counseling. Maybe then he could put his feelings for his dead wife to rest once and for all. She smiled back at him, giving away none of her thoughts, then, just as she reached her family's pew, the couple turned.

At first Savannah thought she was imagining things. She felt the room spin, felt herself go into some sort of shock. She must've stopped right in the middle of the aisle, because someone nudged her, prodding her forward so the rest of the choir could get through the door.

She was not certain how she managed to make it to the front of the church and keep singing at the same time. She felt her mouth move, but she wasn't sure there were any words coming out. She climbed the steps to the choir area and stood, waiting until the other members were in place before sitting. Once more, she sought out the older couple sitting near her children. They smiled at her, and she had no idea how to respond. Besides, she would never be able to smile back with her lips feeling so rubbery.

Her parents? What were they doing there? How'd they

know where to find her? Riley? Had he contacted them? Was that what he was trying to tell her earlier?

The sermon seemed to last forever. Luckily, Savannah was able to concentrate enough so that she led the choir into song at all the right places. She forced herself not to look in her parents' direction; otherwise, she'd grow flustered again. Instead, she focused at the back of the church where most of the teenagers whispered and fidgeted among themselves.

She performed her solo flawlessly while the collection baskets were passed. She was glad for all the hours of practice; she knew the song inside out and upside down. Had she not been so well prepared, she wasn't sure she could have done it.

Finally, the service was over. Savannah was so anxious by that time, she was near tears. Riley was waiting for her in the cloakroom when she arrived. "I wasn't sure they'd come," he said. "Otherwise, I wouldn't have sprung it on you like this."

Savannah's eyes burned and felt heavy with tears. "Why did you invite them here?" she whispered harshly. "You had no right."

Sophie, who'd come into the cloakroom right behind Savannah, must've sensed a problem because she closed the door before the other choir members could enter. Savannah and Riley were alone for the moment.

"I don't like the idea of you and your parents staying mad for the rest of your lives. How would you ever forgive yourself if something happened to them?"

She was angry now. He had enough problems of his own not to be worrying about her. "This is none of your business, Riley," she almost shouted. "My parents turned their backs on me, it wasn't the other way around. I made a mistake, and they couldn't forgive me, *wouldn't* forgive me. Do you know how long I've lived with that mistake? How much guilt I've suffered?" She was crying now. "So now, *now* that I finally have my life together, they're ready to hear my sins and maybe, *just maybe* exonerate me?"

There was a light tap on the door. Savannah swung around and found her parents coming in. Sophie, who seemed to be playing guard, tossed her an apologetic look. "They asked me to let them in," she said, then closed the door once more.

Nobody said a word for at least a minute. Riley looked miserable, as though he genuinely regretted what he'd done.

"You're still beautiful," Savannah's mother said.

"And tiny as a teacup," her father added.

Savannah hitched her head high. "I'm not sorry for what I did. I have two beautiful children as a result."

Her mother's eyes teared. "You don't understand," she said. "We didn't come here to forgive *you*. We came to ask *you* to forgive *us*."

TWELVE

Savannah was glad her parents were riding back to the house in a separate vehicle. After what her mother had blurted out in the cloakroom, she needed time to think. She was vaguely aware of the road in front of them, of the way Riley kept looking at her.

"Mom?" Melody tapped Savannah on the shoulder.

"Yes, honey?"

"Are you going to make up with Grandma and Grandpa?"

"I don't know what I'm going to do," she said wearily. "All I know is I don't ever want to go through another night like this one."

Riley reached over and squeezed her hand, still choking back the guilt that had assuaged him the minute he saw the look on Savannah's face when she'd spotted her parents. Now he felt awful for having wanted to surprise her. "I think you should at least hear them out," he said at last. "What've you got to lose?"

The house looked pretty with the floodlights shining up on it, and it was impossible to tell where the paint was chipping and fading in places. Naturally, Riley was already making plans to have it painted. They pulled into the driveway and waited while Savannah's parents pulled in beside them. Once inside, she headed straight for the coffeepot.

"Riley, why don't you show my parents into the living room while I prepare refreshments," she said as soon as he saw the Cooksons out.

"Oh, we'd just as soon sit at the kitchen table, if it's all the same to you," her father said.

Savannah lifted her shoulders in the barest shrug and went on with what she was doing. When she noticed Melody and David lurking in the doorway, she offered them a brief smile. "You may have an hour of TV if you like." As though realizing it was a hint to make themselves scarce, brother and sister left without a word.

"So, you have other children?" Savannah's mother asked.

Riley nodded. "Twin boys from my first marriage. They're seventeen months old."

"You're divorced?"

"My . . . er . . . first wife died in an automobile accident."

"We're so sorry. That must've been difficult for you and the babies."

The tense lines in his face indicated how uncomfortable he was discussing his dead wife, but there was no way Savannah's parents could know because they'd only just met him. "Yes, well I was lucky to find a woman who loved children," he said. "The boys are crazy about her." He glanced at Savannah, who'd remained standing with her back to them and hadn't so much as tried to join in the conversation. He felt lost, and he imagined she did too. "I probably ought to go check on them," he said, then told himself he was a coward for choosing the easy way out. Still, Savannah needed to work this out for herself.

Savannah carried a tray of steaming mugs to the table,

along with the cream and sugar and a plate of oatmeal cookies. "I'm sorry, but it's been so long I forgot what you take in your coffee." She saw a flash of pain in her mother's eyes and wished she hadn't said it.

"Please sit down, Savannah," her father said. "We're much more interested in you than anything else at the moment."

She took a seat at the far end of the table and gazed at the man and woman who'd raised her. They felt like strangers now. She wondered if they had any idea how they'd hurt her. "So, whatever happened to Reverend Snood?" she asked, recalling the pious man who'd all but convinced her parents to turn away from her, fast seven days a week, and live in poverty. And they had followed every one of his commandments.

Her father wiped his hand down his face. He had a ravaged hound-dog look about him that suggested much suffering. "Reverend Snood left town three years ago," he said, "with the congregation's money."

Savannah was speechless for a moment. "Are you serious?"

Her mother folded her hands in front of her. "We were planning to build a new church at the time. Everybody had given their last dime. Your father and I used all our savings, even mortgaged our house and sold most of the farm equipment. We never suspected Reverend Snood would run off with our money, but now that I look back it seems he did live rather well all those years. I guess you could say—" She paused, and it was obvious her emotions were getting the best of her. "I guess you could say he all but brainwashed us." The tears began to fall. "That's the only excuse we have for turning our backs on our own daughter."

Her father cleared his throat. "We swore we'd never step back in another church. Tonight was the first time. I guess we've been pretty bitter." He glanced at his wife. "Not to mention embarrassed and ashamed."

Savannah was truly sorry for them, especially since they'd never really meant to hurt anyone. Her parents were simple, unsuspecting country folk who'd been taken advantage of by a Bible-toting con artist. "But that was three years ago," she pointed out. "Why didn't you contact me afterward?"

They didn't answer right away. When her father spoke, his voice trembled. "We lost everything, Savannah. Our house, our land, all our belongings. We had to move in with your sister until we could find jobs. Then, when it looked like things couldn't get worse, I took sick."

"Cancer," her mother whispered.

Her father nodded. "I'm okay now; I've been through the surgery and the chemotherapy, and the doctors feel sure they got it all. We're working part-time and living in a little garage apartment in town."

"We didn't want to call you with so much awfulness going on," her mother said. "We told your sister not to say anything until we got on our feet again, and she promised to stay quiet. Getting Riley's letter meant more to us than you can know."

Savannah took a cup of coffee from the tray and stirred cream and sugar into it. Her parents seemed to take it as their cue to do the same. "I don't know what to say," she said after several minutes. "I honestly don't know."

Her mother touched her hand tentatively. "All we want, Savannah, is the opportunity to make up for what we've done to you, and the chance to know our grandchildren."

"I know it's been a long time, Lil' Bit," her father said, using the nickname he'd tagged her with as a child. "You don't have to give us your answer tonight. We're staying at a motel in town. You can call us tomorrow if you like."

Melody chose that particular moment to walk into the

room. Savannah called her daughter over. "Please put fresh sheets on your bed for Grandma and Grandpa. You can sleep on the sofa tonight. And call the General Lee and cancel their reservations."

Melody smiled and reached for the phone book. It was obvious she was thrilled with her mother's change of heart.

Her parents stayed for four days, during which time there was much talking and crying and hugging and making up. They played with the twins, chatted with David and Melody, drank iced tea on the front porch, and helped out with the chores because they refused to be treated like guests. They spent their evenings at the revival, of course, where husband and wife sat beside their new son-in-law and listened to their daughter's solos with tears streaming down their faces.

"I wish ya'll could hang around," Riley said, the morning of their departure. "We've certainly enjoyed having you."

"Yeah, you're nothing like Mom said you were," David blurted out, then reddened when he realized his slip.

A strained silence followed, then sudden laughter from his grandparents. "I think we should take that as a compliment, Daddy," Savannah's mother said to her husband.

"Maybe we can visit again in the summer," he said. "That's not so far away."

Savannah knew they were worried about getting back to their jobs although they would never admit as much. She also knew, then and there, that she was going to help them somehow. No matter what, she was going to get them out of that garage apartment and see they didn't have to work every day for the rest of their lives. She watched them drive away in their old car and hoped it would make the trip home.

The next day she was still thinking about it as she and Riley had their first cups of coffee in their cozy bedroom and waited for the twins to stir. They had just made love, and her cheeks and breasts were still chafed red from Riley's unshaved jaw. Once again, she had waited for Riley to give her some indication how he felt about her, but she had waited in vain for the words she wanted to hear.

"I've been thinking," she said, trying to talk around a wide, unladylike yawn. "I probably shouldn't stay out of the workforce too long. If I do, I'll lose all my abilities." He didn't say anything and she went on. "I was also thinking maybe it's time the twins went to some sort of day care, even if it's only part-time. They need to play with children their own ages. Otherwise, they'll have trouble once they start kindergarten."

Riley, who was leaning on one elbow facing her, nodded in agreement. "You're right. They could develop a nasty personality disorder. Like picking their teeth in public or cleaning their toenails in class."

"You're not taking me seriously," Savannah told him.

"You're right, I'm not." He pulled her into his arms. "Why don't you just come right out and tell me you want to help your parents?"

Her mouth popped open in surprise.

He mimicked her. "I couldn't help overhearing part of your conversation that first night."

"What you really mean to say is you eavesdropped."

"I was worried about you. Why is it so hard for you to come to me when you have a problem?"

Oh, how she longed to tell him. But if she opened the discussion and demanded answers to the questions that plagued her, he might withdraw totally from her. If, on the other hand, he admitted still loving his first wife and feeling as though he were unable to get past that love and the guilt associated with it, well, Savannah would either have to accept being second in his life or leave. She wasn't ready for either consequence. "This problem is different," she said at last. "It involves money."

"Have I been stingy with you?"

"I don't expect you to support my parents."

"You're my wife. If your parents are in need you *should* expect me to help if I can. And I can. We're not hurting for anything. I can afford to put them in a decent house."

Savannah sighed. It was so much easier for him to give her material things than it was his love. But then, hadn't she been looking for security and stability when she'd answered his ad? Only now did she realize how foolish she'd been to think that was all she needed from him. Of course, she hadn't counted on falling head over heels in love with him.

"My parents are proud people, Riley," she said at last. "They won't go for handouts."

"I'm sure Ben can hire your father at the packing house. Give him something to do in the office," he added.

"Are you saying they should move here?"

"How else are you going to make up for all that lost time?"

"You're not suggesting they live with us?"

"No. But I know we can find something reasonable in the area. I have this friend in real estate—"

"Male or female?" she interrupted.

"Female. She's almost sixty. I can ask her to find something for them."

"Let me think about it first, okay?"

He shrugged, then sat up and reached for his underwear. "Let me know what you decide."

Savannah watched him dress, and it struck her odd that she could find every part of his body so perfect. It made sense, though. She was head over heels in love with him. So why did that thought make her feel so heavyhearted?

———————

The call came the following night, only an hour after Riley had picked David up from the school dance that officially marked the end of school. He'd climbed into bed, curled his body against Savannah's, and drifted off, only to be awakened moments later. He groped for the phone in the dark and mumbled incoherently into the receiver.

"Is this the Locke residence?" a man asked from the other end of the line.

Riley felt Savannah stir beside him. "Yeah, who is this?"

"Mr. Locke, this is Principal Petrie at Pinckney High School. Your stepson attended a dance tonight? David Day, I believe his name is?"

"That's right. What's this about?" Riley saw that Savannah had awaken.

"Could you please come down to the school? There's been some vandalism, and we believe David was involved."

Riley glanced at the digital clock. *"Now?"*

"We'd appreciate it, sir. The damage is pretty bad."

Riley hung up and repeated what he'd been told to Savannah.

"David wouldn't do something like that," she said matter-of-factly.

They were on their way ten minutes later, after rousing David from his own bed and leaving a note for Melody.

"What's going on?" the boy asked sleepily from the backseat of the Explorer. When nobody answered he became more insistent. "Did I do something wrong?" he demanded.

"I don't believe this," Riley muttered, certain the boy was trying to con them.

Savannah turned in her seat. She was so upset, it was all she could do to maintain her composure. It was obvious Riley had already pronounced her son guilty in his mind.

"The science lab at your school was vandalized tonight,
she told her son. "Thousands of dollars worth of equip
ment was destroyed."

"Oh, I get it," David said bitterly. "They think *I* did it."

"The letters DD were spray painted on the walls.
student claims he saw you in that area. Did you have
particular reason for being there?" She held her breath fo
his answer.

"Maybe. But who would believe me at this point?
David folded his arms across his chest. "Even if I was stupi
enough to vandalize the room, I'm certainly not stupi
enough to sign my initials. Besides, I'm probably not th
only DD in that school."

The meeting was more like an inquest, leading Savan
nah to believe that nothing much ever happened in th
town of Pinckney, South Carolina. As an officer questione
a sullen David, Savannah found her hopes slipping.

"I'm being framed for a crime I didn't commit," th
boy replied a number of times.

"We've got a witness that saw you try to pick the loc
on the science lab door," a deputy replied. "You denyin
that?"

David had no answer for that.

They were silent on the ride home. No charges ha
been filed against David since there wasn't absolute proo
of his guilt, but it was obvious he was the prime and onl
suspect. The police were merely biding their time unti
they had more proof. Riley pulled into the drive and
parked, and the three of them remained quiet for a mo
ment.

"I didn't do it, Mom," David said before getting out o
the car. "I know it looks like I did, but I didn't."

Savannah stared out the window into darkness. It wa
quiet in the country; no streetlights or traffic. So differen

from the city. "Why were you trying to get into that room, David?"

"I don't know, I guess I wasn't thinking."

"That's not good enough," Riley said.

Riley and Savannah argued long into the night.

"I've tried to support you on everything," he said, "but that boy's guilty, and we both know it."

"That boy just happens to be my son," she said from her side of the bed. "And I believe him when he tells me he didn't do it."

Riley climbed out of the bed and began to pace the floor. "The evidence was there, Savannah. What more do you need?"

Savannah sniffed hard. In the dark, it was not possible to tell she'd been crying, but the crack in her voice gave her away. "I need for David to tell me himself," she said. "Then I'll believe it."

Riley was angry. Not only was his wife refusing to face the facts, her son was making an absolute fool of her. "I can't help you raise your son, if you're going to treat him like a sniveling infant every time he does something wrong. This is serious, Savannah. It involves thousands of dollars. Who is going to pay for it?"

She didn't answer. Time passed, during which they didn't exchange a word. Finally, Riley climbed into bed. Savannah was still trying to decide what to do after he'd drifted off. Unable to sleep, she climbed out of bed and made her way to the kitchen. The overhead light burned dully from the stove. She made coffee, then drank it at the kitchen table.

She thought of what Riley had said. *That boy's guilty, and we both know it.* If she listened to Riley long enough, she would lose her faith in her son.

Riley was too hard on the boy. He couldn't expect David to be a man at fourteen, especially after what the boy had been through. Riley had had a stable and loving childhood with both parents in the home. David hadn't had those advantages. But Riley couldn't see that, *wouldn't* see it. She knew as long as she stayed they would argue about her son. She couldn't have that. David was her child, her own flesh and blood.

The bottom line was, her son was innocent. Nobody was going to convince her otherwise. She was crying by the time she made her decision.

Savannah found a notepad and pencil. Pouring one more cup of coffee, she sat down and wrote:

Dear Riley:
I've thought long and hard about this, and I know it's just not going to work out. I have to believe in my children no matter what. And I have to know I'm first in your life. I can't compete with a dead woman, and I can't stand by and let you make decisions based on guilt over that relationship. There's also the problem with my parents, of course, and I've decided to go back home where I can help them. You needn't worry about finding them a place here. Please don't be angry.

Savannah.

Savannah made her way up the stairs and into the twins' room. Both boys were sleeping on their stomachs, their behinds sticking high in the air. She leaned over Trevor's crib. In the dim light she could make out the contours of his face, a face that looked so much like Riley's, it almost made her cry. Travis was sleeping as well when she checked him, and she found herself wondering what they would be when they grew up.

Still crying, Savannah left the nursery and crossed the

hall. She only had to tap Melody once before the girl opened her eyes. "I want you to be very quiet," she whispered.

"What's going on, Mom?" the girl asked, giving her a sleepy-eyed look.

"We're going to Grandma and Grandpa's. Pack just enough to last a few days. We'll send for the rest."

"Are you sure?" the girl asked.

Savannah hitched her chin up. "I'm positive."

David was harder to wake. It wasn't until Savannah threatened bodily harm that the boy climbed out of bed and stuffed clothes into a duffel bag.

Riley was still snoring when Savannah entered their bedroom and grabbed a few of her own belongings, and she was thankful he wasn't a light sleeper. Although she had very little money and absolutely refused to take the money Riley had offered as part of their marriage contract, she knew she and the kids could sleep on the floor at her parents' place until she found a job and got on her feet again. She glanced at Riley once before she left the room, and she was certain the pain in her chest was her heart breaking.

David and Melody were waiting in the kitchen, their own bags packed. Savannah quietly unlocked the back door and led them out to the detached garage that housed her old car.

"We're not taking the Explorer?" David asked.

Savannah shook her head. "It belongs to Riley."

"He gave it to you, Mom."

"Just get in the car, please. I don't want to talk about it right now." Brother and sister shot each other a funny look but did as they were told.

Savannah hadn't even reached Pinckney before the strange noise beneath the hood of her car began. "What is that sound?" she asked her son.

"Do I look like a mechanic to you?" he asked.

"Don't get smart with me. I just thought—"

"The only thing I know about is bikes. Dirt bikes," he added. "And you made me leave mine behind."

Savannah could feel the beginnings of a headache. "Let's not go into that right now." She crossed the last bridge and arrived in the city limits. Although the town appeared deserted, she didn't have to search long for a service station.

"Sounds serious," a man in blue overalls told her when he heard the noise.

Savannah nodded, then wondered why he just stood there rocking back and forth on his heels. "Can you fix it?"

"Nope."

"Any particular reason why?"

"I'm not a mechanic."

She was trying so hard to be patient. "Okay, could you tell me where I might find one?" she asked, eyes darting toward the station where a lanky teenage boy leaned against the door, arms crossed and looking very bored with the world.

"I reckon he's home in bed like most folks at this hour. He'll be back in the morning around eight. Sometimes he gets in a little later on account he drops by the donut shop first."

"Is there anywhere else I can go?" Savannah asked, her frustration mounting with every breath she took.

"Not in that car," he replied. "Besides, you ain't gonna find a mechanic this time of night. Why don't you just leave your car, and I'll ask Joe to look at it first thing when he comes in."

"What are we supposed to do in the meantime?" Savannah demanded, her weariness making her irritable.

"Mom, it's not his fault," Melody whispered.

"It's not my fault," the man echoed. He glanced behind him where the lanky youth was still standing. "My nephew can take you home in his truck." He pointed in the direction of a pickup truck with tires the size of those found on eighteen-wheelers. Savannah found herself wondering how someone as short as her would ever be able to climb up into the passenger seat.

She glanced around. The General Lee was only a few blocks away, they could walk. "Where do you want me to park it?" she asked.

The man pointed. "You can just leave it right over yonder. Joe'll see it when he gets here. You can call later to check on it," he added.

Savannah could tell she had roused the desk clerk from a sound sleep when they arrived at the General Lee. "I need a room with two double beds," she said, already fumbling in her purse for the money.

The man yawned so wide, Savannah saw the fillings in his back teeth. "Just for tonight?" he asked, then checked the clock on the wall. "Well, it's not night anymore, is it?"

"I'd like to arrange for a late checkout," she told him as she counted out the money. She knew she needed to rest if she was going to drive all the way to her parents' house.

"I won't be needing the room," he said, indicating the empty parking lot. "Sleep as late as you like."

Savannah would have given any amount of money for sleep, but once she laid down on the bed she shared with her daughter, her mind became instantly alert. She wondered if Riley had discovered their half-empty bed and gone to investigate. She wondered if he'd found the note on the kitchen table. She cried at the thought of him reading it, at the thought of the twins wondering where she was.

While David and Melody slept, Savannah pondered their future. She would find a job as soon as she got back home. Somehow, they would have to manage in her parents' small apartment until she could afford a bigger place. She felt a tug of sheer sorrow. Riley had been more than willing to find her parents a house in Pinckney or Gull Island. But as good as he was, the man didn't believe in her son, and she knew they would fight bitterly over the boy as long as they lived under the same roof. He also didn't love her the way she loved him.

Savannah drifted off to sleep sometime later, her tears and worries leaving her exhausted and unable to think anymore.

Riley knew something was wrong the minute he opened his eyes. He didn't even have to read Savannah's note to know she was gone. He sensed the emptiness, the desolation that had been a part of him until she had come into his life and brought love and happiness with her. He checked the twins and found them still sleeping. He hurried out back and opened the door on the detached garage. Her car was gone. She had chosen to take her old clunker instead of the Explorer he'd given her.

Riley poured a cup of coffee and read the note several times before he allowed himself to believe it. He heard the twins and sighed his immense relief at having something to do for the moment.

The phone rang while he was feeding the boys. He snatched it up, hoping it was Savannah. But it wasn't her, it was Mr. Petrie, the high school principal.

"Have I called too early, Mr. Locke?" the man said.

"It's okay," he said abruptly. "What can I do for you?"

"Basically, I'm calling to apologize," he said. "We found the culprits. Seemed one of them arrived home last night with red paint on his slacks. His mother phoned me first thing this morning. Anyway, the paint matched, and the minute the boy knew he'd been caught he started ratting on his friends."

"So why'd they paint DD on the walls?"

"They wanted to get your stepson into trouble. Just for being the new boy," he added. "I'm really sorry for putting you and your wife through this. I'd like to apologize to David personally if I may."

"Uh, David's not here at the moment," Riley said. "You'll have to call back some other time." He hung up the telephone, noting the twins had tired of their spoons, and were scooping their oatmeal up with their fingers and sucking it off. Riley would have found it amusing had he not been so miserable.

"I hope Savannah teaches you boys some manners before you start taking young ladies out."

Savannah. He'd said her name without thinking. *I have to believe in my children no matter what.* He'd let her down. Oh, he'd fixed up the house and given her a decent car to drive and the security she craved, but he'd never once told her he loved her. And he *did* love her. But he was a coward. He'd let past tragedy stand in the way of telling her, simply because he was afraid of being vulnerable again. He had doubted her son when it was obvious she needed him to believe in the boy. But he'd made it worse by voicing his doubts when what she'd really needed was for him to take her in his arms and tell her everything would be okay. How many times had he seen her kiss away the hurts and disappointments where his twins were concerned.

He had to stop thinking along those lines. *His* kids; *her* kids. The children were *theirs*.

Riley saw that the twins had somehow managed to get oatmeal in their hair. "Why don't I clean you guys up?" he said. "Then, we're going to go visit Grandma and Grandpa Day. How's that sound?"

The boys muttered a string of gibberish that made him smile despite his misery.

❖━━━━━━❖

It was coming up to ten o'clock when Riley crossed the last bridge to Pinckney and decided to stop for gas. He pulled in at the first station he came to.

A man in a uniform shirt with the name Joe embroidered on it appeared almost out of nowhere. "Fill it up?" he asked, startling Riley so bad, he jumped.

"Please," Riley said, telling himself to get a grip.

The man ambled toward the back of the Explorer, unscrewed the gas cap, and shoved the metal nozzle in. "Gonna be a nice day," Joe said, ducking his head in the window when he saw the twins. "My, my, what handsome young men."

"Look, I'm in a bit of a hurry—"

"No problem," Joe said. "Want me to clean that windshield for you?" He didn't wait for an answer, just did it anyway, twice, as a matter of fact, then went to the back and cleaned that window. The twins craned their necks around to watch; Riley squirmed in his seat until he feared he'd put a hole right through it. He had to get on the road.

Riley paid him, and Joe went inside for change. He seemed to be moving in slow motion. Riley drummed his fingers against the steering wheel, waiting, waiting. When Joe didn't come back right away, Riley glanced toward the station irritably. He froze when he saw the old clunker sitting in the garage. He was so stunned by the sight, he didn't notice Joe had reappeared.

"Sorry I took so long," the man said. "Most folks don't pay with large bills. I had to break out some change."

"Whose car is that?" Riley asked, motioning toward the garage.

"I don't know. It was here when I came in this morning. All's I know is some lady dropped it off late last night."

"Where is she now?"

Joe looked surprised. "I think she went to a motel. She's supposed to call me once I've had a chance to look at it. I ain't going to touch it till she does. You could write a book on all that's wrong with that car. Why, you interested in buying it?"

"Could be."

The other man leaned closer. "Don't waste your time, mister. It's a heap of junk."

Riley glanced in the direction of the General Lee. She and the kids could have walked there from the station.

". . . Frankly, I'd just haul the old battle ax to the nearest dump," Joe said.

Riley realized he hadn't been paying attention. "Haul it off?" he repeated, then found himself frowning at the thought. Savannah loved that car and planned to give it to David. Poor David. Of course, if Joe hauled it away that would mean Savannah couldn't drive off in it.

He frowned at his own line of thinking. He wanted Savannah to stay with him because she loved him and wanted to be there, not because she didn't have transportation to get out. He'd lived with a woman once who'd considered herself a prisoner, and he never wanted to go through that again.

He had to stop thinking of the past, had to stop feeling guilty. He could not undo any of it. Savannah was his present and his future, and he knew he'd never know another moment of happiness till he found her.

"Do me a favor," he said to Joe, reaching into the glove compartment for pen and paper. "I want you to get that car in tip-top shape. New engine, new tires, new paint job. Whatever it takes."

Joe studied him for a long moment. "You're kiddin', right?"

"And send the bill to me. I'll see that you get a commission if you'll take care of it personally." Riley handed him a slip of paper with his name, address, and phone number.

"Locke, huh?" the man said. "Are you the one who practically owns Gull Island?"

"I don't own it; I just have property there. Can you take care of this for me?"

The man looked impressed as he tucked the paper in his shirt pocket. "Sure, I'll get it all spiffied up for you. You know, Mr. Locke, I got some more junkers out back you might be interested in."

Riley shook his head and started the engine. "No thanks. I'm only interested in that particular junker."

The desk clerk at the General Lee was not too keen on giving out Savannah's room number, at least not until Riley handed him a fifty-dollar bill. With the twins in the car, he didn't want to waste time. The clerk became very accommodating once he saw the money.

The drapes were pulled tight beside her door. Riley tapped on it softly and the curtain was pulled aside. Melody peered out at him. "May I come in?" he asked.

She opened the door quietly. "Where are the twins?"

"In the car. Don't worry, I've got the windows down. I need to talk to your mother."

David came up beside Melody dressed in jeans and nothing else. "Who is it, Mel?" he asked, rubbing his eyes. He froze when he saw Riley.

"Melody? David?" Savannah called out sleepily. "If that's the maid, tell her I've arranged a late checkout."

They stepped back, and Riley walked into the room. "It's not the maid," he said.

The color seemed to drain from Savannah's face. "What are you doing here?"

"Can we talk?"

"I don't think that's wise."

"Just for a second, Savannah," he said, going to her bed. He sat on the edge. She rolled over and offered him her back.

"I'm going out to check on the twins," Melody whispered.

"Mom, you need to listen to him," David said.

"Stay out of this, David, it's between us adults."

"I *am* an adult," he replied, "but Riley's the first person who ever treated me like one."

"You're just upset over the dirt bike," she mumbled.

"It's not just the bike," he told her. "I was beginning to feel good about our life. I like coming home from school and finding you there all happy and relaxed and not torn into a million pieces over how we're going to afford groceries. I know Riley and I argue a lot, but so do Ben and Sam. I think it's normal."

"I've heard that too," Riley said, thankful the boy seemed to be on his side for once. Then he remembered the call from the principal. "I owe you an apology, David. They found out who vandalized the science lab. The kids painted your initials on the walls to make them think you did it."

"Which is exactly what David tried to tell us," Savannah mumbled.

"I'm not the innocent you try to make me out to be, Mom," the boy confessed. "The reason I was trying to pick that lock was so I could get in and find my teacher's grade book. I wanted to know if I'd pulled up my average by doing those dumb terrariums Mandy insisted on having me do. I thought if my grade was better, Riley would let me have the bike back."

Savannah remained quiet. Finally, David stood, pulled on a shirt, and grabbed his sneakers. She heard the door close behind him. She raised up and left the bed. Riley followed, but she hurried into the bathroom and locked the door.

He tried the knob and sighed his frustration. "We're not leaving this room until we settle this," he said.

"Don't come in here and start giving me orders," she replied. "As soon as my car's ready, I'm out of here."

On the other side of the door, Riley rolled his eyes heavenward. "You don't really think you're going to get very far in that thing, do you?" She didn't answer. "You can't escape me, Savannah. I'll follow you all over the country if I have to. I need you." She opened the door. In her demure gown with her hair mussed and her eyes still sleepy, he thought she was the most beautiful thing in the world.

"You don't need me. You've never once implied you did. It's always been me needing you. I was willing to do anything to make it work between us because I was so desperate." She felt tears sting her eyes. "Well, I refuse to feel desperate anymore, and I'm tired of loving a man who might not be capable of loving me in return."

Riley felt his heart swell with emotion at her confession of love. He stepped closer, and she moved back so that they were having the conversation in the tiny blue-tiled bathroom. "Just because I never said it doesn't mean it isn't true," he said. "If I had to get up in the morning without seeing your face, I don't think I'd bother getting out of bed." He shook his head. His eyes were unnaturally bright. "Why do you think I've gone to so much trouble to get the place fixed up?"

"Isn't it because you feel guilty about your dead wife?"

Some of the light went out of his eyes. "At first maybe. But then I realized Kara wouldn't have been happy no matter what I did to the house. I've come to terms with it, though, Savannah. I realize I've been given a second chance, and that means everything to me. *You* mean everything to me."

They were quiet for a long moment. "I *do* love you, Savannah. I guess I should have told you sooner, but it happened so fast . . . I was scared. I didn't want to risk another failure."

She was crying now. He was so big and strong looking, it was hard to believe he had his own fears and insecurities. She wanted so desperately to kiss them away. "I love you, too, Riley, but I still feel the need to protect my children."

"So do I," he said. "But when they do something wrong, we have to discipline them whether we like it or not. Same goes for the twins." He raked one hand through his hair. "I genuinely like your kids, Savannah, and I think I could be a good influence, especially on David. But if we're going to live in the same house, then I have to think of them as my kids as well." She didn't say anything so he went on. "I'll make a deal with you, though. We don't level any form of punishment on them without discussing it with each other first. In other words, we'll be in complete agreement before we ever sit down with them."

She pondered it. "That might work," she said, sniffing hard.

He wanted to go to her, pull her in his arms, but he hesitated. "I don't want the children to rule our lives, Savannah. There's still you and me. That's one of the reasons I was so eager to move your parents here. I figured they could baby-sit once in a while so you and I could spend some time together, maybe even take an overdue honeymoon."

A sudden noise made them peer around the bathroom door. Melody and David walked in, each carrying a crying twin. They saw Savannah and squealed in delight, and she wondered what had ever made her think she could just walk away from them. Or their father.

"Have you guys made up yet?" David said frantically. "Trevor has a dirty diaper, and it's smelling up the whole parking lot."

Riley tossed him a grin. "I think we're close." He

nudged Savannah farther into the bathroom and locked the door behind him. "What do you say? Want to make up and come back home with me? If I think real hard, I'm sure I can come up with new ways to show you how much I love you."

She put her arms around his neck and stood on tiptoe. When he looked at her that way she didn't have a fighting chance. "How soon can we leave?"

He sighed his immense relief and hauled her against him roughly before kissing her deeply. They came out of the bathroom a minute later, flushed with desire. "Let's go home," Riley said, and was instantly greeted with cheers from the teenagers. Even Trevor in his dirty diaper clapped.

THE EDITORS' CORNER

When renowned psychic Fiona hosts a special radio call-in show promising to reveal the perfect woman for the man who won't commit, four listeners' lives are forever changed. So begins our AMERICAN BACHELORS romances next month! You'll be captivated by these red, white, and blue hunks who are exactly the kind of men your mother warned you about. Each one knows just the right moves to seduce, dazzle, and entice, and it will take the most bewitching of heroines to conquer our sexy heroes' resistant hearts. But with the help of destiny and passion, these die-hard AMERICAN BACHELORS won't be single much longer.

Riley Morse creates a sizzling tale of everlasting love in **KISS OF FIRE**, LOVESWEPT #766. He'd been warned—and tempted—by the mysterious promise that his fate was linked to a lady whose caress would strike sparks, but Dr. Dayton Westfield knows that playing with fire is his only hope! When Adrienne Bellew enters his lab, he feels the heat of her need in his blood—and answers it with insatiable hunger. Weaving the tantalizing mysteries of a woman's sensual power with the fierce passion of a man who'd give anything to believe in the impossible, Riley Morse presents this fabulous follow-up to her sensational Loveswept debut.

Victoria Leigh turns up the heat in this breathlessly sexy, faster-than-a-bullet story of love on the run, **NIGHT OF THE HAWK,** LOVESWEPT #767. She'd pointed a gun at his head, yet never fired the weapon—but Hawk believes the woman must have been hired to kill him! Angela Ferguson bravely insists she knows nothing, no matter how dark his threats, but even her innocence won't save her from the violence that shadows his haunted eyes. When a renegade with vengeance on his mind meets a feisty heroine who's more than his match, be prepared for anything—Victoria Leigh always packs a passionate punch.

THRILL OF THE CHASE, LOVESWEPT #768, showcases the playful, witty, and very sexy writing of Maris Soule. He's a heartbreaker, a hunk whose sex appeal is hard to ignore, but Peggi Barnett is tired of men who thrill to the chase, then never seem willing to catch what they've pursued! Cameron Slater is gorgeous, charming, and enjoys teasing the woman he's hired to redo his home. He'd always vowed that marriage wasn't on his agenda, but could she be the woman he'd been waiting for all his life? When a pretty designer finds that a handshake feels more like an embrace, Maris Soule sets a delicious game in motion.

Praised by *Romantic Times* as "a magnificent writer," Terry Lawrence presents **DRIVEN TO DISTRACTION**, LOVESWEPT #769. Cole Creek is almost too much man to spend a month with in the confines of a car, Evie Mercer admits, but sitting too close for comfort next to him will certainly make the miles fly! Sharing tight quarters with a woman he's fallen head-over-heels for isn't such a good idea, especially when a tender kiss explodes into pure, primal yearning. Terry Lawrence knows just how to entangle smart, sexy women with an appetite for all life offers with the kind of men the best dreams are made of.

Happy reading!

With warmest wishes,

Beth de Guzman

Shauna Summers

Beth de Guzman   Shauna Summers
Senior Editor   Associate Editor

P.S. Watch for these fascinating Bantam women's fiction titles coming in December: With her spellbinding imagination and seductive voice, Kay Hooper is the only author worthy of being called today's successor to Victoria Holt; now, she has created a unique and stunning tale of contemporary suspense that begins with a mysterious homecoming and ends in a shattering explosion of passion, greed, and murder—and all because a stranger says her name is **AMANDA.** *New York Times* bestselling author Sandra Brown's **HEAVEN'S PRICE** will be available in paperback, and Katherine O'Neal, winner of the *Romantic Times* Award for Best Sensual Historical Romance, unveils **MASTER OF PARADISE**—a tantalizing tale of a notorious pirate, a rebellious beauty, and a dangerously erotic duel of hearts. Finally, in the bestselling tradition of Arnette Lamb and Pamela Morsi, **TEXAS OUTLAW** is a triumph of captivating romance and adventure from spectacular newcomer Adrienne deWolfe. Be sure to catch next month's LOVESWEPTs for a preview of these wonderful novels.